We Are Broken

Paul Coffey was born and raised in Nottingham, England, and spent almost 20 years working as a journalist before moving into media and communications within law enforcement. His debut novel, *Shadows of the Somme*, was independently published in 2015. He still lives in Nottinghamshire with his wife and two daughters.

Also by Paul Coffey

Shadows of the Somme

We Are Broken

Paul Coffey

For Mum and Dad,
for their ever-lasting love and support

'Where the work of the surgeon is completed. When the surgeon has done all he can to restore functions ... I endeavour by means of the skill I happen to possess as a sculptor to make a man's face as near as possible to what it looked like before he was wounded.'

- Francis Derwent Wood

England, 1919

Prologue

Streaks of winter sunshine streamed through the windows, the rays illuminating the room's drab wood panelling so every knot and blemish shimmered.

Charlie Hobbs brushed past the young nurse in the doorway, her face wearing the smile she'd perfected for every patient; friendly, sympathetic. Her eyes betrayed nothing of the horrors she saw.

'Take a seat, Mr Hobbs, you'll be called when he's ready.'

Hobbs nodded, dreading the thought of eye contact, shuffling uneasily to a row of chairs where two men sat staring at the floor, one of them reaching into his trouser pocket, withdrawing a cigarette case.

'I'm sorry, Mr Barnes, you can't smoke in here,' the nurse said. Her smile was still there but Hobbs sensed it masked something else; irritation, probably.

Barnes pocketed the case, his face reddened from the mild rebuke that saw him slump into his chair, head bowed.

'It shouldn't be too long now,' she added, leaving the room.

The three men waited; an awkward, stilted silence, louder and more intrusive than anything Hobbs could remember. Beads of sweat ran between his neck and the starched collar of the shirt once belonging to someone else.

Barnes fidgeted in his seat, the man next to him coughed, but no one said a word. Hobbs saw particles of dust floating wistfully in the sunlight and imagined if Heaven had a waiting room, would it look like this?

The only sound was the faint ticking of a clock perched above a door and as the minutes ticked by, Hobbs was forced to move to avoid the sun's glare. Shuffling in his seat, he searched for distractions, anything to fill the void.

Above the fireplace in the centre of the wall facing the clock, a portrait of the King hung over the mantelpiece, dominating the room.

Holding a black cane in his left hand, King George V stood rigid, magnificently turned out in full ceremonial uniform, his collar, cuffs and waist adorned with elaborate gold braiding.

Draped over his shoulders was a white and blue ermine cloak, while an array of medals was visible on a sky blue sash running across his broad chest.

The Monarch's piercing blue eyes gazed out beyond the picture and in the sunlight, Hobbs saw his King as an ethereal figure. He wondered how long he had been made to stand there in his regalia while the artist skilfully painted.

And then Hobbs remembered having to sit perfectly still, while an artist of a different kind went to work on him.

'Private Whittaker, please.'

Hobbs didn't hear the name; all he heard was the sound of another man's voice as a door opened. It was enough to break the suffocating silence and his body responded, the muscles relaxing as the relief came.

Whittaker was the third man in the room and Hobbs stole a glance as he rose from his seat, wondering why he was here. His question was answered when Whittaker turned to grab his coat, revealing what was left of the right side of his face.

The eyelid was closed but the skin had been sewn shut. Beneath were a series of ugly scars, pulling the flesh downwards, where it congealed in a messy scrunch of skin that wobbled in the space where his jawbone used to be. Whittaker disappeared into the room, the door closed and Hobbs was grateful for the audible distraction of muffled voices coming from the other side.

Barnes, clearly desperate for the cigarette he was denied, sat cross-legged staring into space peering through his one remaining eye. Half his nose was missing, replaced by distorted, uneven tissue that stretched over his left cheek.

His right leg shook vigorously and Hobbs watched as he idly clawed and scratched at the skin around his disfigurement. He used to do that too; the constant impulse to reach up and touch. But that had long passed.

Now, whenever he touched his own face, Hobbs' skin crawled. Running his fingers down from the forehead, there was a profound inward curve of soft, squashed, uneven flesh where his nose used to be.

Brushing his fingertips over his left eye, he could never quite bring himself to touch the empty socket, the eyelid merely a flap of skin unable to open.

The sensation inevitably triggered a memory, the moment he instinctively raised his hands, his vision blurring, senses obliterated, but still able to feel half his face come away in his hands.

But soon he would have a new face, though not one made from flesh and bone. It would be a face that could never smile, never move, never feel; but it wouldn't age and Hobbs would feel normal once more.

He was alone when his name was finally called, stepping into the room with a sense of dread, knowing how crucial the next few minutes were to the rest of his life.

This room was smaller, its windowless walls giving it a suffocating feel and Hobbs was unnerved by the sight of dozens of faces hanging on the wall, peering lifelessly like the death masks of ancient Rome.

Only these faces were incomplete; a nose and mouth, eyes and a cheek. All had the same ghostly white finish and for a moment Hobbs was convinced he could hear them calling.

'Right, Mr Hobbs, let's get started, shall we?'

Flinching as cold metal touched his skin, Hobbs felt the warmth of his breath as he exhaled. And then his breathing quickened, responding to the unnerving sensation of his face being covered.

The sensory cells in his nasal cavity had been destroyed along with his nose so he would never know of the metallic odour now pressed up against him.

'How does that feel, not too tight?' the man asked, his fingers probing around Hobbs' head, hooking spectacles over his ears. The impulse to speak prompted a wet, low grunt from what remained of Hobbs' mouth.

Even that sounded different, resonating against the artificial barrier now in front of him.

'Now, can you see out of the eye clearly? You may notice a little difference but that's because I've used spectacles, they are perfect for helping concealment. The glass is tinted too, you'll resemble a blind man, but that can't be helped.'

Before Hobbs could answer he was issued with instructions.

'Turn your head for me, slowly; look around the room. That's it, excellent. Now, look up to the ceiling ... and down to the floor. Good, good. Now, stand up and have a walk around.'

As he moved the metal rubbed, making a noise only Hobbs could hear, the warmth from his breath still noticeable.

'You'll soon get used to the sound and, at this time of year, you'll be grateful for the heat around your face,' and Hobbs wondered if his instructor could sense his thoughts.

'I think you'll be happy with the likeness, you've got good skin tone which has made it easier to get the shading right. It blends in very well and, from this distance, it's extremely difficult to tell.'

Hobbs was struck by the man's optimism, which jarred against the desolate, despair of his own life. And yet it acted as a spark, coaxing the embers of hope from deep within. He recalled how little this extraordinary man had reacted when they'd first met, Hobbs having become so used to the gawps of those morbidly fascinated and appalled by his grotesque appearance.

Introducing himself as Francis Derwent Wood, his hooked nose and greased coal black hair reminded Hobbs of a Dickens character. Reading from a folder, Derwent Wood had said:

'So, Mr Hobbs, I see all the surgical work has now been completed and your wounds have healed as much as they can. That's very important because I can't do anything until we get to that stage. Have you brought a photograph with you as I requested?'

Fumbling inside the inner pocket of his ill-fitting, grey, tweed suit, Hobbs had retrieved a small black and white photograph.

In it, his former self stared out from the image, shoulders back, proud to be wearing the uniform he'd been so desperate to wear.

Reaching across, Derwent Wood had examined it closely before looking up to compare the picture with the real thing.

'Ah yes, that shouldn't be too much of a problem, nothing too tricky here. And you're happy with this? It's just that we had one fellow who brought me a picture of Rupert Brooke! I told him, I'm a sculptor not a miracle worker,' and he'd laughed at his own joke.

Back then Hobbs never imagined how long or painful the process would be; the awful sensation of being covered in the suffocating plaster of Paris, the insufferable hours sitting still while this master craftsman created him a new face.

But it would be worth it. Because he knew how utterly repulsive he was, his shattered face leaving him a monstrous deformity of the man he'd once been. Hobbs didn't look or feel human anymore, how could he? To be human meant having two eyes, a nose, a mouth.

'So? Are you ready to have a look?' Derwent Wood asked smiling.

He dreaded having to speak, detesting the pathetic sounds that came from no longer having an upper jaw. His speech defect sickened him and he was repulsed at what emerged from his mouth.

But incredibly, Derwent Wood, hands buried deep into the pockets of his white laboratory coat, was able to understand.

'Good man, now take your time and let me know when you're ready.' Taking a deep breath, Hobbs nodded as Derwent Wood reached for a round, brass vanity mirror and held it aloft.

'Well? What do you think? Is it like looking at your old self again?' Staring at his reflection, Hobbs could only gasp, confronted by the sight of the man he used to be.

'Can I ... can I feel?'

'Yes, yes, of course. Just be mindful that some of the paintwork and finishing touches may still be a little delicate. I'd hate for you to inadvertently pull off one of your eyebrows,' he chuckled.

Tentatively touching his new face, Hobbs watched his fingers in the mirror as they ran over the nose, stroking the mouth, feeling the cheeks. It was the strangest thing to watch himself stroke his face and yet only feel cold, hard metal.

'It takes time, but you'll get used to the feel of it. Now remember, try and avoid getting it wet, a little rain won't harm occasionally but you don't want to get it soaked. And if it's dropped, or it gets banged or chipped, it will damage; just like a real face would, though I'm afraid it's not going to heal itself,' Derwent Wood added, oblivious to the insensitivity of his remark.

He turned his back, reaching for a blue cloth bag.

'Now, when you're not wearing it keep it inside this; it helps prevent scratches and other damage. To clean it, simply use a damp cloth but don't use soap as it can bring off the paintwork.

'Remember to use the wadding underneath or it will chafe. Any problems, you know where I am.'
Derwent Wood had already opened the door and for a moment Hobbs was hesitant, unable to believe this was it. He wasn't ready yet, he needed more time ... there were questions, he couldn't simply walk out, not like this ...

'It's been a pleasure meeting you, Rifleman Hobbs. I only hope I've been able to help in some small way and that you're now able to live a full and happy life. I wish you the very best of luck,' and Derwent Wood offered Hobbs his hand, unable to see the panic on his patient's face thanks to his own cosmetic creation.

Hobbs avoided the handshake by picking up the cloth bag in his right hand, sweating profusely now, his heart racing. He had no thought of how odd it must be for Derwent Wood to hear him speak but not see his mouth or face moving.

'Thank ... you ... for everything,' he mumbled, feeling the spit and saliva run down his chin.

His footsteps echoed as he strode along the corridors of the former asylum that was now the Third London General Hospital. Passing two nurses, they barely noticed the man in the dark glasses with the impassive face.

Coming to another door of the imposing Gothic building, Hobbs opened it and stepped outside, ignoring the sign on the wall which read: *The Masks for Facial Disfigurement Department.*

1

There were two this side of the park, both overlooking the lake.

They were far enough away from the road not to be seen and unlike the dull, brown benches dotted around Kelsey Park and beyond, these were painted bright blue. Both were empty.

Close to the water, a young mother was pushing her perambulator, smiling at the precious cargo inside, a watchful eye on her toddler son trying to chase pigeons. He tottered awkwardly, and the inevitable tumble followed.

'Up you get, Peter, you'll be fine,' she said encouragingly, as the boy got to his feet and set off in pursuit. But the cumbersome birds took to the skies with inelegance, leaving their young pursuer to gaze upwards pointing.

'Here you go, Peter, feed the ducks,' his mother urged, retrieving a brown paper bag from beneath her pram, and watching her son grab it eagerly before heading to the water.

'Be careful, sweetie, not too close now.'

Dipping into the bag, the little boy ripped chunks of bread, tossing them into the lake, the floating morsels attracting the ducks.

'Make the pieces smaller, Peter, they like that don't they?' his mother said, idly rocking the pram.

Facing the lake, she didn't spot the man in the grey overcoat staring at them from the blue bench. He took a pear from his pocket, biting into the fruit, all the time watching.

It was when the young boy toddled after a mallard that clambered out of the water, that something else caught his mother's gaze. She was drawn to the man on the bench; the way he looked, even from afar, there was something different, something strange.

And then her son saw him, and he too stared at the man with the pear.

'Peter, Peter, come here, darling,' she was suddenly wary, sensing danger.

Moving closer she caught sight of his face, horrified to see he had no features; it gave the appearance of having melted.

He had no lips, which meant when he opened his mouth to eat, his front teeth and gums were exposed, giving him a strange, almost skeletal appearance. Grimacing, she turned away.

Yet, her boy carried on staring and the man noticed. Wiping his mouth and smiling, he beckoned him closer. But the grin exaggerated his distorted features and now the little boy was frightened.

'Peter, come to Mummy, quickly' and he turned, hurrying back to his mother, who lifted him into her arms, pressing his face into her chest. She didn't want him looking at the scary man on the bench.

'Not to worry love, I don't bite,' he said.

One hand still on the pram, the other cradling her son, she was unsure how to respond.

'I'm ... I'm sorry, it's just ... he's never seen; I didn't want him getting upset.'

There were few people around and her maternal instincts were yelling *'leave, leave now.'*

'That's all right love, I know he don't mean no harm. How old is he?' and now he stood, and then he was heading towards her.

'What? Oh, he ... he's three. Listen, I'm sorry to have bothered you but we must be on our way.'

But closer he came, and she saw his entire face had been destroyed by burns; the skin left hideously wrinkled, like rubber.

'It's not Florence is it? Florence Preston?'

'Please go away, you're scaring me,' and she shook her head.

'Well, you look just like her, all the boys fancied Flo when we were at school.'

That made him laugh, his face contorting into creases, his eyes wild, and it unnerved her more.

'I'm Freddy, Freddy Lucas. So, you er ... you married then? It's just I know a lot of women who are on their own now, if you know what I mean.'

'What? Oh my God, is he really doing this?

'Yes, yes I am married,' she lied. 'Look, I ... I really ought to be going.'

'Ah, that's a shame; I'm not surprised though, good looking girl like you. Might have fancied me chances asking you out for a drink otherwise.'

'How dare he? How could he possibly think she would ... oh, the affront of the man, he was hideous.'

'Look, I feel sorry for you, really I do … what you boys had to face and all but … but you shouldn't come here, not when there's children about,' and she turned swiftly, hurrying away, her young son's face peering at him from the safety of his mother's shoulder.

'You prissy cow, I was only being friendly.'

Freddy returned to the bench muttering to himself, picking up his half eaten pear and hurling it into the lake.

Once, she'd have been eating out of his hand. She was nothing special, it's not as if he fancied her.

But when had that ever mattered?

No, he just loved women; and what he could do to them. The gift of the gab his mates used to call it, the knack of being able to talk himself under the petticoats of even the shyest of girls.

And then, once you'd got that far, well, nothing could stop him. Some had tried, especially the frigid ones who were 'saving themselves'.

But they yielded soon enough, either from the threat or the feel of his fist. Until that too soon became part of his pleasure.

He felt a stir in his groin as he imagined taking the woman in the park roughly from behind.

'Bet you love it like that, don't you,' he muttered aloud, watching as she hurried from the park pushing her pram, her little boy struggling to keep up.

'You're all the fucking same.'

And Freddy pictured women turning their heads when they caught sight of his face. They didn't hide their revulsion like men did and he hated them for that, feeling for his cigarette lighter in his pocket.

A flick of his thumb and the flame appeared; and he cupped his hand, shielding it from the breeze.

He wondered how the young mother would cope with a disfigured face, if her pretty little features had been melted by flames.

She'd be desperate for someone to fuck her then.

And Freddy stared into the flickering flame smiling.

2

Feeling the tip pierce the skin, he was careful not to thrust too deep; in one swift movement the blade was drawn and the abdomen sliced open. Reaching inside, he grabbed the innards, yanking hard until they came away from the flesh.

Solomon Wheeler didn't flinch. He'd done this numerous times; the sight of spilled entrails and his bloody hands never bothered him.

Picking up the knife he held the gutted fish firmly before slicing off its head, tossing it into a bucket of several more. Solomon paused, staring at the lifeless eyes that gawped at him, open mouthed, seemingly unable to comprehend their violent fate.

Wiping both sides of the wet blade across his chest, he smeared more blood on his already stained apron, his nostrils numbed to the odour of fish and guts.

When only the fillet remained, Solomon placed it on top of the others, piled on a bed of ice, before reaching down for another of the abundant mackerel crammed into a large crate on the damp, concrete floor of J.E Wilson & Son Fishery.

'I need you to get a shifty on, Sol, I've got a load of herring needs sorting. Sol? Sol? 'Fucking hell, Sol, are you going deaf?'

The voice was that of fishery foreman Billy Draper, a look of annoyance on his unshaven, pockmarked face that he was having to bawl out his best man in the middle of the busy fish hall.

'Do we have a problem, Sol?'

Solomon remembered the man who once used to sit on his bench as a young boy, watching with fascination as the fish were gutted; he would even let young Billy have a go himself from time to time.

Draper was a likeable boy then; but his days of calling him 'Uncle Sol' had long gone. Since the death of his father, Draper had morphed into a foul-mouthed, bastard of a boss since rising to foreman, his heavy gut suiting the swagger he relished from being in charge.

'If only your father could see you now, Billy,' and the thought depressed Solomon, as so much else did nowadays.

'No problem here, Billy,' he replied, digging deep for a cheery tone, unsure if he found one. 'I've almost finished the mackerel.'

Draper's eyes narrowed and he was about to say something else, but hoots and cheers from the other side of the hall distracted him as a young lad slipped, sprawling on the wet floor, an upturned crate by his side, fish and ice spilt everywhere.

'Oh, for fuck's sake, get this lot cleaned up NOW!' Draper yelled, spitting in the eye-line of the skinny lad who'd tumbled.

'And what are you lot laughing at? That's good money right there, and we're not made of it … now clean that

mess up and any lost mackerel, it'll come out of your pay,
you dozy idiot.'

Ignoring the commotion, Solomon took another
mackerel and sliced open its belly, his fingers slipping
inside, feeling the wetness. His stomach groaned, craving
the food he had been denying himself. He hadn't eaten
properly for days, the inevitability of what was coming,
crushing his appetite.

'Here you go, Sol, Mr Draper sez' you're to start on the
'erring,' it was young Amos, a scrawny, red-haired boy,
who always looked like he was about to throw up. He set
the box on the floor, his bony fingers red raw from the
cold.

With the mackerel finished, Solomon sighed, gazing
down at the dozens of gutted herring, scattered with ice to
preserve their freshness. It occurred to him how much he
dealt with death; for in that moment the fish ceased to be
food in Solomon's eyes and became instead portents of a
world about to end.

He was meticulous in his work, able to gut and fillet a
fish with his eyes closed. Yet now, on this day, he
imagined how an undertaker felt, preparing corpse after
corpse, day after day. And the bile rose in his throat, his
eyes watered and Solomon shuddered with rage at the
injustice of it all.

'Mr Wheeler, Mr Wheeler, Sir … me Mam says you have
to come quick, you have to come now … she says … she
says it's…'

The boy was out of breath, his cheeks flushed, smearing
a dirty hand across his face, staring wide-eyed at
Solomon. He put a hand to his forehead, lifting his untidy
fringe and the old man saw fear in his youthful eyes.

Dropping his knife, a gutted fish stared lifelessly up from the table as Solomon wiped his bloody hands on a towel.

'What is it, lad? What's happened?'
But he needn't have asked. He knew the time had finally come.

The boy bolted for the door, Solomon following, hoisting his bloody apron over his head and letting it fall to the floor. Draper moved to stand in his way, but his expression changed on seeing Solomon's ashen face, and he stepped aside. Solomon didn't see him. He didn't see anyone; no, that's not true. He saw her, and then his entire life about to come crashing down.

Home was a twenty minute stroll. In his younger days he could do it in ten. Now, though he hurried, it took him almost fifteen, jogging breathlessly through the streets, every step bringing a sense of dread, a belief that the collapse of everything he held dear would soon be upon him.

Forcing himself on, he arrived home, gasping for breath, the panic taking hold now, the creeping fear of the inevitable. He only hoped he was in time.

The boy was already there, waiting at the door, looking nervous, embarrassed even. Brushing past him, Solomon climbed the stairs two at a time to find his neighbour, Patricia Donnelly, coming out of his bedroom, tears streaming down her face.

She didn't speak, her eyes only confirmed what he already knew. Pushing open the door Solomon stepped into more than just a bedroom; it was a sanctuary, their sanctuary; within these four walls was a lifetime of love and intimacy he'd never taken for granted, but one he'd never allowed himself to think would ever end.

His nose detected the sickly sweet smell of death. The curtains were drawn and he could hear voices in the street below, knowing the window must be open.

The final steps now, he was almost at the end of the world.

At the bedside he dropped to his knees; it was an awkward action but he ignored the discomfort in his joints. And then, letting out a slow and heavy sigh, he saw her lying still before him.

Maud Wheeler's face was sunken, the Pallor Mortis giving her a ghostly appearance. Solomon's hands were cold but he tenderly stroked his dead wife's face, she was still warm.

There was a tap on the door and the round figure of Patricia Donnelly appeared wringing her hands in front of her buxom frame.

'Oh Mr Wheeler, I am so, so sorry for your loss. Maud was such a wonderful woman, salt of the Earth she was.'

Hearing her soft Irish accent was strangely comforting and yet Solomon's eyes remained firmly on his wife:

'Thank you Pat, that she was. Were you with her at the ... at the end?'

She approached the bed and amidst his grief Solomon could sense her unease.

'I'm ... I'm sorry, Mr Wheeler, truly I am,' and her face crumpled, hands over her mouth. 'I nipped in first t'ing this morning as I always do ...'

'Go on, Pat.'

'Maud, she ... she was still with us, all peaceful and calm she was. I promised to pick up some tailoring for Mrs Dawes, it's her legs you see, she can't get about as much as she used to. When I came back, well ... it can't have been any more than half an hour, Mr Wheeler.'

Nodding, Solomon rose stiffly, a hand on the mattress to steady himself, careful not to press down on Maud. Wincing from the pain in his knees and back, he got to his feet and reached for his neighbour's hand, holding it in his own.

'It's quite all right, Pat. You've done more than enough for Maud, she thought a lot of you and your boys.'

And with that she broke down sobbing and Solomon was doing the comforting as tears rolled down Patricia Donnelly's crimson face.

'Oh, wudja look at me, getting all upset, t'inking of myself. It's you who should be comforted, God bless ya,' she said, pulling a handkerchief from her sleeve. 'Now, you let me know if you need anyt'ing, I mean that. I'll pray for you, Solomon Wheeler ... and for your beloved Maud. She's with the Good Lord now, you mark my words, no more sufferin' for her, God rest her soul ... just eternal peace.'

Solomon ushered her gently from the room, following her downstairs to where her eldest boy, Niall, who'd come to fetch him from the fish hall, was sitting on the doorstep throwing pebbles against the wall.

'Just remember what I said now, anyt'ing I can do, anyt'ing at all ... well, you only have to ask. God bless ya, Mr Wheeler.'

One more sympathetic smile and the door was closed. It was just the two of them now, just him and Maud, like it had always been. But it was never like this.

Solomon drew the curtains, shutting out the light. Trudging back upstairs he stopped outside the bedroom, swamped by a sadness that threatened to crush his very soul.

And suddenly he was afraid to push open the door, to see her lying there. There was hesitation and … fear, yes, fear of what was in that room, their room. Reaching for the handle he didn't open it; instead Solomon pulled it towards him, determined to trap death inside.

And then he slumped to the floor at the top of the stairs, feeling more alone and afraid than he'd ever been before. He wanted his Maud, to hold her, to look into those beautiful green eyes once more.

Solomon was incapable of stemming the inevitable descent into grief that followed, his vigil only broken by the sleep that finally came in the dead of night, a fractured, tortured sleep, where the demons tormented him and he woke more exhausted than ever.

He never did turn the handle and open the door again; not while Maud was still lying there. When they came for her he stayed out the way, unable to look as they carried what remained of the woman he'd fallen in love with more than forty years ago, down the stairs of the pokey, two up, two down house that had been their home.

He couldn't bear to see the cruel, ruin of the once sparkling woman who defined his life. Instead, he resolved to remember Maud's laugh, her intoxicating smile, the scintillating eyes, her spirit.

Staring into nothing, Solomon heard the horses trot away carrying her body.

3

The small brown teddy slumped forward, teetering precariously over the edge; but the little girl was quick, tucking it back into place, a gentle pat on the head for her beloved bear.

Thirza Moran was sitting next to a rag doll at the wooden toy chest she was using as a table.

'We're so happy that you're home, Daddy, we've missed you so much haven't we, Hugo?' And she gazed at her teddy, smiling at the imagined reply.

Thirza's voice was nasally; she had a speech defect which made it difficult to pronounce some words. Earlier, she'd set four places, sneaking tea plates out of her mother's kitchen which she now used to 'serve' the colourful building blocks she pretended were cakes.

'Would you like some more? We baked this especially for you as a coming home present. Oh, you want some more too, do you? Well, that's your last piece, Hugo, or there'll be none left for Daddy.'

Staring at an empty chair, her face broke out into a wide smile:

'It's the best cake you've ever tasted? Oh, thank you, Daddy. Did you hear that, Hugo? Daddy loves the cake we've made him.'

Her head was a thick mop of red curls and the ringlets gently bounced every time she moved. She picked up a fork too big for her small hands, held it to her open mouth and mimicked eating, freckles wobbling on her pale cheeks.

To a rag doll perched on a pillow, she said: 'Mother, you don't have to put me to bed tonight, Daddy can do it. Will you tell me a story, Daddy? Like the ones I remember?'

And for a moment she gazed longingly at the empty chair, her smile fading, an anxious, pained expression appearing on her young face.

Thirza frowned, trying to concentrate, thinking really hard ... but it was too late, the panic was dissolving her memories now.

Scrunching her eyes shut, she willed herself to try harder; but there was nothing. Her eyes watered, the tears came and she grabbed her teddy, sobbing into its musty fur.

'Thirza? Thirza, supper's ready.'

When her mother called a second time, Thirza sat up, wiped her nose on a sleeve and rubbed her eyes. She reached for Hugo just as her bedroom door swung open.

Wearing a plain blue apron-style dress, Mary Moran was drying her hands on a tea towel when she breezed in. Her dark, wavy, brunette hair was tied up in a pin; not as immaculate as she used to do it, but then there were lots of things she didn't do any more.

Mary's slim face only highlighted her drawn features and amidst the frown lines the eyes that once sparkled were tired and distant.

There was irritation in those eyes on seeing the kitchen items her daughter had squirrelled away upstairs but that dissolved when she saw Thirza's blotchy, tear-stained face.

Mary dropped the towel, wrapping her arms around her little girl.

Now the tears came again, for both of them, and they clung to each other sobbing. When the grief finally passed, both were quiet and Mary relaxed her hold, kneeling beside her daughter, gently wiping tears from Thirza's cheeks and sweeping the curls away from her face.

'There, is that better?'

Thirza nodded.

'What's made you so upset, sweetie, did you remember something? You know it's fine to cry, it shows how much you loved your father. I remember little things all the time. Sometimes they make me sad but other times they make me smile, remembering the happy times.'

She could see Thirza was about to start crying again, but sensing it, Mary tenderly stroked her face.

'Shhhh, there, there, Thirza. It's going to be all right.'

'No, it's not, Mother … you don't … you don't understand.'

A flash of anger, so unlike her little girl; and Mary hid her surprise.

She never heard the speech impediment when her daughter spoke. For her, it was the most natural thing in the world.

'Understand what? Tell me, darling.'

'I can't.'

'Yes, you can, you can tell me anything'.

'No, I mean I can't … I can't remember, Mother,' her bottom lip trembling.

Confused, Mary rocked back on her knees, gently caressing Thirza's hands.

'What can't you remember, sweetie?'

Her mother had delicate fingers, a soothing touch and Thirza found it relaxing, before answering softly:

'His voice. I can't remember Daddy's voice anymore.'

Mary swallowed hard, her lip quivering, a silent scream at the pain her daughter felt. It wasn't fair, it was cruel. There were many times she'd questioned her faith, unable to find any solace or comfort from a God that allowed a young girl to be so cruelly orphaned.

She pulled Thirza close, kissed the top of her head, the two of them taking comfort in the embrace.

Mary was sick of the way grief toyed with them; wasn't it enough that it crushed every last drop of happiness she'd ever known? Or that it hid in the most innocuous of things, ready to leap out, relishing the agony it inflicted.

No, that was expected. She could cope with that because she knew, she'd been promised, that the light would slowly emerge and with it, brighter days.

What she hated was the way grief callously crept up on them both, sadistically imposing itself on their mundane, day to day routine.

Biting her lip, she took a deep breath, eyes peering upwards, lest her little girl should see her struggling to hold back more tears.

'You know, before you were even born your father would sing to you.'

Thirza burrowed into Mary's chest, but a mop of curls emerged and she peeped out, a puzzled expression on her young face.

'When you were growing inside me he would lay beside me stroking my tummy and yes, he would sing to you.'

She saw the sign of a sparkle returning to Thirza's eyes:

'What did he sing?'

'Oh, he'd sing an old song he always said reminded him of me,' and for a moment Mary's face betrayed her own thoughts that drifted to days long gone.

'What was it called? Can you sing it to me, Mother, please!'

'Oh, Thirza you know I can't sing.'

'Please, Mother.'

Stroking Thirza's hair, Mary smiled. How could she resist that? Gazing adoringly into her eyes she sang softly:

'The pale moon was rising above the green mountain,

'The sun was declining beneath the blue sea;

'When I strayed with my love to the pure crystal fountain,

'That stands in the beautiful Vale of Tralee.

'She was lovely and fair as the rose of the summer,

'Yet 'twas not her beauty alone that won me;

'Oh no, 'twas the truth in her eyes ever dawning,

'That made me love Mary, the Rose of Tralee.'

A kiss on Thirza's forehead ended the song as Mary thoughts were for the man she once could never have imagined her life without.

'Mary … it's a song about you, Mother … Is that why Daddy liked it?'

'Yes, I think it was. He would sing it to me when we first met. Your father had a lovely singing voice.'

'I'd like to learn it too, Mother, then I can sing it to you like Daddy did.'

And with that Mary hugged her again and felt she would never let go.

4

On the doorstep, Charlie Hobbs carefully removed the spectacles holding his mask in place, before sliding his tin face inside the cloth bag given to him by Derwent Wood. A deep breath, a turn of the handle and he stepped inside.

He'd deliberately stayed away until late, relieved the house was quiet. Only one person knew where he'd been; he wasn't yet ready to share his new face with everybody else, especially not Freddy.

Listening for noises in the hallway, Hobbs slowly wriggled free of his coat, hanging it on a hook alongside the others.

Number sixteen Gladstone Street, or the House of Horrors as Freddy dubbed it, was home to five men. It had few visitors and the occupants rarely ventured out. When they did it was through necessity; preferring it when the weather worsened, so they could cover their faces with scarves, or walk with their heads down.

Hobbs and Freddy were the newest tenants. They met in opposite beds in Queen Mary's Hospital, Siddcup, undergoing painful treatment on their broken faces. Speaking to another man without a face had become the most normal thing in the world and the two would compare injuries, amusing each other by shocking the nurses with their gallows humour.

It didn't matter that Hobbs had been in the Army while Freddy was an airman. Or that Freddy had a darker side and had come to rely on his friend a little too much.

All that mattered to Hobbs was he knew how Freddy felt when he saw his reflection or when people turned away in disgust, not bothering to hide their own horrified faces.

Hobbs knew because he felt the same way.

When they left hospital the two men went their separate ways, drifting from one place to another, never being allowed to settle by people who found it all too uncomfortable to be around them.

And then, by chance, sitting in a soup kitchen to escape the rain, they met up again and soon afterwards heard about a home for injured veterans in nearby Bromley, Kent, funded by a grieving father who had lost one son in the war and seen another left horribly scarred.

A week later they arrived in Gladstone Street, greeted by Stanley Finch, a war veteran himself, but of the South African campaigns of another age.

'Make yourselves at home, lads, you've got the top two rooms next to each other. Now, it's up to you how much you want to get to know the other boys but we do try and have one meal together once a week, how does that sound?' he'd said, never once flinching at either man's appearance.

Freddy had nodded nervously, his hands fiddling with his lighter.

'That's fine … Mr Finch,' Hobbs replied for them both.

Learning to speak with his facial deformity had been the biggest struggle. The ability to form words without the upper part of his mouth meant he had to speak painfully slowly so people could try and work out what he was saying. Even so, Hobbs knew he was difficult to understand.

'Call me Stan, everybody else does,' came the reply, a smile emerging from beneath the bushy, grey moustache dominating the old soldier's face.

Producing a small notebook, Hobbs had then scribbled something with a pencil, before showing it to Stan.

'We're pleased to meet you. This is Freddy Lucas, I'm Charlie Hobbs.'

'Nice to make your acquaintance,' and Stan had thrust out a hand.

The gesture unnerved Hobbs who hated handshakes. He avoided it by reaching into his pocket and pulling out the letter which confirmed their tenancy.

If the older man noticed he didn't say anything

'Right, that's all in order. Now, I'll leave you both to it. I would take you up and show you around but I never have quite fathomed using stairs with these buggers,' and Stan had lifted his trousers to reveal two wooden legs.

'Jesus Christ! The bastards got you too, did they?' Freddy asked, speaking for the first time.

'What? Hell no, it was our lot that gave me these. The bloody Field Artillery.'

Hobbs listened to the old boy's story, while Freddy's eyes were constantly on the move, taking in his surroundings.

'We were moving our battery during a rainstorm outside Stormberg in South Africa when the limbers slipped in the mud; one of the fifteen pounders toppled over pinning me to the ground. That was the end of my Army life … and my legs,' Stan said.

Hobbs scribbled again in his notebook.

'How did you end up here?'

'I served with Captain Lewellyn and he's been good to me since the day they sent me home. I knew both his boys, Ted and Archie. Affected him badly when Archie was killed in Nineteen Fourteen. Then Ted was badly wounded too. It didn't surprise me when he wanted to do something to help other boys who'd suffered. Just angers me that there's even a need for it … all you boys should have somewhere of your own. It's what's due to you.'

Hobbs had since grown close to Stan so it was only natural that he confided in him about his frequent visits to London as a patient – or was that guinea pig? – of Derwent Wood.

Now, standing in the same hallway, his mask hidden in its cloth bag, Stan appeared from the back room.

'I wondered where you'd got to. So, come on then … let's see it. I'm surprised you're not wearing it,' he whispered.

'Not here,' Hobbs muttered, and with a flick of his head gestured towards the kitchen.

'You can't hide it forever, Charlie, otherwise what's the point in having it?'

Hobbs bristled. He wasn't hiding it but he had to be careful. Only Stan knew the real reason he'd gone through with this. And he hadn't told Freddy yet.

He reached into the bag, embarrassed and self-conscious, fiddling to put it on properly; he needn't have worried.

'Is that supposed to be what you looked like? You look better with it off! I'm only joking, Charlie,' and Stan laughed.

Stepping closer, he peered into Hobbs' face, fascinated:

'Blimey, you can't tell from standing here. Amazing what they can do nowadays ain't it?'

'Really? You ... really ... think so?'

'Yes, absolutely. Though she's not always going to be standing this far away from you ... you know that right?'

Both men were silent while Hobbs whipped out his notebook, resting it on a lifted leg to write.

'I know that, but she'll look at me and won't be repulsed.'

Stan pulled a chair from under the kitchen table, falling into it, his paunch hanging over his belt, trouser legs concealing his wooden limbs. Leaning back he rubbed his chin in that odd way people do when they're thinking.

'I still reckon you should have been to see her before now. Believe me, I'm no expert, Charlie, but you're taking a huge gamble. I don't want to sound harsh but how do you know ... well, you know, that she's even waiting for you?'

'She's waiting. I know she is. And she'll understand ... I just couldn't let her see me before.'

'Well, good luck to you, Charlie, you deserve it. I only hope she appreciates what you've been through. And I hope she's worth it.'

Removing his mask, Hobbs glanced across at his friend.
'She is, Stan.'

'Right then, I'm off to bed. Oh, before I forget, Freddy's not been good today. Something about a woman in the park was all he said but he was in a foul temper when he got home, I know that much.

'Is he ... all right?'

'As much as Freddy can be. You're the only one he listens to, Charlie. I know it's hard but he's got to try and keep it together.'

'I'll … talk to him.'

'Aye, I know you will. But you're not always going to be around, Charlie. He's got to try and put it past him. Like you and the other lads.'

He was never going to be able to do that thought Hobbs. All of them were condemned to live with it, every single day.

5

What more could she do to preserve her little girl's memories before they inevitably dissolved forever? It was a question Mary wrestled with, day after day.

Now, lying in bed waiting for sleep to come, she was mulling it over yet again. Thirza's memories of her father were fading fast and Mary knew it was merely a matter of time before he was little more than a photograph on the mantelpiece.

The moment Thirza had forgotten the sound of his voice was inescapable, as was the memory of him playing with her, reading her stories, his laugh, his smell. Every lingering trace of James Moran was dissolving from her daughter's consciousness and there was nothing she could do to stop it.

Yet, Mary was determined to fight a battle she couldn't win, it was the stubbornness she got from her father, the unshakeable belief that if you kept persevering, remained steadfast, you could achieve anything.

It's why she and Thirza had spent the morning wrapped in thick coats walking through the woods where James used to take his little girl.

All the while Mary was constantly talking to her in the
hope it would trigger or rekindle her memories.

'He'd take you out early on Sunday mornings; in the
autumn you'd collect horse chestnuts, he said he always
knew the best places where the largest trees were,' Mary
said, watching Thirza poke leaves with a stick.

'And then you'd both come home laden and you'd sit by
the fire while he showed you the best way to string them
up ready to play, remember?'

'Hmm … I'm not sure … I think so,' Thirza replied, her
eyes scouring the undergrowth.

'I'd toast crumpets for you both and then the three of us
would count how many you'd collected.'

But those days had been more than three years ago
when Thirza was only five. Mary tried thinking of the
youngest memory she had as a girl, recalling a Christmas
when it snowed heavily. She'd been sledging on Christmas
Eve, her father making a makeshift sledge using pieces of
timber from his woodshed.

How old would she have been? Eight? Nine, even? She
couldn't remember exactly but she knew it wasn't five.

Staring up into the darkness, she sensed every new day
was a little easier than the last; yet each was another step
into the future, a future where only vague, hazy memories
of James remained.

She also knew how fragile Thirza would be, vulnerable
to the swathe of new memories she'd make for herself,
until they consumed every last trace of her father.

Yet, stubbornly Mary refused to yield to the inevitability
of time. Tomorrow she'd open the box, the one that
contained everything precious to her; the letters she and
James had written to each other in those heady,
intoxicating first months; the napkin from the restaurant

on the night he proposed; the small, battered tobacco tin full of French soil … he knew how much she'd always wanted to visit France, sending it home with his first letter.

Smiling to herself, she closed her eyes, allowing her own memories to flood in. There he was, standing tall at the door in his uniform, that devilish look on his face, the one that got her every, single time.

Then he was leaning forward, their faces almost touching; and she saw his eyes close as his mouth opened moments before they kissed. Even now she could recall the thrill of it, his taste, the excitement, the feelings it stirred.

But her mind moved on, exploring the contents of the box as she lay in the dark; the official letter … her thoughts always coming back to that damned letter.

'Dear Madam, I regret to have to inform you that a report has been received from the War Office to the effect that Lance Corporal James Moran of the 2nd Battalion, the Duke of Wellington's Regiment, was posted 'missing' on the twelfth of October 1916.

'The report that he is missing does not necessarily mean that he has been killed, as he may be a prisoner of war or temporarily separated from his regiment. If any further information is received it will be communicated to you.'

But there was nothing else.

Every day for almost a year she hadn't known whether to grieve or to hope. Sometimes she yearned to know, even if it meant her worst fears were true; anything to end the agony.

Yet, no news fed the hope that he might still be alive, cooped up in a prisoner of war camp somewhere, unable to write and let her know.

All that came to an end on the eighteenth of August, Nineteen Seventeen. She couldn't recall what he looked like, or even his last name; Reg something wasn't it? He'd stood suitably sombre, cap in hand, when she answered the door.

He was a friend of James; in the same battalion they were; they were sent to Geudecourt on the Somme; she remembered thinking what a ridiculous name it was; pretty bad up there it was, he'd said; they'd attacked and he'd seen James fall; caught by a machine gun which accounted for several others lads; it was quick and instant Reg reckoned; they'd marked where he fell but it was shelled to pieces days later.

And that was when Mary began grieving for the death of a man who had died more than a year before.

Telling Thirza had been the hardest thing she'd ever had to do. At first, she refused to believe it and even now, Mary harboured suspicions that her daughter still hoped it wasn't true; that one day James Moran would walk through the door.

She heard a thud in the darkness and the bedroom door swung open, quickly followed by Thirza scrambling into bed next to her, clutching her teddy. Coiling her small body around Mary, she was asleep in an instant.

Mary knew she'd come, just as she had every night since they'd heard about James. Her little girl felt safe and secure wrapped around her. As did she.

Kissing Thirza gently on the forehead, Mary snuggled up to her and allowed sleep to take her too.

6

Rain streaked down the glass in erratic lines and when the wind whipped, it sounded like hundreds of tiny pebbles slamming against the window.

Like the persistent rain there was now a dull, monotony to Solomon's life; optimism was missing from the grey, day to day routine which enveloped itself around him, crushing what little remained of his spirit.

Rubbing his socked feet together to keep them warm, his clothes reeked of fish and stale tobacco, the odours soaking into the walls and what little furniture there was.

An oblivious prisoner to a life devoid of vitality, hope or cheer, the lights Solomon extinguished in the minutes following Maud's death also snuffed out the optimism that had once defined his character.

There had been no conscious decision made, no vow to live a life of relative solitude consumed by grief; without knowing it, he simply succumbed to an acceptance that his life, as he once knew it, was now all but over.

Hours became days, weeks became months, yet Solomon no longer noticed time; not in the way he used to. He still went to work, slicing open fish for J.E. Wilson & Son, but the everyday banter with the others was gone.

Solomon withdrew into himself, going days without a meaningful conversation.

That Billy Draper had been bordering on civil since Maud passed was no consolation, nor something Solomon even noticed. He knew the other lads kept their distance, finding it too awkward to talk about death and grief.

But they expected time to heal as it did for most people, and the banter in the fish hall slowly returned; the crude jokes, the lewd comments about the Wilson girls, that men only aired in front of other men.

Wearing a nightshirt and wrapping himself inside a blanket that still smelled of Maud, Solomon clutched a mug of strong tea, his weathered hands clasped around it. In the fireplace a faint orange glow ebbed amidst the burnt coal as the embers died.

He considered throwing another shovel on to resurrect the flames but it was the early hours now and in a couple more he'd be leaving for work.

Instead, supping his tea in silence he lit another cigarette and waited, the noise of the rain strangely comforting. Sleep came in fits and starts. Some nights he dozed off within minutes of coming through the door, usually waking in the early hours famished.

Other times he couldn't sleep at all. No longer fighting it, he simply brewed up, sat in his chair and waited for the new day. This was one of those nights.

He hadn't ventured upstairs since Maud had gone. He'd been in the room just once, to close the open window and empty his drawers and wardrobe.

Ever since, the bedroom door had remained closed, the inside left untouched since the day she died. It never occurred to Solomon to go back in. He didn't need her scent, her clothes, her things, to remind him of Maud. He only had to close his eyes to recall every tiny detail.

That had been their room and it was the most natural thing in the world to shut the door on it forever now she was gone.

Downstairs was where he spent all his time, his clothes an untidy heap on one of the two faded armchairs he and Maud would spend their evenings sitting opposite each other, neither of them wanting for anything else.

On the floor in front of the fire was a makeshift bed that faced the door into a small larder kitchen. The back door led out to a yard, where a row of toilets for the terraced houses stood.

A glance at the clock and Solomon rose wearily, dressing in silence before shaving in a bowl of lukewarm water. Every scrape of the razor against the bristles on his face was as tiresome as the next.

He'd have preferred nothing more than to sink into the black abyss that consumed his every waking moment. Only the reluctant promise he'd made to Maud in her final days stopped him from doing so.

For breakfast he forced down a hunk of bread and leftover herring he'd wrapped in paper from last night's supper.

Bending down into the fireplace he retrieved a grey stone next to the coal scuttle, taking it into the kitchen.

For the next two minutes Solomon ran the blade of his fish knife up and down the sharpening stone before rinsing it in water, wrapping the knife in a cloth and slipping it in the pocket of his overcoat.

He trudged through puddles in a journey he'd repeated hundreds of times, the streets of Bromley murky and bereft of people. Solomon used to love this time of day, when it felt like he was the only person in the world.

Now, he dreaded it; the deserted streets a pathway to the purgatory he convinced himself he had to endure.

The nearer he got to the market place, the more it came alive, bustling with early morning traders. Delivery wagons pulled by horses competed for space with large motorised lorries as traders rushed to off-load boxes and crates, one or two bellowing instructions. Solomon stepped into the road to avoid having to stop as a flower seller busied himself arranging his stall.

The rain had stopped now and the smell of freshly baked bread drifting from Morley's bakery, took him briefly back to more contented times. He turned the corner where the fruit and veg sellers were unstacking their crates, the smell of fresh fish growing stronger.

Moments later he was putting his apron on, standing at a large wooden bench, stained with the remains of countless fish, despite its daily scrub down.

'Morning Sol,' Billy Draper shouted. 'I'm putting you on mackerel and herring again today. You're my quickest man and there's plenty of 'em coming in.'

Solomon nodded. So, what, if Draper was suddenly playing nice, it didn't change how he felt about him.

If anyone had known it's doubtful Solomon would have been able to explain why it was that hours later, following a tea break in which he sat listening to Sid Parker bemoaning his luck with women, that he made his decision.

But make it he did, slicing the fin and head off another gutted herring. Finishing for the day, Solomon meticulously washed down his bench, removed his bloodied apron and threw it into a basket with a pile of others.

After washing his knife and wrapping it in the same cloth, he put his coat back on and left. Only, he didn't go straight home. Instead, Solomon set off walking to nowhere in particular.

Home was now simply a roof over his head where he'd live out his final days. It held no comfort for him and he preferred to wander the streets for hours on end to avoid spending any more time alone than he had to.

When he finally returned, he reluctantly opened the door, hesitating before stepping inside. Because the house he'd shared with Maud for so many years was no longer a home. Instead, it was a tomb to a life that had long since disappeared and where emptiness reached out, dragging him inside.

7

'Jesus, Charlie … you weren't even there, you didn't see how she looked at me. And then having to listen to the patronising pity she came out with. There was a time when a frumpy cow like her would have been desperate for me to fuck her … she was no oil painting, Charlie,'

   'Freddy!' Hobbs had heard enough.

   The rebuke saw Freddy's shoulders slump and he leaned back against the window, looking down at the floor.

   They were in his room overlooking the street, Hobbs rising early to brew tea for his friend.

   He finally planned to tell him about his visits to Derwent Wood, knowing he had to tread carefully, that his friend was … erratic.

   But Freddy had other ideas, launching into a tirade about the woman in the park as soon as Hobbs knocked on his door, holding tea.

   Hobbs didn't want to do this now, he had his words prepared about Derwent Wood, his mask, why he hadn't said anything before. He didn't need any distractions and he certainly didn't need Freddy agitated.

'You need to calm down, Freddy,' Hobbs said, retrieving the notebook and pencil from his back pocket and scribbling quickly, tearing a sheet from the book and handing it to his friend.

'I'm not saying you were in the wrong but you can't always have a go at people.'

'Have a go? I was ready to throttle the prissy bitch, Charlie,' and he was off again, ranting.

As Freddy vented, his figure silhouetted against the light from the window, Hobbs knew he had no choice but to let him be; at least he was contained here, just the two them.

Finally, Freddy talked himself out, took a breath and was silent. Hobbs summoned up the effort to both speak and make himself understood.

'Listen to me, Freddy. People will … never, ever … understand.'

Freddy watched Hobbs intently, his beady eyes peering from his rubber-like, scarred face. The damage done by the burns had not only destroyed his features but erased any ability for facial expression.

There was no hair, no eyebrows and his ears were unrecognisable; what remained of his lips were puckered and scarred while his complexion was lifeless and dull.

There was silence as Hobbs scribbled again:

'They'll never know what it was like, Freddy. Never. And as for how we look? Well, it's the same … how can they possibly know?'

It was Hobbs' turn to watch Freddy now, as his friend scanned the notebook reading silently:

'There are going to be those who turn away so they don't have to confront it. Everyone wants to forget and move on. Except we can't. But we have to try … we owe that to all those who never came back.'

There was a heavy silence and Freddy turned to the window. When he ventured out he often wore a wig underneath his hat but here, Hobbs was staring at the back of his friend's crinkled bald head.

'Why do we?' Freddy asked, not bothering to turn round. 'We don't owe them a sodding thing, Charlie.'

Hobbs didn't reply.

'They're fucking dead, Charlie. We came back and we should be treated like Kings, messed up faces or not. Instead, they treat us like fucking freaks with not so much as a thank you. That's not what they promised us, Charlie and you know it!'

Hobbs sighed, he'd seen Freddy like this many times, knew it was an outlet, a valve to release the anger. Moments later his demeanour changed.

'I still see it you know, it won't go away; it's in there all the time,' and Freddy prodded the side of his head with a finger, all the time fiddling with his lighter.

Hobbs had asked him about it once, wondering why he carried it despite never seeing him smoke.

'It belonged to my dad,' was all Freddy would say.

He was still gazing out the window and Hobbs was surprised to hear him talk about *that* day.

'I felt invincible up there … nothing could touch me, Charlie … it was just me and the sky.'

Hobbs shuffled awkwardly, he didn't want to do this again.

'Come on, Freddy.'

But Freddy wasn't listening.

'I never saw him … to this day I don't know how I didn't see him, Charlie, I really don't. I just felt the sudden shake and then … and then the flames.'

There was a slight pause and Hobbs wondered if he'd done.

'You know, when they pulled me out … from the wreckage? They told me I kept trying to reach for my revolver. I'd have done it too, the pain was so bad I just wanted it to stop,' and his voice was breaking.

'Freddy, Freddy … they were dark days … but you've come a long way,' Hobbs said, hoping to placate his friend.

'I could feel it Charlie … could feel myself burning … my face on fire, the skin literally cooking … and the smell … the stench of burning flesh; it's still there now … yet I can't smell a fucking thing any more,' and a strange, forced laugh followed..

'Look at me … look at both of us. What sort of life is this, Charlie? A year ago I was flying aeroplanes … those incredible machines. I was fucking flying, Charlie! How many people in the world have ever done that?'

He didn't wait for an answer.

'And now? Now, I can't get even get a job cleaning other people's shit or sit on a park bench without scaring some silly cow.'

Hobbs was quiet. He wasn't trying to think of something to say, he was only half listening now; his mind was elsewhere.

Because Freddy's outburst was the trigger for his own descent back to a time and place he'd do anything to forget.

8

The imposing three-storey houses that dominated Beckenham Road, Bromley, all had a pointed gable with a dormer window at the top. Below, the bay windows on the ground and middle floors jutted outwards, giving the appearance of a row of square-jawed brick guardians.

Dressed in a grey coat and matching hat, with a handbag swinging in the crook of her arm, a squat, prim looking woman climbed the three steps up to the stone porch housing the door to number forty-one.

Using the brass knocker, she rapped loudly, smiling when she heard an excited young voice on the other side.

When Mary Moran opened the door, Thirza scurried downstairs, flinging her arms around her grandmother.

'Granny, Granny … I've missed you,' she squealed breathlessly.

'Oh, my beautiful Thirza, let me have a look at you. My, I think you must have grown again since I last saw you. You'll soon be taller than me, my dear.'

'Hello, Mother,' and a smiling Mary greeted Evelyn Barrett with a kiss on both cheeks and in that brief moment she caught a look of disappointment on her mother's face.

'Mary, you look tired.'

Thirza was pulling on her grandmother's arm, leading her into the house.

'Come and see what we've made, Granny, a jam sponge cake and I did most of it on my own didn't I, Mother?'

Over the next hour or so Thirza's giggles as she entertained her grandmother brought a smile to Mary's face and a warm feeling inside.

'She's a delight, Mary, she really is,' Evelyn said later, walking into the kitchen where Mary was preparing supper. 'I've left her upstairs playing.'

'Thanks, Mother. It's lovely to see her smiling and hear her laugh. She's still finding it so difficult.'

'She's strong, she always has been. It's always been difficult for the girl, what with, you know, how she is and everything.'

Mary hated that. She'd never allowed Thirza to think of herself as different. Her hare lip was part of who she was, her speech defect, the struggles she'd overcome so far in her short life. … there was nothing different or unusual about these for Thirza, because she'd never known life without them.

Mary loved her mother; she'd loved both her parents equally but following the death of her father, Sidney, more than a decade ago, and then the loss of James, she had grown ever closer to Evelyn.

It was why she tolerated her mother's sudden brusqueness and her somewhat insensitive comments, making allowances for a woman who had been widowed for so long.

But it made for some awkward moments, not least the time she introduced her to James. While she thought it a little glamorous that her fiancé had lived in America since he was a teenage boy, her mother was suspicious.

'How do you know he's going to stick around? And what if he wants you to move over there? I might never see you again,' Evelyn had said.

But James had won her over, just as Mary knew he would. Evelyn never did know that they had planned to move to the States. But then the damn war had come. And that had changed everything.

Now, looking across at her mother sitting in the kitchen, Mary dismissed her comment about Thirza.

'What is it, Mother? Something's wrong, I can always tell.'

Evelyn fidgeted slightly, embarrassed at her daughter's shrewdness.

'I don't like having to say this, Mary, but you've asked so I'm going to. You're not in mourning dress anymore. I find that surprising and … I have to say disappointing.'

Mary could scream. Peeling vegetables at the sink, she spun round, knife in one hand, a half peeled carrot in the other.

'Mother, it's been more than a year now. Two actually, when you think of when James was reported missing.'

'Eighteen months I wore mourning dress when your father passed away and not a day less,' her mother said curtly. 'Margaret Baines lost three of her boys. Her curtains remain drawn and she still wears a veil after more than two and a half years.'

'But I'm not Margaret Baines! Do you know what it's like, Mother? For both of us? Thirza and I? I grieve every single day for James, we both do. He was the love of my life and father to the most precious thing in my world.'

If Evelyn was shocked by her daughter's riposte she didn't show it.

'There are some days when I have no idea how I'm going to carry on without him, when I wake up and can't bear the thought of another day knowing he's gone.'

Mary was tearful now, wafting the knife in the air as she spoke, her voice breaking.

'But that little girl,' she said, pointing to the ceiling, 'deserves to be happy. Goodness knows she's had more than her fair share of pain for one so young. And I'm going to do everything I can to give her a normal, happy life. I want her to remember her father for as long as she can but I know that soon she'll have forgotten him completely. The thought of that breaks my heart. When James died, a part of me died too. So, I don't need to wear black, Mother, my heart will be forever broken.'

An awkward silence lingered, punctured only by Mary's sniffles and the sound of the knife scraping against the vegetables.

It was Evelyn who gave in first:

'Seems the whole country's grieving. The wretched war's changed everything. Have you heard from James' mother lately?'

'Yes, she still writes once a month,' Mary replied, regretting her outburst now. 'The letters are for Thirza mainly, she tells her about James's life as a boy living in America. Thirza loves reading about that.'

'No plans to come over and see you then? I'm surprised, I thought she might want to get to know her granddaughter now that her son has … well, you know.'

'Mother, please! Do you know how far away Boston is? It's not as if she and Mr Moran can just hop on a boat and pop over for a visit.'

'Why not? It's not as if they can't afford it. I just know if it'd been my son, I'd want to come.'

Mary wearily rubbed her brow and sighed.

'James's father is not in the best of health and wouldn't be up to the trip and it wouldn't do for her to travel alone. Anyway, we may go over there and see them … I think it would be good for Thirza.'

She didn't need to look up from the sink to picture the expression now on Evelyn's face.

'Go over there? To America? But when? How long for? Oh, Mary, I'm sorry if I've offended you, I miss him too, he was a lovely young man, God rest his soul. But you can't leave England … what would I do?'

Mary knew the reaction her comment would provoke but it didn't give her any pleasure seeing her mother's sudden vulnerability.

'Oh, Mother, nothing's definite. Mrs Moran suggested it in one of her letters, that's all. As I said, I think it would be good for Thirza. I want her to meet her father's family, to get to know them. But she's got a wonderful grandmother here who she adores. And she'll never want to be away from you for very long.'

Reaching out Evelyn squeezed her daughter's hand and more was said in the silence than could ever be spoken.

9

Ladling hot soup into four bowls, Patricia Donnelly carried them to the table on a tray before slicing thick hunks of bread from an oversized loaf.

'John Junior, Niall, come down here ... your supper's ready,' and her voice reverberated through the pokey, terraced house.

'Boys! Come on now ... don't let me ask again.'

Solomon smiled as his neighbour rolled her eyes at the stomps and thuds coming from above.

Seconds later, John and Niall Donnelly appeared at the bottom of the stairs.

At fourteen, John was the eldest, a few inches taller than his twelve-year-old brother. Both had their father's looks; red hair, pale complexion and freckles covering their faces, though Niall had his mother's eyes.

The two boys sat at the table, eager to tuck into their supper; but their mother had other ideas.

'Boys ... aren't we forgetting somet'ing?'

They shared a glance and it was a sheepish John who replied:

'Sorry, Mother. Hello, Mr Wheeler.'

'Good evening, boys. It's good to see you,' Solomon said softly.

'D'at's better,' Mrs Donnelly said, her hands clasped together, elbows resting on the table. Looking at her boys to make sure they followed suit, she closed her eyes, resting her chin on pointed fingers.

'For what we are about to receive, may the Lord God make us truly grateful.'

The four of them said Amen, the two boys waiting for the nod from their mother, the signal that they could begin eating.

'Fergus Finn's family don't say Grace no more. He says his mother won't hear of it,' John said casually, reaching for a slice of bread and ripping it in two.

'While you're under this roof, John Patrick Donnelly, you'll say your prayers and t'ank the good Lord for every day you're alive,' and his mother's eyes narrowed, glaring at her first born.

'Fergus says they've stopped going to church too ... all since his brother, you know, didn't come home and all,' John continued, unconcerned by his mother's reprimand.

Slamming a hand on the table, Mrs Donnelly's patience snapped.

'Enough, John Junior. Now ... I know Carmel Finn will forever grieve for the loss of her son, God rest his soul and I'm sure she's got good reasons for her actions ... but this family will never walk away from the word of God. Do you understand me?'

John's cheeks reddened and he stared into his soup bowl, idly stirring with his spoon.

'I said do you understand me, John Donnelly?'

'Yes, Mother.'

'Good, now eat your supper and let's not hear another word about it. Mr Wheeler doesn't wanna hear talk like 'dat at the dinner table.'

Solomon thought it best to say nothing, though he agreed with Carmel Finn. He couldn't worship or even believe in a God that had stood by while the love of his life crumbled and wasted away, her remaining days spent racked in pain.

He admired his neighbour's faith; maybe she needed it to cope, bringing up her two boys alone. Or more probably she simply believed in the afterlife. He wasn't sure what to believe any more. If he had faith, and he used to, it was snuffed out little by little in the weeks and months watching Maud suffer.

He wondered why Pat's faith hadn't faltered; she hadn't had it easy. All Solomon knew of John Donnelly senior was what his wife had told Maud during their chats hanging out washing in the yard.

A hulk of a man, John Donnelly's size and strength had meant he never had trouble finding work as a labourer. But as Patricia Donnelly confided in Maud, as good a worker as he was, John liked the taste of Irish whisky.

Maybe that's what caused him to slip and his lose his footing, way up on the roof of a house he was helping to build. Whatever, it didn't matter once doctors confirmed the big Irishman wouldn't be labouring again, not with a permanent limp and a useless left arm.

According to Maud, Mrs Donnelly had harboured dreams of opening a family grocery store thanks to a small pay out from her husband's sympathetic employer.

But the dream died with John's drinking, every penny gone on whisky as the big man drank himself numb to forget he was a cripple.

Sometime later John Donnelly walked away. Some say he took a boat to Canada and lives there now, others that he returned to Ireland.

Solomon pitied the woman who doted on her sons but, like him, would probably now never find love or companionship again.

Finishing their supper, the two boys thanked their mother, cleared the table without being asked and were given her blessing to go off and play.

Pouring tea from a pot, she asked Solomon:

'So, how have you been, Mr Wheeler? I've not seen much of you these last few weeks.'

Solomon sipped his tea. She had a good heart and her affection for both him and Maud could never be mistaken for being nosey.

'I do wish you'd call me Solomon, Pat,' and he saw her cheeks redden. 'I've been all right … working mainly.'

He wondered whether she sensed his awkwardness but he knew she wouldn't dare say anything.

'I'm … I'm going away, Pat, I've been thinking about it for a while now,' and he shuffled uneasily in his chair.

'Oh, right … where, where are you off to, if you don't mind me asking an' all?'

Solomon's eyes went down to his mug; he couldn't help but wonder if she already knew or maybe suspected.

'Oh, you know … here and there, Pat. I just think it's time for me to get away … you know, what with Maud.'

'I don't want to pry Mr Wheeler, it's not my place. But I've always t'ought a lot of you … and Maud. And I know she'd want me to make sure you were all right.'

He didn't reply. Instead, setting his mug down, Solomon rose slowly, his knees creaking.

'You're a good woman, Patricia. But I need to go ... the house ... there ... there are too many memories.'

'Do you know how long you will be gone?'

'I ... I don't know yet,' he lied.

Halfway to the door and he already regretted saying anything. It was suddenly uncomfortable between them and he wished he'd kept quiet.

'Maud's things ... I've ... I've not been through them yet. I was wondering if you ...'

'Oh, of course I will. Like I said, anyt'ing you need me to do, you only have to ask.'

'Thanks, Pat. There are some ... some bits of jewellery. I'd like you to have them ... I know Maud would want that too.'

She clearly wasn't expecting that and he jumped in again before she could decline.

'Please, Pat ... I've got no use for them. I'd much rather a friend have them ... please?'

His pleading eyes had the desired effect and he saw her eyes watering.

'T'ank you, Mr Wheeler. I'm honoured ... it means a lot. When are you leaving?'

'I'll be gone tomorrow.'

'So soon? Oh, please take care of yourself, Mr Wheeler and don't stay away too long now, you hear me?'

'Goodbye, Pat. And thanks again for supper.'

He spent the rest of his evening going over things one final time, making sure all was ready, until only thing remained.

Sitting at his table, Solomon began writing .... '*To whom it may concern, this is the last will and testament of Solomon Jacob Wheeler.*'

10

Hobbs was at the bedroom window, waiting for Freddy to emerge in the street below. How had it come to this? More raised voices downstairs, a slam of the door and then he saw him.

It was clear Freddy was in a hurry, but from Hobbs' vantage point high above, he could see his friend had nowhere in mind to go. He just needed to get away.

Down in the street, Freddy turned and Hobbs watched him stumble as he glared up at his bedroom window.

Hobbs beckoned him to return with a wave of his hand but Freddy bent down, picked up a pebble and hurled it up at the window.

The pebble cracked against the pane, causing Hobbs to flinch. Luckily, the glass held but when Hobbs looked out he saw Freddy striding away. Seconds later he was gone.

'Charlie, you bloody idiot.'

His conversation with Freddy had gone horribly wrong. It didn't help that his own dark memories had returned, shutting out anything his friend was saying.

By the time he'd snapped back to the present, Freddy was sitting on the floor, clutching his knees, sobbing uncontrollably.

'Hey, Freddy. Come on now, pal,' Hobbs had said softly.

But Freddy was inconsolable, his disfigured face crumpled in pain, saliva dribbling from his mouth as snot ran from what was left of his nose.

'It's going to be ok, Freddy. I promise it is.'

Smearing a hand across his mouth, Freddy had peered at Hobbs through fearful eyes.

'Who wants to look at something like me, Charlie?'

Kneeling beside him, Hobbs put an arm around his friend's slumped shoulders.

'I can't … live like this anymore. I … I hate the feel of my own face, Charlie. I can't bear to touch it. How can anyone live like this?' and he'd looked at Hobbs, searching for an answer.

'There's … always hope, Freddy.'

As Freddy sat head in hands, Hobbs had stood up and written again in his notebook, thrusting it under Freddy's nose.

'There are things out there … things they can do. Not now maybe, but in a few years, there'll be other treatments, you're not alone.'

'No, Charlie … there's no hope … for either of us. We can't be fixed. Our lives are over …, we're fucked, pal. And we're going to die alone.'

It was that final, heartbreaking comment which prompted Hobbs to do what he would later regret for months.

He scrawled another message:

'We're not alone, Freddy … I'll prove to you there are people who care and they are doing remarkable things.'

Returning to his own room, Hobbs had reached for the cloth bag and removed his mask. He stood facing the small oval mirror on the wall next to his door, putting it on, adjusting the position until he was satisfied.

And then he walked back into Freddy's room, and stood there, looking at his friend.

That was thirty minutes ago. Now he was sitting downstairs with Stan and it was the old soldier trying to make *him* feel better.

'Look, Charlie, it was a shock for the boy that's all. You can't blame yourself, he's troubled. If you ask me he was never going to take it well.'

'He's … my friend Stan. I should … have told him … sooner.'

'Maybe that's why you didn't tell him. Look, he just needs to let off some steam, he'll come back when he's calmed down … and hungry. You've got your own life to live, Charlie. You haven't gone through these past few months doing what you've done for nothing.'

Stan paused, waiting for Hobbs to say something. When he didn't, he tried again.

'You ought to be going off and finding that gal of yours and then trying to make a new life for yourself.'

But Hobbs was only half listening. He was picturing the look of utter betrayal that appeared on Freddy's face.

Stan had another go:

'Freddy's going to have to make the best of things, just like the other lads here are trying to do. They've all got their troubles, Charlie and they're doing their best to put the past behind them.'

Hobbs knew the old soldier was right, but it didn't make him feel any better. Finally, he mumbled: 'Neither of us have got any family, Stan. Freddy and me … we've become like brothers these past few months. I just want to help him but I don't know how.'

He could feel the warmth of his breath around his face and removed the mask, laying it down carefully on the table.

'We're just going to have to be there for the boy, that's all we can do,' Stan replied, as Hobbs stared at the lifelike tin face looking up at him.

11

Thirza toyed with the bow on the front of her school dress, hoping her teacher would pick her out.

She used to be nervous speaking out loud but thanks to the help of Miss Hesketh, it was no longer a worry.

Her classmates had long gotten used to her appearance and speech defect and, though one or two of the boys still took the mickey occasionally, she was well schooled in the art of ignoring insults.

She had her mother to thank for that; and Miss Hesketh. Her teacher was a slim, attractive woman whose delicate features hid a steely resolve that ensured she ran her classroom fairly, but firmly.

Thirza suspected she had a soft spot for her, that much was obvious from the time she had spent helping with her speech.

Dropping her fountain pen in a hole next to the ink pot on her desk, Miss Hesketh stood to address her class.

'Good morning, children. Today, we will continue our study of verbs and their use thereof. You will remember I told you yesterday how important verbs are and that we cannot form sentences without them.'

Thirza listened intently, watching her teacher scribble on the blackboard.

Miss Hesketh then asked her class to arrange the words into a grammatical sentence.

'When you have finished, you will then write down ten different verbs, using their base form or either past or present tense, putting these into sentences.'

Thirza loved school and learning. She'd always been curious, wondering about the world she lived in, how things worked. Why didn't a boat sink? What made a balloon fly? Why did her tummy feel funny when she thought about her dad? Instead of bedtime stories she often just asked her mother questions, one after the other, and always a 'last one, Mummy, I promise' when it was time to go to sleep.

Fifteen minutes later she was the first to finish the task and sat with a contented smile on her face, hoping to catch her teacher's eye. Desperate to be picked out, she sat upright, willing her name to be called.

'When it rains I like to *jump* over puddles,' said a boy's voice.

'Excellent, Daniel.'

'Now, let's see how the rest of you have got on with coming up with your own verbs and sentences.'

Glancing around the room, her eyes fixed upon a blonde haired girl at the front of the class.

'Muriel, please share one of yours.'

The girl's cheeks glowed crimson, a yellow ribbon in her tousled hair. Reading from her workbook she'd hardly said a word before an irritated Miss Hesketh cut her off.

'Muriel, you must speak up, we can't hear you. Now, project your voice.'

With the entire class staring, Muriel's face reddened further. Then, raising her head she said aloud:

'My Dad *died* in the war.'

Thirza gasped, as did others, and their teacher was caught off guard.

'Erm … yes, thank you, Muriel, that is … erm, a correct use of a verb. Now, who wants to,' … but she was interrupted, this time by a boy holding an arm aloft:

'Excuse me, Miss.'

'Yes Michael? What is it?'

'My Dad died in the war too.'

'So did mine,' chirped a small, skinny girl with plaits in her hair.

Suddenly, she was looking at half a dozen hands in the air.

'Miss Hesketh, my older brother John didn't die but his best pal William Morris did. John's really different now,' said another boy.

She wasn't overly strict but Grace Hesketh knew how to run a disciplined classroom. She would never normally tolerate pupils speaking out unless invited to do so but this required delicacy. She wouldn't chastise them.

'Children, children, settle down,' and she lifted her hands, held them open in front of the class, before lowering them to illustrate her point.

'So many brave men died in the Great War. It was ghastly; but your fathers and brothers, cousins, uncles and friends … they died for you, for all of us, for their King and their country. We should be very proud of them,' she added, hoping that would be enough to bring them back to verbs and grammar. Yet, more hands went up.

'Yes, Michael. What is it?'

'They told my mum that my dad was missing. It was only months later they said he'd died. But where did he go? And how do they know he's dead if they don't know where he is?' he asked puzzled.

'Michael ... children, listen to me. There is a lot about the war that is difficult for you to understand, for all of us to understand,' and this time she spoke in a softer, gentler tone.

'But how do they know he died if he went missing, Miss?'

'I know it must be terribly hard for those of you who have lost loved ones but ... I'm afraid I don't have all the answers.'

Thirza wanted to speak out too, she had questions, lots of questions. Maybe Miss Hesketh could answer them. But she saw the look on her teacher's face; it was one she'd seen so many times in her mother's eyes.

After school, she made a beeline for Michael Gregory, hurrying to catch up, tapping him on the shoulder.

'My ... my father went missing too. They didn't tell my mother anything else. Then one day she told me he'd died.'

For a moment the boy said nothing, Thirza saw him looking at her lip. She used to hate her lip, how it lifted upwards, it was horrible. She used to pray every night for her lip to look like everyone else's the next morning. But it never did and now she couldn't even remember the prayer.

Michael Gregory finally spoke, running a hand through the fringe of his untidy, brown hair.

'Yeh, mine too.'

She found herself walking alongside him until he suddenly stopped.

'You know what? I don't believe it. There's no way that many people simply go missing. I reckon my dad's still alive … and yours probably, too.'

Thirza stared with wide eyes, her mouth open.

'You … you really think so?'

'Yeh I do. I reckon my dad was probably on some secret mission or something. Or maybe he's in hiding somewhere and doesn't realise the war's over. Anyway, whatever the reason he'll come home one day, I know he will.'

'Do you … do you think my father will too?'

'What? Oh, yeh, maybe. All I know is my dad wouldn't simply disappear. And I bet yours wouldn't too. Right, see you tomorrow, I've got to go,' and with a skip he set off running down the road leaving Thirza to believe that maybe her father wasn't dead after all.

12

Wearing his only suit, Solomon downed the last of his second pint before returning to the bar with an empty glass. It was Friday night and the Railway Inn was packed as people drank to mark the end of the working week.

Waiting to be served before catching the landlord's eye, he returned to the table near the window as a passing train roared by, rattling the glasses and bottles stacked behind the bar.

A glance up at the clock, it was nine forty. In less than an hour the overnight Royal Mail express would pass by. But this time Solomon wouldn't be inside to hear it shaking the windows.

There was time for at least two more drinks. He'd made his decision days ago and nothing would change that now. But he couldn't do it sober.

As he drank he took out a small photograph of Maud which he'd tucked inside a plain white envelope. Next to it was a folded piece of paper on which he'd written his name, address and where to find his will.

He gazed at Maud, allowing the memories to flood in and Solomon sat contented, reliving his life with the woman he loved. The noise from the pub dissolved in a haze as he tumbled headfirst into a memory where Maud was laughing as he playfully chased her through a wood, the ground profuse with bluebells.

And then they were strolling across Southend Pier, was there ever a more beautiful day? Had he ever felt happier than at that very moment? When she'd told his younger self she was falling in love with him?

The cocktail of memories and alcohol put a smile on his face and Solomon appeared just another happy drinker.

In his haze he couldn't hear anyone else, he was oblivious to the rowdy cheers which erupted when a barmaid dropped a tray of glasses and he didn't see the landlord brush past him carrying a pint of beer to a small table in the corner, close to the back door.

****

'There you go lad, that'll be fifep'nce.'

Freddy Lucas fumbled in his trouser pocket, spilling a pile of coins out on to the table. Using his finger to slide five pennies into his hand he handed them to the landlord, picked up his beer and grunted 'cheers' under his breath.

'That's four you've had now, lad. Best make that the last one, eh?'

Freddy's eyes met the landlord's.

'And what if I don't want it to be my last one.'

Wiping his hands on a small towel tucked into his belt, the landlord moved closer and leaned in.

What was left of his hair was now swept back with grease, his face and forehead glistening with sweat. Freddy thought he could smell the man's body odour, though he knew that it was impossible, his sense of smell was nothing but a memory.

'Look, lad, you should just be thankful I let you drink in here at all.

There was a menace to his voice as he whispered: 'There's many a landlord who wouldn't let you through the fucking door looking like you do. Now, you can't help that … and yeh, I know you've done your bit. 'But,' and now he leaned in even closer, making sure Freddy would hear him above the noise.

'So, have thousands of others. Now, I suggest you finish your pint like a good lad and then piss off. Is that clear enough for you?'

Freddy said nothing as the landlord walked away but felt for his lighter, repeatedly flicking the flint beneath the table and imagining the man's face as it burned.

'Wanker,' he muttered to himself, before his profanity triggered a memory and this time Freddy was far away, back in a time and place when the entire world was aflame.

The estaminet was only half full and the mood amongst the punters was subdued. It hadn't taken long for news of the failed French offensive to reach the town and now everyone wore the same weary, resigned expression.

'So, what do you think'll happen now, Johnny?' Freddy asked quietly, the two airmen drinking at a table.

Johnny Burke emptied his glass with one long gulp before lifting the bottle and refilling it with cheap wine.

'Now? Well, until the Americans get here we're on our own, Freddy. This lot are finished,' he said, deliberately raising his voice knowing full well everyone would hear.

'Keep your voice down, Johnny, this place is full of Frenchies!' whispered Freddy nervously.

'I'm only telling it like it is, pal. Look, Freddy,' and his voice rose again, the locals now looking at him.

'This lot couldn't fight their way out of a paper bag. Why do you think they needed our help in the first place?' Freddy had no intention of replying and Burke didn't wait for him.

'Because the much vaunted French Army isn't much cop that's why.'

He wasn't looking at Freddy now; instead he was addressing the faces of the dozen or so middle-aged men and women staring at him inside the pokey bar. Sitting with his back to the door, he didn't hear it open or see the two French Pouli step inside.

'Your famous élan has got you nowhere. You'd be beaten already if it wasn't for us. And now we'll have to kick the Hun out for you. Well, you'd better be bloody grateful,' he said, wagging a finger to make his point before clicking his fingers to beckon the barmaid.

'Mam'selle … another bottle.'

Burke had a smirk on his face as he peered into his glass but the expression changed when he saw Freddy looking ashen.

'You have a lot to say, Englishman.'

Spinning round, the two French soldiers loomed large. Their long, sky blue field coats were caked in mud, their bearded faces dusted with the white chalk of the trenches.

If Freddy didn't know any different he'd have sworn they had both come straight out of the front line and into the bar.

The sight of two grizzled infantrymen standing over him unnerved Burke who recoiled back in his seat as the larger of the two men stepped closer.

'I know what you are. You think you are brave flying around the sky in your strange machine huh?' and he spat the words out in a heavy accent.

'Shooting at the Boche from afar is one thing … but I've killed dozens of those pigs up close,' and he drew his bayonet from the scabbard hanging on his belt.

He brought the blade up close to Burke's face: 'I've seen their faces and felt their last breath after thrusting this into the chests of those dirty Boche pigs. Do you know what they do? What they say when they're dying?'

Burke was pale, too stunned or afraid to speak. Freddy said nothing.

'They cry out for their mothers … 'Mutter, Mutter' they say,' and he mimicked a German accent, and his companion, who hadn't uttered a word, laughed.

'That's right, Englishman … they squeal like the pigs they are. They are nothing special the Boche … they bleed like you and I. You see this?' and he reached into his pack retrieving a small leather pouch, stained heavily with a dark, reddish brown.

With bayonet still in hand, he fumbled to undo the clasp.

'I took this from a young German officer when I ended his life. The last thing he ever saw was my face as I cut the pig open.'

There were murmurs of support from the others in the bar as he told his story.

'He was wearing this around his neck,' he said, opening the pouch, reaching inside with blackened, gnarled fingers.

'I bet he wore it for luck … pas un porte-bonheur pour ce cochon huh?' and there was a ripple of laughter in the bar.

Burke and Freddy stared as he held a lock of blonde hair in his fingers.

'From his girl,' the soldier said mockingly.

'The little slut probably doesn't even know he's dead yet. Well, he's in the clay now … another dead Boche. And now I'll wear this. And that whore of a pig will never know,' he said laughing.

And then his face changed again and he was so close now that Burke could smell his stale breath.

'France is not finished. France will never be finished. Not until every last one of those dirty, German pigs has been made to pay. Understand that you merde,' and he glared into Burke's eyes with a fury that drained the colour from the Englishman's face.

'Vin rouge pour mon camarade et moi,' he said loudly, and the French soldiers sneered at Burke and Freddy before taking a seat at the bar.

'You all right, Johnny?' Freddy asked quietly.

But Burke was seething.

'Let's go,' he said, glancing at the backs of the two French soldiers now deep in conversation with the locals.

'Wanker,' he hissed under his breath, as the pair of them got up and left.

Rising unsteadily, Freddy glared at the landlord who was too busy serving to notice. About to walk out the rear entrance of the Railway Inn, he turned and deliberately pushed his way through the crowded pub towards the front.

He relished the looks on their faces as they glimpsed his disfigured face and he pictured them all dying horribly, trapped inside a burning building, their terrified faces at the window as a ferocious blaze raged.

Stepping out into the fresh air, the sign above the pub squeaked and swayed in the chill breeze.

Looking up Freddy saw stars and a crescent moon. The bridge that crossed the railway line was in silhouette and as he headed towards it he thought of the times he'd played there as a boy, dropping sticks on to passing trains from the railway bridge near home.

13

Half an hour later, Solomon pushed open the same doors of the pub, stumbling on the steps outside, almost losing his balance.

He'd never been a big drinker and now, after five pints of ale, he was unsteady on his feet, heading towards the lights of Bromley Station. There were no more passenger trains tonight, which meant the surrounding streets were reassuringly quiet. The mail train was still to come but Solomon knew it didn't stop on its route through.

He shivered wondering what speed the train would be doing, trying not to think about it. All he hoped was it would be going fast enough that he wouldn't feel anything.

Recalling other options he'd briefly considered, Solomon smiled, remembering how he'd ruled out water straight away. Long enough to be excruciating he decided.

If he'd had a gun he could have shot himself but even that had its drawbacks. He'd never fired a gun in his life and he feared doing it wrong, leaving himself severely wounded but not dead.

No, he needed it to be immediate and this was the best way to end his life. He'd dreamed about it last night;

watching from afar, hovering high above, seeing himself stand in the middle of the track.

And then he'd felt the impact as the train smashed into him, time slowing to a crawl as his body shattered into a thousand pieces.

The recollection caused him to shudder and he pulled his collar up higher as he entered the final few minutes of his life.

Earlier he'd finalised his will, leaving everything he owned – and there wasn't much of it – to Patricia and her boys.

The wooden fence separating the railway line from the pavement came to an end, replaced by iron steps leading up to a footbridge that crossed the track.

Pausing to catch his breath, Solomon gripped the railing to steady himself. And then he climbed, ignoring the pain in his knees, a hollow, deathly clanging sound accompanying every step, the stairs a tangible metaphor for an ascent to oblivion.

'I won't be long now, my dearest,' he said out loud, and the need to hear himself was crucial if his body was going to submit to this.

'I'm coming, Maud.'

The walk to the middle of the bridge was a reticent one. Solomon's heart raced and he wondered if his body could somehow sense the mortal danger his brain had decided upon.

The bridge was uncovered but its two sides had iron girders crisscrossing lattice style. It's why Solomon had chosen it because he knew, at his age, that he could use the gaps as footholds to climb up and over.

Turning his back on the station he faced the direction the train would be coming. It wouldn't be long now. His hands were already numb with cold as he clasped the freezing metal and he wished he'd worn gloves before telling himself how ridiculous that was.

Another step up and he paused, wondering whether to climb all the way over and stand precariously on the ledge, or wait until he could hear the sound of the train. He decided on the former but changed his mind again, swinging his leg over, sitting astride the long girder which ran the length of the structure.

And now suddenly he felt foolish, sitting on top of a bridge in the black of night and Solomon hoped no one would spot him.

'Careful, Sol,' he told himself, smiling at the absurdity of his remark.

Peering into the darkness he could just about make out the track which weaved its way into the blackness beyond. Nothing stirred, there was hardly a sound.

The more he stared the more his eyes adjusted to the dark and now Solomon could make out clumps of trees in the distance, a small building trackside.

His eyes followed the line as it got nearer to the bridge and he found himself trying to count the sleepers. And then something made him stop. His eyes darted back. What was that? A shape … something moving up ahead.

Squinting, he leaned forward, clutching on to the bridge to remain still. He must be mistaken, there was nothing … wait! There! He saw it again.

There was something out there. No, there was *someone* out there; the outline of a man. What was he doing? For a moment, Solomon feared he'd been spotted and his own plan ruined, and he lowered himself, hugging the bridge.

He looked again to make sure he wasn't seen; surely they'd be heading this way if he had? Solomon's eyes fixed on the figure, trying to work out what it was the man could be doing.

And then the realisation dawned.

'Oh no ... oh, God no.'

His mouth fell open as the stranger, cloaked in darkness, knelt down in the middle of the track, head bowed. Solomon was angry, this was his time to die. It was of his choosing and he was incredulous that someone else planned to do the same thing at the very same time and place.

But then everything changed because in the distance he heard the rumble of a train. And that's when the humanity in Solomon seized control.

'Hey! You there,' he shouted. No reply.

Clambering awkwardly back on to the middle of the bridge, he hurried across and down the steps to the other side of the track. The train was getting closer, he could see lights now, looming nearer.

Adrenaline surged through his body, its effect sobering him up as Solomon ran along the grass verge beside the track.

'Hey! Hey you!' he panted breathlessly. But his voice was drowned out by the roar from the train.

Increasing his pace, he stumbled and fell, his face hitting the soft grass. Scrambling to his feet, wiping mud from his eyes, he spat soil from his mouth.

The light from the train appeared round a bend, shining down the track, illuminating the man who was now kneeling with his arms outstretched. There was no use shouting now, he was too out of breath anyway. Solomon kept running.

It never occurred to him to simply stop and stand in the middle of the line, awaiting the finality he had so meticulously planned.

Instead, he strained every sinew to reach whoever it was calmly waiting for death to come. Closer and closer now; he could see the man was wearing an overcoat. The uneven grass verge was slowing him down and he moved onto the track, running towards the oncoming train.

Maybe he would die tonight after all. But for reasons he could never explain, he couldn't let that happen.

The lights from the locomotive were dazzling and he felt the air rushing past amid a deafening roar.

There was no time to pause, to stop or to speak. At the final moment Solomon hurled himself forward, smashing into the stranger from behind, the impact sending them both sprawling into shrubbery at the side of the track as the train hurtled by.

14

Solomon spat out more grass and soil, gingerly lifting himself to his hands and knees. The noise from the train faded and he could hear groans in the nearby gloom.

'Hey … can you … can you hear me?'

He crawled on all fours towards the murmurs, groping around in the dark until his hand touched a leg; it moved.

Through the blackness he saw the man's body, moving closer, his hands pawing the wet grass.

Peering down, even in the darkness, he noticed something different about the stranger's face.

Freddy writhed in agony, clutching his right side. He felt a hand on his leg, aware of someone up close.

'You've broken … my fucking … ribs!' he gasped through gritted teeth.

'I'm … I'm sorry. I … I was trying to … I mean, I couldn't let you do that.'

'What, fucking … business … is it of YOURS?' Freddy yelled, struggling to sit up before falling back on the grass.

'Hey, try and keep still … I'll go and fetch help.'

'No! no help.'

'But you're in pain, you need medical attention,' and Solomon watched incredulous as Freddy, groaning in agony, started crawling away.

'What are you? … What are you doing? You need help … please, let me help you?'

Solomon saw Freddy drag his injured body across the ground. He only got a few yards before slumping face down into the dirt.

'Please … I can help you. At least let me help you get home.'

'I don't … need your help,' Freddy snapped, still inching himself forward, clutching his side.

'Wait. Look, I don't know you. And I have no idea why you want to end your life … but I understand. Truly I do.'

Freddy lifted his head and in the gloom Solomon saw part of his disfigured face.

'You had … no right … no fucking right. Do you hear me? Now, fuck off and leave me alone,' he said, hauling himself to his feet.

'I'm sorry but I saw you, when I was perched on the ledge of the footbridge. I was … I was waiting to leap off into the path of the same train.'

There was a yawning silence.

'You? … You were going to kill yourself?'

Solomon found himself smiling.

'Yes … yes I was. I had it all planned. My affairs were in order and I was going to be together again with my Maud, God rest her soul. Do you know how many times I've come down here and watched the overnight mail train roar past?'

Freddy said nothing.

'Four. Four times ... and I haven't seen hide nor hair of anyone or anything. And then ... when I choose my time, you appear.'

'I didn't know you had to book a slot to top yourself,' Freddy sniffed. 'Is that why you stopped me? Didn't want me muscling in on your death ride?'

'What? No ... no, not at all. I stopped you because ... well, because I couldn't stand by and watch you end your life. Why do you think I chose somewhere so quiet for myself? Because I didn't want anybody doing the same for me.'

'What? So, you didn't want anybody stopping you, yet you had no qualms about stopping me from doing what I wanted?'

'Committing suicide isn't something you want to do.'

'You're kidding me, right?' And Freddy was laughing. 'This coming from a bloke perched on a bridge ready to end it all. What the fuck do you know about me? You haven't got a clue ... you have no idea what my life's like. Why don't you leave me the fuck alone? Go and kill yourself old man ... maybe I'll see you on the other side, wherever that is.'

He turned and hobbled away, still clutching his side.

'Look, wait. Are you hungry? I'm famished,' Solomon said. 'Didn't think I'd be eating again see. Best fish 'n' chips in Bromley are just around that corner. If we're going to have a last supper, let's at least eat together. I owe you that much.'

His outstretched arm leaning against a tree, Freddy looked at the old man, weighing him up.

'You wouldn't want to be seen with me, not if you knew ... if you saw me, my face I mean.'

Solomon saw an opening and came closer.

'I'm an old man, with few friends. Appearances aren't important to me, chum.'

Freddy wondered why he called him that. They weren't pals, they'd never met.

'The best you say?'

'You'll never have better.'

'I guess I could eat something.'

'Solomon, my name's Solomon Wheeler.'

'Freddy ... Freddy Lucas.'

Ten minutes later the two men were sitting on a bench under a gaslight, eating fish and chips out of paper, the steam rising in the cold air.

'So, am I right?' Solomon asked, holding a piece of battered fish in his greasy fingers.

'Aye, they are ... pretty good,' Freddy said, wincing through every mouthful on account of his aching ribs.

'Look, Freddy, you need to get yourself looked at.'

'Cracked ribs heal on their own.'

Stuffing a chip into his mouth, the vinegar catching the back of his throat, Solomon added:

'A whisky might help. There's half a bottle at the back of my sideboard. Maud and I would always have a tipple at New Year ... her dad was a Scotsman you see.'

He knew the young man was considering the offer.

'Come to think of it I could do with a glass myself; my neck's right playing up. What do you say, Freddy?'

'If you think you're going to change my mind you're mistaken. This changes nothing.'

Solomon was thinking of something else to say when Freddy turned to him and said:

'But I'll have that drink.'

15

Hobbs knew Stan was right; Freddy was a big boy, he could look after himself. But still, there was that nagging thought that something was wrong this time. Where was he? He hadn't returned to the house and two hours walking the streets looking for him had led nowhere.

'He's big enough to look after himself, Charlie,' Stan had said, exasperated. 'You're letting him hold you back.'

Hobbs was riled by that.

'No, Freddy is my friend and I refuse to give up on him.'

But again, he knew the old soldier was right.

Stan continued: 'You've been given a second chance, Charlie. And if that thing,' he said, pointing to Hobbs' tin face, 'helps you do that, then all the better. Now, you get out of here and start living your life. You've made her wait long enough, lad.'

Hobbs' destroyed features had long lost the ability to smile properly but behind his mask, what were left of the nerves in his face tried to.

Then his thoughts turned to her; what would she say? What would he say? He'd gone over it in his head so many times, yet the carefully rehearsed explanation always faltered at the same point ... his face.

How on Earth could he ever show her? It was the reason he'd had the mask made. He knew that if they were to ever be together - and he wanted that more than anything - then at some point Grace was going to have to see him without it on.

'Well? Are you going or what?'

'What? Err ... yes, yes I am, Stan.'

'Good lad. Like I said, don't worry about Freddy. When he decides to drag himself back here, I'll keep an eye on him.'

Scribbling in the notebook that was now such an everyday part of his life, Hobbs showed the open page to Stan.

'I know I don't look it but I'm smiling right now ... or trying to anyway.'

Half an hour later Hobbs was walking along Bromley High Street, heading for the station, a stiff wintry breeze blowing through him, whistling around the metal covering his face.

It still astonished him, the lack of stares from people who would have gawped in fascination or turned away in disgust if he hadn't been wearing it; though he still felt acutely self-conscious.

Peering through the tinted lens covering his one good eye, Hobbs scoured the faces of passers-by, convincing himself they were looking at him. But all they saw was a man in dark glasses; no one seemed to have spotted the peculiarities of his face.

His real problem was talking. At first, he'd tried turning his head, pretending to look at something else lest they would notice his face remaining perfectly still when he spoke.

The speech impediment though, was impossible to hide. He knew most people thought of him as 'feeble minded' and it didn't seem to matter that he always wore his silver war badge to show he was a disabled veteran.

It's why his notebook was so important; that and a small card he would show, on which Hobbs had written: *'I have difficulty speaking. Please be patient.'*

He was relieved to see Bromley railway station quieter than usual. As a boy he used to love trains. Now they triggered dark reminders of rumbling through the French countryside, insufferably packed with men, united in fear of their dreaded destination.

Climbing aboard the London-bound service, he looked for an empty compartment and was relieved to find one in the rear carriage of the train. He hadn't been to the city properly since the war. But if he was going to see Grace, like Stan said, he'd better look the part.

How long had it been since he bought a new suit? He had no idea; but Stan told him where to go and as steam enveloped the platform, Hobbs visibly relaxed as the train pulled away.

It hadn't even left the station when the carriage door slid open and a breathless man clutching a folded copy of the Daily Express, his overcoat under his arm, sat opposite.

'That was close. For a minute there I thought I was going to miss it,' he said, breathing heavily and fiddling with the brim of his hat resting on his lap.

Hobbs detested the enforced captivity of a railway carriage, dreading the very idea of being up close to strangers.

'I've got a sweat on now. I haven't run like that since I was in France,' and the stranger dabbed his brow with a handkerchief.

Hobbs rested a hand against the side of his face, surreptitiously covering his mouth.

'Where were you posted? Your silver badge ... I hope you don't mind me asking.'

Hobbs was sweating now. His silver badge was usually enough to prevent awkward conversation from strangers who didn't want to talk about the war. His instinct was to get up and change seats but inside the moving compartment he was trapped. The anxiety came, his heart pounding.

'Read your sodding paper, just leave me be.'

'Don't want to talk about it? No problem, pal ... I'm just making conversation.'

Hobbs reached into his coat pocket, feeling for the card about his speech difficulties. He watched the stranger's reaction from behind his spectacles.

'Oh I'm sorry, pal... I didn't realise. I was ASC by the way. Lucky really ... I spent most of my time in the channel ports driving lorries. I was a driver before the war so that's where they put me. If it was up to me I'd have been at the front.'

'Shut up, just shut up.'

'Driving lorries was all right mind and me old man tells me I've done my bit ... but I wouldn't have minded having a proper go at the Hun, if you know what I mean.'

Hobbs had heard enough; taking the notebook from his pocket, he scribbled quickly, thrusting out an arm when he was done.

'I was a rifleman with the Royal Fusiliers, London Division. If it was up to me I'd have been driving lorries in the channel ports.'

His point made, the two sat in silence.

At the first stop, there was a crowd on the platform waiting to board; moments later the compartment door opened and two red-faced, tired eyed women bundled four children inside.

The three boys and a girl shoved past each other in the rush to get to the window, pressing themselves up against the glass. They giggled loudly while their mothers struggled with bags.

'Here, let me help you, ladies,' and the stranger opposite Hobbs was up, lifting their cases into the luggage rack.

'Thank you, much obliged. Children, come away from the window please.'

'But we want to sit by the window!'

'Boys! Do as I say and come and sit down.'

'It's all right, they can sit here, I've seen the view plenty of times,' and Mr Blue Suit, as Hobbs had now christened him, moved to the end of the seat nearest the door.

Hobbs was desperate to be ignored but now felt compelled to move. He got up and went to move in the small space between a sea of legs.

'Don't look at me, please don't look at me,' and he scratched the side of his ear, another conscious effort to conceal his face.

The two women were immersed in conversation as he stepped over their legs when suddenly the carriage swayed as the train rounded a bend. Hobbs' right leg was off the floor and he lost his balance, flinging out an arm to steady himself. It was too late.

His body lurched forward, and as he fell, the mask came away from his face as the top of his head hit the compartment door, the screams of the women and their children echoing through the train.

16

'Come on, mate, let me give you a hand up.'

The women's screams subsided but they were hugging their sobbing children as Hobbs felt Mr Blue Suit's arm, ushering him out into the corridor.

Other passengers were milling around, attracted by the commotion and he heard mutters and gasps as they saw the man with no face.

'Excuse us, let us through,' and Mr Blue Suit was polite but firm, guiding Hobbs along the carriage.

He was dazed; not from the fall but from the flashback which followed. And he could feel the stares.

'My ... my mask ... where is it?'

Mr Blue Suit was surprised Hobbs had spoken ... or tried to. But he had no idea what he'd said.

Taking a deep breath, Hobbs forced himself to slow down.

'My ... mask ... where is it?'

'Oh yes ... yes, of course. It's right here, I've got it here.'

Hobbs snatched it from him, it looked ridiculous, pathetic even. Half a tin face and a pair of dark glasses.

'I ... I don't think it's too bad ... though the glass is cracked in the left spectacle.'

He couldn't stay here, not with all these people gawping. Moving down the train, the stranger followed. But Hobbs just saw more faces staring and panic set in, sweat running down his disfigured face; there was nowhere to go, he was surrounded.

The door to a lavatory opened and the occupant, a portly woman, shrieked when she emerged to be confronted by Hobbs.

Pushing past her, he locked himself in the cramped space, oblivious to the chatter from passengers on the other side. Dropping his shoulders, he crouched to look in the small mirror fixed to the door.

He brought the mask up to his face, hesitating briefly, lowered his arms and gazed at his reflection; he would never get used to his appearance. It was grotesque and the sight of his face repulsed him.

Slamming a fist hard against the door, he stared at the pained expression on his mutilated features, hating what he'd become.

'Are you ... are you all right in there?'

Mr Blue Suit was hovering outside, unsure what to do. He considered waiting but heard nothing from the man in the lavatory.

'All right ... well, you ... you look after yourself, pal,' and he turned back twice before stepping through the door into an adjoining carriage.

Hobbs' body swayed with the rhythm of the train as he stood there holding his mask. The paint had chipped on the tip of the nose; it was only small but it would be noticeable.

Cursing out loud he lifted it to his face, hooking the spectacles over his ears. In the mirror he saw the cracked glass in the left lens, grateful it wasn't over his good eye.

The thought of opening the door and sitting amongst people with their embarrassed stares was too much. Instead, he sat on the toilet waiting for the train to stop. Abandoning the idea of going into London, he decided to get off at the next station.

He had to.

Twenty minutes later he was walking briskly, head down, his only desire to get out of there, to get away from these people. Hobbs turned into a side street exiting the station, relieved it was empty.

He knew exactly where he was. He used to come here with Grace on days drenched in sunshine; the two of them strolling through Bromley's streets, browsing the shops that skirted the edge of the park.

Hobbs thought of that now, remembering the little book shop she would always drag him into, its musty smell of books piled high on shelves from floor to ceiling.

His first instinct was to head for the sanctuary of Gladstone Street and attempt to fix his damaged mask.

But there was a welcome familiarity to where he now found himself, and he craved more of these warm memories. He wanted to linger, hoping the recollection of happier days would give him the strength to carry on.

It was almost midday, the late morning sun bathing Beckenham High Street. The spring air was cool but Hobbs didn't feel the chill. Instead, he was sweating; a mixture of walking and the stress of the train.

Maybe it was the sight of the Baptist church tower pointing towards the heavens or seeing shoppers clustered around Lumsden's grocery shop, its baskets teaming with fruit and veg, that made Hobbs yearn for an England that appeared lost forever.

He thought of the final letter he'd written to Grace but never had the courage to send; how he regretted that now. And then the weeks spent in hospital, at first unable and then afraid to write, not knowing how to put down on paper that he had changed; devastatingly so.

He'd toyed with writing to say he didn't love her anymore, that he'd met somebody else. But he couldn't lie. So, he did nothing.

It was the mask and Stan's encouragement that changed things; but the incident on the train had crushed his optimism and the doubts were emerging with every step.

What was he thinking? Grace would never forgive him, he knew that now. And when she looked at him, she'd be disgusted.

He came to a stop, sitting on a low wall with iron railings, feeling the hardness of the metal against his back.

There, he heard children's voices, he was outside a school. Hobbs watched them play, envied their happiness, their innocence. The door to the main building opened, a woman emerged, wearing a long blue skirt and white blouse, pulling a shawl around her shoulders to keep out the cold.

She rang a large brass bell, the noise corralling the children to form a line.

'Silence as you walk inside. Hang your coats up and take your seats quietly,' Miss Hesketh said.

And a chill ran through Hobbs on hearing her voice.

There she was; there was Grace.

And he watched in astonishment as she led the children back inside.

17

Holding a pencil, Thirza drew a stick man with a huge smile on his face and an oversized gun protruding from one hand.

Next, she sketched a smaller figure with a triangular body and round face, topping it off with curly scribbles and a beaming smile.

She picked through a pile of coloured crayons, choosing a yellow one to draw a large sunshine, unaware her teacher was watching.

'Very good, Thirza, what is your picture about?'

The children's task for the afternoon had been to draw something they wished for.

'It's my father and me … we're holding hands and we're really happy because he's finally come home,' Thirza replied.

Grace Hesketh liked the little girl with the hare lip. She knew the difficulties Thirza had faced, yet she'd also heard some children with the condition could be mentally challenged. Thankfully, Thirza hadn't been afflicted in that way, yet it still saddened her to think of the girl's future, tainted by her appearance.

She suppressed a smile, the teacher inside her surfacing: 'My Father and *I*, Thirza … my father and *I*.'

Ever since Michael Gregory had spoken of his missing dad, Thirza had thought of little else. She too now believed her own dad was still alive, convinced that one day he would return home. He had to. Michael was right, people didn't simply disappear. It was simply ridiculous.

No, Thirza was sure it was only a matter of time before he returned. And when he did, she'd be the happiest girl alive.

She didn't tell her mother, nor anyone else. Michael was right. For some reason grown-ups had either given up or didn't want to talk about it. That made her suspicious.

Instead, she kept silent, busying herself in preparation for the day it happened. She'd already begun collecting things to give him, keeping them hidden in a keepsake box under her bed.

In it were numerous sketches and colourings, a wooden crucifix she made out of twigs for Easter and the red notebook she'd been using to write down everything her father had missed; like the day her first tooth fell out, what was in her Christmas stocking and the time she found an injured Blackbird in the garden, as pleased as punch when she nursed it back to health with her mother's help.

She knew her mother had a special box too. Was she also collecting things ready for his return? The thought made Thirza feel warm inside and she started thinking of other things to put in hers.

When Miss Hesketh dismissed her class, Thirza swung her satchel over a shoulder and set off for home. It wasn't far away but she never rushed and, despite Mary insisting she go straight home, Thirza sometimes joined friends in the park to play tag or French skipping.

Out the school yard and into the street she passed a blind man in a long, heavy overcoat leaning against a wall next to the iron monger's.

Hobbs had spent the afternoon in a daze, wandering up and down, his body using the time to fight a battle of nerves over whether to finally face Grace or walk away. The skin around his mask itched like crazy, his mouth was parched.

He watched the last of the children depart and then saw her emerge, not quite able to believe it was Grace. She wasn't tall, even at five foot nine he'd towered over her. She had a slender frame in keeping with her character; not naïve, she was never that. But Grace had a softness, a delicate side that he'd fallen for, from the moment he first saw her.

His heart pounded as he watched her pause at the door, taking a small mirror from her bag and using a finger to dab her face. He wanted to be closer, needed to be closer; to see the sparkle in her eyes, the sparkle she hid behind her spectacles, until she was ready to trust.

'I'm doing this, it'll be fine, you can do this, Charlie.'
And then he stopped.

Something was wrong; even from a distance he sensed it. There was something different about her, she wasn't the same Grace anymore.

Hobbs stood motionless, sweat pouring, the urge to scratch his face overwhelming. He couldn't do it, not this, not now.

'Look at you, you've got half a face and you're wearing a tin mask.'
He could almost hear Freddy saying it and his heart sank.

Behind the mask, the dark lens of his spectacles painting a shaded world, he stood and watched Grace go, recalling that afternoon she lay with her head in his lap, the giggles, her smile and his belief they'd be together forever.

How naive he'd been, to think she'd put her life on hold, that she'd wait for him. Clenching his fists, he kicked a pebble across the street, picturing Grace with another man. A small part of him was willing him to follow her.

But the fear of rejection was too strong. Instead, Hobbs turned and walked away, head down, disconsolate, ashamed when he felt the relief wash over him.

At least he knew now. This was the end; the moment Grace had gone forever.

From behind his glasses the tears came, but Hobbs had sobbed with anger, frustration and despair so often that he no longer wondered why his missing eye still had the ability to cry.

'Charlie? Charlie Hobbs? Oh, my word is that really you?'

The woman was frail, elderly, dressed head to toe in black, her wrinkled face visible beneath the wide brim of a hat, withered hands clutching a bag of groceries.

'Edie... Edie Chambers ... your mother and I lived opposite,' she said, jogging Hobbs' memory.

'You and my boy Fred used to pal around when you were younger. How are you, my boy? I was sorry to hear about your mother ... I know how much you loved your mam.'

Hobbs knew he'd have to speak. But when she heard his voice and saw his mouth not moving ...

'I assume you were over there? My Fred never came home, God rest his soul. Killed in November last year he was ... a week before the wretched thing finally finished.'

She paused again.

'What's the matter? Cat got your tongue, Charlie?'

Fumbling in his pockets, Hobbs searched for his card. It wasn't there, he must have dropped it on the train. He had no choice but to speak.

'What was that?'

'Breathe, damn it, breathe...'

'I'm ... sorry ... about Fred.'

'Are you? Are you all right, Charlie?'

'My voice ... I was injured.'

'Oh, you poor boy and there was I thinking you'd come through unscathed.'

The afternoon sun disappeared behind a thick, rolling mass of angry clouds and the sky was menacing. Large raindrops spattered on the ground in a prelude of the deluge to come.

They landed on Hobbs' face, sounding like water splashing into an empty bucket.

His instinct was to look up but he was unnerved by the sound of more rain falling on the tin.

Scurrying away, he turned to look at Edie Chambers who thought it odd that the young man's expression had never once changed.

18

Running for cover to escape the downpour, Thirza felt the rainwater splash up the back of her legs.

She took shelter under the red and white striped canopy above Dannett's chemist shop, staring in the window, waiting for it to stop.

Ruffling her hair to shake the water from her head, she read a poster for an invigorating hair tonic 'guaranteed to encourage new growth.'

Scanning the window at the array of assorted bottles on display, she saw half a dozen or so identical tins piled neatly in a pyramid below a sign: 'Brand's Invalid Calf's Foot Jelly.'

In the middle of the window was a large poster, showing a pencil-drawn boy and his mother in silhouette.

Thirza recognised the product - Calvert's Carbolic Tooth Powder - and it made her think of its distinctive flavour.

The rain slowed to a persistent drizzle, enough for her to leave the shelter of the chemist and head for home.

Crossing the road, she leapt a large puddle before heading through the open gate into the park, where the daffodils were starting to open and the cherry blossom was about to bloom.

She took a shortcut using the footpath which snaked around the park before descending the gentle slope that led down to the duck pond. The rain had emptied the park of people except for someone sitting alone under the bandstand.

He looked vaguely familiar and Thirza remembered the blind man she'd seen when leaving school. She wondered if he'd always been blind, and tried to imagine what it must be like, closing her eyes briefly as she walked.

Daring herself to get closer without him knowing, she softened her steps, heading towards the wooden chairs the brass bands used when they came to play.

He was wearing a long overcoat and sat with his elbows resting on his knees, hands clasped together as though in prayer.

Confident she remained undetected, Thirza's right foot felt for the bottom step and she leaned forward, peering closer.

His face hadn't moved and she wondered if he might be asleep behind those dark spectacles.

But then he turned, was looking right at her and she blushed, a little afraid at the unfriendly expression on his face.

'I'm … I'm sorry,' she said.

Her voice surprised Hobbs; why did she speak like that? And then he saw why.

'I … I thought you were blind. I wasn't staring, honest.'

Maybe it was because of how she looked that Hobbs momentarily forgot about his own appearance.

'I'm used …. to people staring,' he replied.

Thirza was convinced his mouth didn't move. And why did he sound like that?

'How ... how do you do that? Speak without moving your mouth? Is that why you sound ... different?'

Her red curls had turned a dark, rusty colour in the rain and now hung like a cluster of sparkling ringlets on top of her head. Her cheeks wore a reddish glow but it was her mouth Hobbs was looking at.

He saw the distinctive sign of hare lip, the gap, or split, in her top lip which curled upwards until it met the base of her nose.

'I sound different because of this,' Thirza said, pointing to her mouth.

Hobbs stared, knowing he was doing the one thing he found so uncomfortable in others. But he couldn't stop himself.

Thirza was unsure what to do next. He hadn't spoken again and he didn't look very friendly.

'I was ... in France. I was ... injured,' Hobbs said. He didn't elaborate, that's all she needed to know.

Climbing the three steps up to the bandstand, Thirza came closer, peering at Hobbs who watched from behind his spectacles. Her eyes narrowed, she was searching for clues.

'I saw a variety show at the seaside once ... there was a ven ... a ven-tor-ist who could make his dummy speak without moving his mouth. Are you a ven-tor-ist?'

If he'd thought about it, Hobbs would have tried to remember the last time he'd laughed.

But laugh he did, ignoring the saliva that dribbled down his chin. He reached for his notebook, adding to Thirza's curiosity.

Sadly, I'm not a ventriloquist. Though you may have given me an idea to earn some money! My voice was damaged and now people struggle to understand me. It's easier to write things down.'

She handed the book back.

'Oh, so you're not blind then? And isn't writing everything down tiresome? No! Don't answer that … it's a silly question. Of course, it's tiresome.'

She was annoyed with herself and Hobbs laughed again, writing:

'I'm blind in one eye and you are very perceptive. My name's Charlie, what's yours?'

'Thirza … my name's Thirza,' and she struggled to pronounce the first two letters. 'My daddy was in the war. He went to France too. Maybe you knew him?'

'I … I don't … think so.'

'His name was James. James Moran … though I think his friends call him Jimmy.'

'Sorry, no … I don't … know him,' and Hobbs wondered if she could understand him.

'Are you sure? I could run home and fetch a photograph, you might remember if you saw his picture.'

So much of his time was spent trying to get it out of his head; the last thing he needed was a schoolgirl talking to him about it. Hobbs got up, he needed to go.

'Are you going?' I'm sorry … it's just … well, my daddy's not come home yet.'

Hobbs stopped, staring at the floor, his left foot perched over the step leading down from the bandstand.

'I'm … sorry.'

'Don't be,' she said, chirpily, leaping on the wet grass in front of him. 'He'll come home soon, I know he will. They told my mother he was missing and now they're saying he's dead … but they're wrong. I know they are.'

It was raining again and Hobbs retreated back under the cover of the bandstand.

'I've got to go home now. It was nice to meet you, Charlie,' and she held out a hand, just like she'd seen grown-ups do.

Hobbs was swamped with nausea triggered by a memory. Thrusting his hands deep into his pockets, he muttered: 'Nice to meet … you too.'

Thirza didn't notice his reluctance to shake hands; she simply waved cheerily before jauntily skipping off through the park.

Hobbs watched her go, imagining her father's head being blown off by a whizz bang. He thought of James Moran staring at his own bloody innards; the last thought not of his daughter but the grotesque sight of his own body.

19

They'd never discussed it; Solomon hadn't offered and Freddy didn't ask. But in the month or so since that night on the railway line, Freddy had been staying in the old man's house.

He slept upstairs in a small room overlooking the back yard, and opposite the bedroom Solomon and Maud had shared but was now locked away forever.

Freddy never asked why Solomon preferred to sleep downstairs. He rarely spoke at all and when he did, it was usually to answer what he wanted for supper.

Solomon knew it wasn't his place to pry. A man's life was his own and if Freddy wanted to keep himself to himself, that was just fine. He had questions, of course he did; but the thing that struck Solomon was just how much he'd changed.

He couldn't explain why, but his melancholy had lifted. Tracing it back to the moment he shoved Freddy out of the train's path, he felt energised, as though his whole being had been illuminated with a renewed purpose.

Back on that night, while Freddy had downed three glasses of whisky before falling asleep in the chair, Solomon had felt strangely alive.

He'd never been religious, he left that stuff to Maud; twice a year he was the reluctant worshipper, hopelessly trying to sing along to hymns he didn't know.

So, it wasn't God's will that had saved him that night; not in Solomon's mind anyway. Though a part of him liked the idea that maybe Maud was looking out for him.

No, he was simply of the view that some things couldn't be explained while most things were just meant to be.

And for Solomon Wheeler that meant it wasn't his time yet.

The next morning, he'd gone back to work as though nothing had happened. He didn't notice the puzzled looks he got until someone told him later they'd heard him whistling.

Returning home, Patricia Donnelly had been in the yard hanging out washing. Solomon greeted her with a cheery smile, her eyes filling with tears almost as if she knew.

'I'm fine, Pat. Really I am.'

What he hadn't expected was for Freddy to still be there when he opened the door.

But he'd concealed his surprise, cooked them a supper of fried eggs and ham and told his guest there was a single bed upstairs in the small bedroom, should he want to stay.

That was as near to talking about it as the two men got. They never spoke about that night, though Solomon supposed Freddy was a man who couldn't face the thought of living, looking like he did.

Freddy hadn't asked for help and nor would he. But Solomon's mind was already made up. It was because of Freddy he was still alive; and in return, he was determined to show Freddy Lucas he did have something to live for.

He wouldn't force it, Freddy was troubled, that much was clear. Instead, he gave him no reason to leave. There were no questions, no idle conversation; he simply treated him as a house guest.

Given time, he'd open up at some point. Patience and time were key and Solomon had plenty of both.

It no longer felt awkward when they sat in silence eating at the small sitting room table. Cutlery against plates was the only sound, Solomon resisting the temptation to look in fascination at Freddy's face as he ate.

Until one evening, when the younger man suddenly spoke.

'Would you ... would you post a letter for me please, Mr Wheeler?'

'Solomon ... please, call me Solomon. Or Sol ... everyone calls me Sol.'

Freddy saw the old man smiling warmly. The thought never occurred to him to smile back.

'I can pay you ... for the stamp I mean. I just need it posting.'

'Don't you fancy a walk out yourself? Supposed to be nice tomorrow,' and Solomon was aware of the need to tread carefully, finally sensing an opportunity to talk.

'Forget it.'

'Freddy, of course I can post it for you, and I will. I just thought you might fancy some fresh air, that's all.'

There was no reply.

'You writing to your family?' and Solomon regretted being so direct.

'No.'

Gently does it, Sol.

'I'm sure I've got a stamp somewhere, Freddy. It's no trouble, I'll be going out first thing in the morning as usual ... if you need it posting tomorrow, let me have it tonight.'

After supper Freddy left a small, white envelope leaning against the salt before disappearing into his room, like always. Solomon tucked it into his coat pocket, curious about its contents and the recipient.

Lying in bed later, waiting for sleep to come, he waited for Maud. She came to him occasionally throughout the day but always at night. As ever he was careful to select the memory, they were strolling along the pier, holding hands, her smile radiant.

And then screams shattered the memory.

Clambering out of bed, Solomon hurried to the foot of the stairs; Freddy was yelling now, his words incoherent.

There was a hesitancy before Solomon went up, he'd had plenty of nightmares himself, but he'd never heard anything like this. Was Freddy crying? Solomon thought so.

He stood outside his room, listening to the murmurs coming from the other side. And then it went quiet, the nightmare was over.

Solomon was halfway down the stairs when the screaming erupted again.

But this time was different; there was menace, anger, something thrown, breaking glass, the crash of furniture.

Solomon was afraid but he had to go in. A deep breath and he opened Freddy's door, his eyes adjusting to the dark. The bed was empty; squinting, he searched for Freddy.

'Freddy? Freddy, it's me, Sol … you're having a nightmare. Can you hear me, Freddy?'

The bed was shoved up against the wardrobe facing the window and Solomon could make out an upturned chair. He stepped on something sharp, winced in pain, and then heard whimpering from behind the door.

   The huddled figure of Freddy was crouched in the corner, head buried between his knees.

   Even in the dark Solomon could see him shaking. Kneeling, he put a hand on his shoulder, feeling the shake of his sobs.

The old man eased himself to the floor, ignoring the pain in his knees and his foot. Tentatively, he put an arm around Freddy who leaned against him, burying his face in the old man's chest.

20

It was dark when the rain finally stopped, prompting Hobbs to poke his head out gingerly from beneath the bandstand before moving out into the open, looking up in the night sky.

The journey back to Gladstone Street was depressing but uneventful; Hobbs unable to stop himself looking at his reflection in passing windows.

His mask had been on for hours and it was irritating his face. The skin itched and he lifted the tin away from his face, scratching the squashed flesh where his nose had once been.

He kept thinking of Grace, ashamed of himself for not having the guts to face her. His mind wandered, he delved into his memories and pictured them kissing, desperate now to recall her scent.

And then she was with another man; Grace was laughing, they were holding hands; and then she was naked beneath him, her eyes closed.

This was Hobbs' future now. Condemned to live like a freak in a mask, tormented by memories and visions of a woman he couldn't bring himself to face.

He strained to think of something else, recalling the young girl in the park and he wondered how long it would be before she accepted her father was dead and was never coming home.

Edie Chambers' son Fred wasn't coming home either and now Hobbs was picturing the tall, lanky boy they'd nicknamed 'Runner Bean' on account of his skinny physique, remembering him as a real mummy's boy when they were kids.

Hobbs heard the words of Edie Chambers ... 'he died a week before the wretched thing finally finished.'

He hoped 'Runner' hadn't suffered; maybe his size had done for him and a sniper had been unable to resist taking a pot shot at the lanky lad. But most of the dead had suffered. He'd seen enough of it to know it was never painless.

Unless 'Runner' had been obliterated by a Jack Johnson and his mates had been 'lucky enough' to scrape the bits out of the mud, then it was more likely he'd died in agony, probably clutching his guts as they spilled out of his ripped stomach.

And all the while 'Runner' would have been screaming for his mother.

The house was in darkness when he got home and going up to his room, Hobbs paused at Freddy's door. If it wasn't so late he'd have knocked.

Tomorrow; he'd have to sort things out with Freddy tomorrow.

Across Bromley, Mary Moran couldn't sleep. Staring into the blackness, a sleeping Thirza coiled around her, she listened to the gentle, rhythmic breathing of her little girl as her own thoughts wandered.

Like all mothers she worried about her daughter. The future was an uncertain one and she fretted over how Thirza would cope in a changing world. Her appearance hadn't yet been an issue but Mary knew as Thirza got older, she'd have to confront it. She was the most beautiful child a mother could ask for, yet Mary knew how men would look at her daughter.

And she said a silent prayer that her baby wouldn't be condemned to a life without love because of her looks.

It was the thought of Thirza being alone, of having no one to share her life with, that Mary hated most. And that made her angry with James for dying. How could he have been so foolish, so stupid, so selfish?

He'd left them both and her dreams of a brother or sister for Thirza had died with him, in a place she had never heard of.

And now another fear surfaced to keep her awake; dying young and leaving Thirza alone.

Yes, she had grandparents but two lived in America and they had never even met; while her own mother was in her mid-sixties and had never been in the best of health.

Thirza murmured, flinging a sleepy arm over her mother's face. Mary gently moved it away, kissing her forehead. And she saw James' face. He was smiling, arms out and at that moment Mary knew what she had to do.

Together, she and James had dreamed of emigrating, raising a family in what she still thought of as the 'New World.'

She remembered James telling her stories of America's vast open country, its mountains, huge, winding rivers and forests the size of England.

Her mind was made up. She and Thirza would move to the United States and begin a new life there.

She was excited and nervous but Mary felt reassured knowing James' parents would be there for them. Telling her mother would be hard but this was something she and

Thirza had to do. There was nothing here for them now, nothing but dark, painful memories.

Mary played out the conversation with Evelyn in her head, imagining the older woman smiling, saying that she understood and supported her daughter's decision.

But deep down Mary knew her reaction wouldn't be like that.

Instead, she focused on the things that excited her; telling Thirza, the huge adventure it would be, and watching her little girl grow up away from the memories of a war that had so cruelly taken her father.

A surge of excitement pushed sleep even further away. Mary lay thinking about the voyage across the ocean, smiling in the dark as she imagined standing on the deck of a huge passenger ship, the sea breeze wafting through her hair.

Tomorrow, she'd begin preparing for their new life. First, she would write to James' parents in Boston and tell them, knowing they'd be thrilled.

The distant relationship she had forged through the letters exchanged with Howard and Laura Moran, meant they could never be called strangers. There was a closeness, a bond that had only grown deeper following James' death. The grief that only a mother could feel about losing a child would reduce Mary to sobs as she read Laura's letters.

They were desperate to meet their granddaughter, more so as Thirza was a living link to their dead son. Mary smiled, knowing the joy she'd bring to them both.

But then thoughts again turned to her own mother and the excitement dissolved, replaced with guilt as Mary finally succumbed to sleep.

21

'I still can't believe it, after all you've done for the lad. The bloody idiot.'

Stan Finch was furious, pouring boiling water from a kettle which moments ago had been whistling furiously, blowing steam across the kitchen.

Hobbs said nothing. Sitting at the table, he stared at the letter waiting for him on the doormat when he'd come downstairs.

Finding no sign of Freddy at home, he'd spent most of the previous day looking for his friend, only returning home in the late afternoon when it started raining again.

No one else in the house had seen him and Hobbs's anxiety was growing, despite Stan telling him not to worry.

'He'll be fine, Charlie, you've got to stop worrying about the lad. He's big enough to look after himself and I expect he's just letting off steam somewhere. You're not his keeper,' Stan had told him.

But Hobbs knew Freddy better than anyone. And he knew his disappearance, even for a couple of days, meant something was wrong.

At least it stopped him thinking about Grace as he spent a restless night racking his brains where Freddy might be.

Yet, despite the lack of sleep Hobbs was up early, determined to find his friend.

The letter was a surprise at first. He couldn't think of anyone other than Freddy who knew he lived there.

And then he realised who it was from.

'It's a letter … from Freddy,' Hobbs had said, lifting the flap of the envelope with his finger as he walked into the kitchen.

'See, what did I tell you? He's probably letting you know he's all right and not to worry.'

Sometimes Stan would forget the permanent expression on Hobbs' face was made of tin.

He couldn't know what the young man was thinking as he read Freddy's letter. It was only when he didn't reply to his question, he knew something was amiss.

Hobbs slowly lifted his head and for a split second Stan thought he could see real emotion on his friend's face.

'Charlie? What is it? Everything all right?'

Hobbs didn't reply, he wasn't even listening. Stunned by what he'd just read, he slumped back in his chair, the letter falling from his hand.

'Charlie? What's wrong, lad? What does it say?'

When Hobbs still didn't answer, Stan hobbled over to the table, reaching for the letter. Freddy's handwriting was erratic, almost illegible in parts, but Stan had no trouble interpreting it.

'I fucking hate you Charlie. Did you read that? With your one eye? I said I fucking HATE you! I thought you were my friend. How stupid you must think I am.'

'I won't make that mistake again. The difference between us Charlie is that I know what we are … we're both repulsive to look at and we always will be.'

'Do you know how ridiculous you look wearing that piece of metal over your face? You can't run from it Charlie. You're deformed, you have no face! Either live with it or be a man and kill yourself.'

'But you won't do that, you haven't got the guts. They should have left you to die where you fell. You're fucking deluded if you think that piece of tin is going to make people treat you normally.'

'There's nothing normal about you Charlie. You're a freak, we both are. At least I know it. Two-faced Charlie … how fucking appropriate.'

'God, I hate you. I wish you were fucking dead. If I never see you again it will be too soon. So go on, live out your pathetic life wearing your tin face until you die someday, alone. No one's going to mourn for you.'

'Jesus Christ,' Stan muttered.

He felt awkward having read it, as though he'd interrupted a private conversation, and he let the letter slip through his fingers, returning to the stove, thankful to have something to do.

Hobbs sat quietly, his mug of tea with a drinking straw left untouched.

Stan broke the silence, the shock of Freddy's vitriol turning to anger.

'The ungrateful bastard,' he muttered. 'He's the one who'll end up alone, Charlie, mark my words. And if he ever shows his face around here … well, wooden legs or not, I'll kick his arse, the little shit.'

Hobbs reached for the letter, folded it twice and tucked it into his trouser pocket.

'You're not … you're not keeping that are you? You should rip it up and chuck it on the stove,' Stan said.

Hobbs rose, heading for the door.

'Charlie, you can't let it get to you. He's not worth it and what he's said … well, it's bollocks, all of it.'

Hobbs returned to his room and sat on the edge of the bed. His window overlooked the back yard; a grey, uninviting space cluttered with dustbins and empty crates.

The room was small; opposite the bed was an oversized wardrobe that looked out of place. It housed what little Hobbs had. There was a bedside table, a chair facing the window and a mirror hanging above it.

He removed his mask and stood peering at his reflection. As much as he detested his appearance, there was a gruesome fascination about his disfigurement that compelled him to run his fingers over the soft, spongy flesh that now made up the middle of his face.

On his right cheek were the lines of three scars that merged together, ending underneath the tip of what used to be his nose; the rest of it was at a right angle, pressed flat as it ran up against the socket of his missing right eye.

For some reason he recalled the moment doctors removed the bandages, warning him to breathe slowly, hearing the anxiety in their voices as he detected light coming through.

The first time he saw himself he found it hard to breathe, stumbling backwards, a doctor holding him steady as he and another man tried their best to be upbeat, telling him how lucky he was to be alive.

But Hobbs didn't feel lucky, then or now.

Freddy was right, he should have died where he fell. At least he'd have been spared this.

He thought of friends he'd lost and the tens of thousands more who never came home; how revered they were; the heroes, the ones who'd paid the ultimate sacrifice.

The country wept and mourned for the dead. But no one wept for men without limbs, the boys driven insane by the savagery, reduced to quivering, shuffling wrecks.

No one cared about them.

There was no place for men without faces. There was no place for him. It had taken the poisonous letter of his only friend to make him realise that.

It wasn't the vile abuse that left Hobbs crushed by Freddy's letter; but the realisation he was now completely alone.

And that every word his friend had written was true.

22

Safe in the knowledge their mother was out for an hour or so, the two Donnelly boys ignored her demand not to play football in the back yard after she'd caught John Junior kicking a ball which slammed against Solomon's back door.

'In the name of Jesus what on Earth do you t'ink you're doing?' She'd yelled.

'You could have broken a window doing that. And let me tell you now, John Junior, I don't have money to spare paying for your stupidity.'

But now their mother had gone, her warnings were forgotten and the boys resumed their game.

'Betcha can't hit old man Wheeler's door again,' Niall challenged his older brother.

'Easy, watch this.'

Launching himself at the ball, John Junior smashed the ball through the air where it hit Solomon's window, leaving a crack in the glass. The smile collapsed from Niall's face.

'John you idiot, you've broken the bloody window, Ma's going to kill us.'

His older brother said nothing, going up close to inspect the damage. There was a six inch crack running diagonally from the top right of the window.

'Maybe ... or maybe the old man won't notice. It's in the corner, I don't think you can tell without looking.'

Niall stood next to his brother, standing on tiptoe to peer through the kitchen window.

'Ma reckons old man Wheeler now lives downstairs since his wife died. I heard her telling Mickey Dobson's mum.'

'Maybe she's not dead after all,' his brother replied mischievously. 'Or maybe he's keeping her body upstairs and he goes up there now and again to see her.'

'Ewww, John that's horrible, stop it!'

'Or maybe he killed her and he can't bear to go upstairs again and return to the scene of his crime.'

'Stop it, John, it's not funny!'

But John Junior was laughing loudly, amused how easily he'd spooked his brother.

'Wait! What was that ... that noise,' Niall said suddenly.

'Nice try, brother, but I'm not falling for that one.'

'No, John, listen. There's someone inside, I just heard something.'

'You're imagining it, Ma said the old man's at work.'

'I'm telling you, John, there's somebody in there. And if it's old man Wheeler, he'll know we've done his window.'

Stepping closer, John Junior put his face up against the glass. He thought about turning the tables on him, pretending he'd seen something ... instead, Niall saw his older brother recoil backwards, a look of terror on his face.

'John! What is it? What's wrong?'

But John Junior didn't reply, he was staring up at the window, his mouth open and his eyes wide.

Turning to look, Niall saw someone … no, something … staring back at him. It had eyes and a mouth but its gruesome, featureless appearance convinced the young boy it wasn't human.

'Come on, let's go,' and John yanked his arm, dragging him away, the pair of them running back into the house and slamming the door.

'John, what the hell was that? What did we just see in old man Wheeler's house?'

Niall was tearful, looking to his brother for assurance. John Junior paced up and down the cramped living room, waving his arms wildly, gesturing for his brother to be quiet.

'Look, whatever it is,' he whispered, 'it's on the other side of that,' and he flicked his head to the wall dividing the two houses. 'So, keep yer ruddy voice down and let me think.'

'John I'm … I'm scared. Did you see its face? It didn't … it wasn't, I mean whatever that was, it wasn't human, was it?'

John Junior knew his little brother was terrified; so was he. But he tried not to show it.

'Look, we stay quiet, keep the doors locked and wait for Ma to get home.'

'But what's she going to do? We're not seriously going to let her go round there are we?'

'I don't know. Now we need to calm down, let me think.'

'Well, you can think all you want but I'm not staying here, I'm going to find Ma,' and Niall bolted for the door.

'Niall, wait!'

The two boys froze and for a moment there was silence. Then John Junior said: 'I'm coming with you.'

The door opened slowly, the boys glanced at Solomon's house before John Junior slammed the door behind him, shouting:

'Niall, run ... come on!'

23

Four times Hobbs made the journey to see Grace, each time loitering from a distance, watching her leave the school gates and then following discreetly.

She would walk along the main road, always wearing the same blue coat, navy hat, black ankle boots and a long skirt. Once she stopped at a florist and Hobbs stared as she picked a bunch of tulips, before getting on the number sixteen trolley bus.

And that was where he'd let her go, watching the bus disappear over the hill. He couldn't risk getting on it, fearing Grace might see him or a sudden jolt would send him flying, his mask coming away from his face like it had on the train.

Yet, in a way he was strangely content with the distant, voyeuristic relationship he felt he now had with her, even feeling a closeness to Grace that he'd craved.

Until the fifth time.

The red bricks of the school building had taken on a rusty hue in the afternoon sunshine as Hobbs watched the children pour out the main door and spill into the streets.

From his regular vantage point near the post box, he knew it normally took ten or fifteen minutes for Grace to emerge.

But this time she didn't show.

Unsure whether to cross the road for a closer look, he hesitated long enough for a grey haired woman with a walking stick to ask if he was lost.

The question unnerved him and he crossed hurriedly without answering.

And then Hobbs saw him; smartly dressed, he was older, a thin moustache on a face that wasn't broken, not quite a smile but a contentment as he strode confidently through the school entrance, removing his hat as he disappeared from view.

A moment later he emerged, smiling broadly now as Grace clung to his arm, giggling, her eyes wide as they gazed at each other. Hobbs could do nothing but watch as his world crumbled and the two of them strolled away.

He slumped against the wrought iron bars surrounding the school.

'You're pathetic.'

'You all right, mate?' asked a workman in a flat cap and overalls.

'Leave me alone, for Christ's sake.'

Hobbs scurried away, his pace quickening to avoid more unwanted encounters. Turning off the road he emerged on the path leading into the park, seeking sanctuary under the bandstand where he'd sheltered from the rain.

He couldn't stop thinking about it, that smile as she embraced another man. And it served as a trigger, conjuring lurid images of the woman he loved, writhing beneath a stranger.

A stranger he knew nothing about. But he didn't need to; the only thing that mattered was that he had a face and Hobbs didn't.

Kicking a stone, it skimmed across the ground, disappearing in the shrubbery. Hobbs wanted to disappear; there was nothing left now, nothing of any consequence. And it occurred to him how right Freddy had been.

Approaching the bandstand, his heart sank seeing someone sitting there. It was a child, a girl. She looked familiar, a mop of red curls covering her head, holding a school satchel.

Faded memories flashed before him of a life he'd once known. Shutting them out he looked again. Hobbs was sure it was her. What was her name? He couldn't recall. She was facing the lake, her back to him.

He changed direction, wanting to avoid another conversation, but he heard her crying.

'Walk on, Charlie, you're no help to a weeping child.'

'It's … it's you, the ven-tro-ist man,' Thirza said, spotting him.

Hobbs was struck again by her voice, wondering if she ever thought about her speech defect or simply accepted it as being who she was.

'Hello again, Charlie,' she said, smearing a sleeve across her face.

It was habit that made him reach for his notebook and pencil. But Hobbs stopped, he wanted to speak instead.

'You remembered my name,' he replied, trying to sound as 'normal' as he could, hoping she'd understand him.

'Of course, I did. Do you remember mine?'

'Sorry,' and Hobbs shook his head.

'It's Thirza, and don't worry, there's no reason you should remember me.'

He regretted the lapse and resting the notebook on his right thigh, wrote.

'Of course, I remember you, it was only your name that escaped me. Why are you crying?'

'It doesn't matter.'

'Is it … is it your father?' Hobbs said aloud, surprising himself that he'd chosen to speak again.

She was staring hard, searching for signs of movement on his still face.

'No … I mean yes, well … not really, oh I don't know,' and Thirza reached for a pebble, hurling it in the lake.

Hobbs was silent, he had no idea what to say.

She picked up a stick and poked around in the undergrowth between the bandstand and the water's edge.

'It's my mother … she says we have to move to America.'

Hobbs hadn't expected that.

'America huh? That's … that's good isn't it?'

'No, it's not good, it's horrible, everything about it is horrible,' she snapped, the tears coming again.

'I'm … I'm sorry,' and Hobbs was mortified he'd made her cry.

'My mother says … America is amazing and we'll … we'll be happy there. But I don't want to go! This is my home.'

Hobbs imagined Thirza's mother, a grieving widow desperate for a fresh start. There were too many memories here for her to be happy. He didn't need to know her to realise that.

'You can always come back when you're older,' he said, finding himself helping a woman he'd never met.

'But that will be too late! Why are we leaving him now?'

'I'm sorry?'

'Daddy! Why would she want us to leave daddy?' and she prodded the stick into the soft earth, flicking mud into the water.

'Why does my mother want to go and live in America before my father comes home?' and she looked at Hobbs pleadingly.

How could he truthfully answer that? The easiest thing would be to ignore it but the little girl had a fragility and innocence he'd forgotten existed.

And protecting that suddenly became precious; to tell the truth didn't always mean to be right. He'd learned that the hard way.

So, what if she believed her father was still alive.

Better that than to know the truth.

And he pictured Thirza walking the fields of Armageddon, stepping over the bloated, rat-eaten corpses, forlornly calling her father's name.

'How long has your father been …,' he was about to say missing but stopped himself, 'gone?'

'October, Nineteen Sixteen. I was five.'

Hobbs winced, knowing it was unlikely she could even remember him.

Yet, to his astonishment she said:

'I can still remember him you know; a little anyway. I remember him carrying me up the stairs to bed.'

She was looking at him but her eyes were elsewhere.

'He was wearing his uniform … I remember his smell. He put me over his shoulder and was singing to me; then tucked me into bed and kissed my head.'

Hobbs' silence allowed the memory to linger.

'I know my mother thinks he's never coming home, but she's wrong! I know she is.'

'When does your mother want to go?' Hobbs asked, hoping to steer the conversation away from her father.

'I don't know, she says we have to sort things out here first but I hope they never get sorted.'

The skin underneath his mask itched and Hobbs was desperate to scratch.

'Can I ask you something, Charlie?'

Hobbs nodded.

'Why doesn't your mouth move when you're talking? I know you said you were injured ... but how?'

He was surprised how calm he felt at being asked the question he'd dreaded; he thought for a moment and then wrote in his notebook, feeling a ripple of relief at finally admitting the truth.

'I was shot in the face and I don't look the same anymore ... so I wear a mask; to stop me scaring folk.'

'Your face is a mask? Really? That's silly ... it's not possible.'

The expression on her delicate face told Hobbs she didn't know what to believe.

Still holding the pencil, he lifted it towards his head and tapped the side of his face.

Thirza stepped back, shocked by the metallic sound.

Hobbs did it again.

'See ... a mask.'

Gingerly, she came closer.

'It's made of tin.'

'Can I ... can I feel it?'

Without waiting for a reply, Thirza reached out a hand and touched Hobbs' cheek, gasping as her fingers stroked metal.

'Gosh, that's amazing,' she said, her hand gently tapping his face. 'So, your whole face is a mask?'

'No, just around my nose and mouth,' and Hobbs traced a circle in front of the middle of his face to illustrate.

'What's underneath, can I see?'

Hobbs recoiled quickly.

'An ugly face … and you don't want to see that.'

'Some people call me ugly because of this,' and Thirza pointed to her lip. 'I guess they're right but it's the only face I've got. Mother tells me I'm beautiful but I know she's just being nice.'

Her maturity astonished him, as did the acceptance of how she looked. In that split second Hobbs realised she was right.

'Your mother is telling the truth, you are beautiful. Don't let anyone ever tell you you're ugly,' he said, raising his hands to lift his spectacles and bringing the mask away from his face.

'Because this is what ugly looks like.'

24

'Come on, Billy, the boy needs a leg up. No one will touch him on account of his looks. How's that fair after all he's given?'

Billy Draper's face gave nothing away as Solomon pursued his quest to get Freddy a job. It was only out of respect for the old man, who'd worked alongside his father for years, that Draper was prepared to hear him out.

'I don't know, Sol. For a start, if he looks as bad as you say, I don't want him putting the customers off … or the rest of the lads.'

'He can work in the back with me, the customers will never see him.'

'But can he do the job, Sol? Fish ain't for everyone, you know that. And we can't afford to hire someone just because we feel sorry for 'em.'

'Look, Billy, you've come a long way, you've done much better than I or your dear old dad did,' Solomon said, hoping to soften Draper by brushing his ego. 'Of course, you've got to do right by the business, the customers and all the lads. But think about it. Once word gets around that Wilson's have taken on a war veteran, and one as badly scarred as Freddy is, well … it won't do the firm any harm that's for sure.'

Draper was silent, thinking it through and Solomon knew he was getting somewhere.

'Well, the boss did say the Chamber of Commerce has been pushing firms to take on more ex-servicemen.' 'There you go then, this is the perfect opportunity to demonstrate we won't forget the sacrifice those lads made.'

Draper rubbed his chin and Solomon resisted the temptation to say anything else.

'All right Sol, we'll give him a go. But it's a two week trial and if he doesn't cut the mustard he's gone, scars or no scars. Bring him in tomorrow, he can start with loading and then we'll put him on packing.'

Draper was already walking back through the fishery when Solomon replied: 'Thanks, Billy, I appreciate it. And Freddy won't let you down, trust me.'

'It's on your head if he does Sol,' Draper yelled, disappearing into his office.

Solomon smiled; all he had to do now was persuade Freddy to take the job. He had to get him out of the house; work was good for the soul, at least that's what his father used to tell him.

He knew the young man was struggling, the constant nightmares told him that; as did Freddy's mood swings. One minute quiet and polite, the next in a rage, cursing and yelling. Solomon knew it was a risk. If it went wrong, he'd be held responsible, no matter how far back he went with Billy's dad.

But he refused to waver in his belief that Freddy had simply lost hope and that if he could help him realise life was still worth living, then he could be saved from himself and his demons.

He rehearsed what he planned to say on the walk home, hoping there hadn't been a repeat of the incident with Patricia's boys. Solomon recalled his agitated neighbour waiting for him when he'd got home a week ago, whispering to him as he stepped out into the back yard.

'Solomon, can I have word please?'

She was worried, he could tell from her face as she beckoned him over, head peering out from behind a half open door.

When she recounted the tale of her sons coming face to face with a 'monster' at the window, Solomon's first instinct had been to laugh. But he'd suppressed his amusement seeing how worried she was.

'Patricia, there's no need for you or your boys to be alarmed, there's a perfectly simple explanation. I happen to have a guest staying with me at the moment.'

He'd ignored the look of surprise on his neighbour's face and continued:

'Now, I don't know all the details but he's a young man who suffered terribly in the war. His face … well, he was very badly burnt. He's staying with me for a while, I want to help him.'

He didn't need to see the flush of her cheeks to know she was embarrassed.

'Oh Solomon, I'm so sorry. But when the boys came running to me … well, to listen to them I didn't know what to t'ink.'

Reassuring Pat Donnelly was one thing; dealing with Freddy, yelling and cursing as he stepped into the house, had been another.

'Fucking kids, staring at me like a freak. Don't know how lucky they are … the little bastards.'

But Solomon was learning how to placate Freddy. He made a mug of tea, listened to him vent and then simply spoke to him, quietly and calmly.

'They're just boys, Freddy. They don't mean any harm, they just didn't expect anyone to be here that's all.'

Now, as the old man made his way home, he felt confident that he could talk Freddy round and get him to accept the job. If he could do that, then Freddy would be taking his first steps on the road to resuming a normal life.

A contented Solomon stepped out into the road as a group of women filed out of the Methodist Church hall, and he tipped his hat.

One of them was Mary Moran.

'Well, I do so hope you found today's meeting informative and helpful, Mrs Moran,' the woman said, spectacles perched precariously on the end of her nose.

'Oh yes, it was extremely useful. Your speaker was very knowledgeable. I was unaware such an organisation existed until I saw your pamphlet advertising today's meeting. It's almost as if it's meant to be.'

'You'd be surprised at how many women are considering emigrating. Some for reasons such as yours, others because they can't get work now the war's over.'

'And yet there's a shortage of manpower Mrs Kingsley was saying in her talk,' Mary replied.

'Oh, absolutely. And not just at home but abroad too. Mrs Kingsley is giving similar talks all over the county. The British Women's Emigration Association has never been busier.'

'I wouldn't have known where to start. But Mrs Kingsley says the association will assist me with all the arrangements, including booking trips for our voyage. That's a huge weight off my mind.'

'Maybe we'll see you at another of our Mothers' Union meetings in the future?'

'Well, that very much depends on how long we'll be here. But yes, I'd like that. Thank you, Mrs Armitage, it's been lovely to meet you.'

'Likewise, my dear,' she said, clutching Mary's hand. 'God bless you and your daughter ... and good luck.'

On the bus home, Mary fizzed with excitement at starting a new life in America, a place free from the dark memories of James and the war that had taken him from her. But she was worried about Thirza. It had never dawned on her she would be so against going.

'I'm not going and you can't make me,' Thirza had yelled, followed by tears, lots of tears.

Mary thought of her mother. She'd expected her to be the angry one. Instead, Evelyn's reaction was just as heart breaking.

'You're my only child, Mary; Thirza and you are all I have left. But do what you believe is right. I'll always love you, wherever you are,' she'd said, resigned to losing them both.

Mary wondered how doing something she believed was so right could upset the two people she loved more than anything else in the world. The contrasting reactions of Thirza and her mother had given her second thoughts and for a moment she'd almost changed her mind.

But after sleeping on it Mary knew it was the right thing to do. She and Thirza would leave England to begin a new life in the New World.

Walking from the bus stop she wondered if they had trolley buses in America. And she smiled with excitement at the thought of finding out.

25

Hobbs couldn't decide if he was more stunned by what he'd done or Thirza's reaction; or the lack of one.

Even as he'd lifted the mask away from his face he was regretting it. Yet, the little girl never flinched or grimaced as she saw the real him.

'You look … funny,' was all she'd said, followed by: 'Can I look at it? Your mask I mean,' seeming more curious about that than his shattered face.

Hobbs was hesitant before handing it over:

'Please be careful … I don't have another one.'

The weight surprised her, she expected it be to heavier.

'It's supposed to make me look like I used to,' Hobbs said.

There was a fragility to it and Thirza held it delicately, afraid she'd drop it. The metal was cold yet its realism caused her to shiver as the lifeless face stared up from her hand.

Hobbs was surprised how comfortable he felt without it on and he savoured the cool air on his skin.

'It looks … so real. Do you wear it all the time?'

'Only when I'm out,' he replied.

She brought the mask up to her own face, looking at Hobbs through the dark lenses of the glasses.

'Hello Charlie, it's your face speaking,' she said, adopting a deep voice and giggling.

Hobbs laughed too, saliva dribbling from his mouth.

'Does it hurt? Your face I mean,' Thirza asked, handing the mask back, much to Hobbs' relief.

'Sometimes, if I forget to put the wadding underneath.'

'Is that what you really used to look like then… before you were injured?'

His lower jaw ached, he wasn't used to talking so much. Hobbs nodded.

'I think you look better without it. Your real face looks … friendlier.'

Hobbs found her honesty refreshing and unsettling. Did Stan feel the same way but was too polite to say?

'Do you wear it because people stare at you?'

'Aye, something like that.'

Perched on the outside of the bandstand's perimeter fence, she held on and leaned back, tipping her head backwards.

'People stare at me all the time. Mother says it's because I'm beautiful but I know it's because of my hare lip.'

Hearing her refer to it surprised him. And the more Thirza spoke, the more Hobbs got used to her voice, though he still struggled to make out some of what she said.

'I wish I could wear a mask sometimes,' she added.

Hobbs scribbled in his notebook, tore out a sheet of paper and gave it to her.

'People will always stare, don't let them bother you. And your mother is right, you are beautiful.'

She looked up at Hobbs smiling. He wasn't lying, she was beautiful. And not even the crude opening in her top lip could take away how magical that smile was.

'You're nice, Charlie. I like talking to you.'

He hadn't expected that and was unsure how to answer.

'I have to get home soon. Will you be here again, Charlie?' and she looked at Hobbs with wide eyes.

'I … I don't know,' he replied honestly, seeing the disappointment on her face. 'Would you like me to be?'

'Yes, yes I would. Tomorrow after school then? Bye, Charlie,' and she skipped off across the park before he could answer.

For the first time since he could remember, someone was treating him normally. Was it that? Or was it because Thirza reminded him of someone else? Someone Hobbs shamefully hadn't thought about for a long time.

It was both and he knew it.

She wasn't repulsed when she saw his real face; no child could, or would hide that. But it was how alike to his sister she was that struck him most. How long had it been now? Ten years?

There was shame and embarrassment at how little he thought of Ursula. But Thirza had brought her back. And that alone was reason enough to be in the park tomorrow, waiting for her under the bandstand.

His walk home was different, the anxiety gone. Bromley's streets were busy as usual but Hobbs didn't look to hide. He was simply another pedestrian.

In that moment he felt something that had vanished in the unbearable minutes Hobbs and eight hundred other men of the Royal Fusiliers had been ordered up the line in readiness to attack; calm.

There was no shortage of breath, no racing heartbeat or the flood of anxiety that usually ripped his nerves to shreds.

Hobbs was aware of an inner peace, a calmness acutely exaggerated by its sudden reappearance.

All that because an eight-year-old girl wasn't repulsed at the sight of his face.

No, it was more than that. It had to be.

He passed the train station, a gaunt veteran balancing on crutches coming the other way. His right leg missing, Hobbs watched as he awkwardly swung himself forward.

Before turning the corner, he glanced back to see the cripple leaning against a wall lighting a cigarette, oblivious to all around him.

26

*'This, gentlemen, is the Scout Experimental number five …
we call it the SE5 for short; not very original I grant you,
but there we are,' and the officer walked ahead of the
seven men across a field.*

'Did he just call us gentleman?'

*'Aye Eric, I think he bloody well did,' Freddy Lucas
replied.*

Stopping in front of the biplane, he turned to face them.

*'Now, we've only just started to see these coming in but
they're a beaut to fly. I took one up last week for the first
time and believe me, it's a dream to handle compared to a
DH5 or even the BE2.'*

His spiel was interrupted by a Tommy with his hand up.

*'Sir … I've only been up in a BE2. Are these … much
different?'*

*The officer's boots shone in the grass, wet from the dew.
Lifting his head he smiled and said: 'Trust me, once you've
flown one of these beauties, you won't want to go near a
BE2 again.'*

*His black hair remained still in the breeze, sleeked to his
head in grease. Clean shaven, his square jaw jutted out
beneath wary eyes.*

'My name is Captain Anthony Parr, welcome to thirty-two squadron. Now, I'm aware you all passed the pilot's test at the first attempt and you've had some time up over England admiring the countryside.'

Clasping his hands behind his back, Parr's eyes scanned this latest assortment of recruits to the Royal Flying Corps.

'Some of you may think that you're ready to take on Fritz but believe me, he'll have other ideas. Now, has anyone here got more than the recommended fifteen hours up?' he asked.

Freddy stepped to the front.

'I have, Sir.'

'Good man, how long?'

'Well, I spent three weeks as an observer with seventy squadron, going up in Camels, so in excess of twenty hours under my belt, Sir.'

Parr's sanguine expression changed and his irritation came out in the reply: 'Solo man ... I'm not interested in how long you've sat looking down at Fritz while some other bugger does all the work. How many hours have you got flying?'

There were sniggers from the others and Freddy felt his face redden.

'Er ...three and a half dual .... and nine solo, Sir.'

Parr stared into Freddy's eyes, as he though could read his thoughts.

'Right, well you're all going to have listen carefully, watch ... and learn bloody fast. Lieutenant Crosby?' and he shouted over their heads.

Freddy and the others turned to see a pilot walking towards them, fixing his flight cap into place as he strolled across the field.

'Lieutenant Crosby here is going to show you just what the SE5 can do. I'll be blowed if I'm letting any of you lot near one of these things until I have to. But don't fret, you'll get your chance soon enough.'

Freddy and the others watched as Crosby pulled down hard on the propeller blade of the single seater aircraft. The engine spluttered into life, quickly settling into a steady drone

Climbing into the cockpit, Crosby fiddled with the controls, pulled his goggles down and gave a thumbs up to his audience, as the plane set off trundling over the grass.

Freddy was in awe of this ridiculous looking machine; so incredible, yet so flimsy, so delicate.

The wings of the khaki coloured plane swayed gently as the SE5 gathered speed across the field, its two blue, white and red roundels visible on the top wings.

Suddenly, it lifted off the ground and Freddy's head tilted back, his eyes following the winged wonder up into the air.

'Oy! Are you listening to me, boy, or am I wasting my time?'

Billy Draper was incensed, annoyed that his newest employee appeared to be in a world of his own.

'Look, I took you on as a favour to Sol, so the least you can do is to listen to what I'm bloody well telling you. Is that clear?'

Glaring at Freddy, Draper was revolted by his appearance. When Freddy simply stared back, the foreman's patience snapped.

'Sol? Sol?' and his voice carried above the noise of the chilled warehouse.

Solomon came running, wiping bloody hands on his apron. Draper didn't wait for him to get near before yelling:

'Does your chum want this job? Because if not he can fucking well pack up now.'

Solomon glanced at Freddy, a blank, vacant look in his eyes.

'Yes, Billy, of course he wants the job and he's very grateful to you for giving him the opportunity. Ain't that right, Freddy?'

To Solomon's relief Freddy nodded.

'Well, he'd better start acting like it. I won't accept shirkers, Sol, you know that.'

Turning to Freddy, Draper walked up close and hissed:

'No second chances, Lucas. Buck your ideas up or you're gone.'

A glare at Solomon and he walked away, barking at a young lad mopping the floor.

'Freddy, come on pal, you've got to help yourself. Billy's not everybody's cup of tea but he's fair and he expects a decent day's graft.'

Freddy said nothing but his eyes spoke to Solomon.

'What is it, Freddy? Come on, you can tell me.'

'He … he wants me to move that,' and Freddy's voice was so quiet, Solomon had to lean in close to hear.

Solomon saw the bloody guts, entrails and fish heads, piled so high they were slipping over the side.

'It's just fish, Freddy … that's all,' and he stooped down to pick up the crate. 'I'll get rid of these, you go and wash down the benches.'

He returned from dumping the waste to find Freddy scrubbing a wooden bench, the soapy water mixing with the blood to create a pink foam that frothed and bubbled, the suds dripping to the floor.

'When you've finished up here go and take your break; there's some tea out the back where the other lads are having a smoke.'

But Freddy wasn't listening. He continued scrubbing, his right arm moving slowly back and forth, but he was somewhere else now.

'Cheers for the lift, mate,' he yelled, jumping from the ambulance as it juddered to a halt. But the driver was already out and round the back, helping an orderly who was opening the canvas from the inside.

Standing in front of what was left of the white stone building, Freddy stared at the rows of wounded lying pitifully out in the open.

He wondered why they weren't being taken inside for treatment, as a lone orderly stood amongst them studying a clipboard.

Freddy was careful, stepping over the stretchers, searching for the entrance. It had been a farmhouse once. Now it was a shattered carcass, an appropriate metaphor for what was inside.

The whitewashed walls had faded to a greyish hue and the stone was pockmarked by shellfire. There were no doors and glass had long gone from its windows. Surrounded by rubble and piles of dirty earth, the Advanced Dressing Station was as broken as the men it sheltered.

It was the nearest Freddy had been to the front on foot and the distant thump of shells whose scream got louder as they exploded close by, was enough to make him nervous. But he'd come this far; he couldn't, and wouldn't, go back.

The groans and cries from the wounded grew louder and he hesitated at the doorway before stepping inside.

The smell of iodine was overwhelming, mixed with vomit, faeces and a pungent odour he knew to be the inside of a human body.

Clamping a hand over his mouth, Freddy moved through a mass of bodies, several leaning or slumped against walls, others lying on the floor.

Those who were conscious shared a desolate, ghost-like appearance, their faces caked in chalky clay and blood; silent stares punctured by retches and coughs.

He searched his way through the building from one end to the other, calling his name in desperation.

'Eric? Eric Jarvis?' It's me, Freddy.'

He peered into a room, the light was poor but he saw enough to know at least a dozen men were crammed in there.

'I'm looking for an airman … Eric Jarvis. Any of you seen him?'

No one spoke.

Still calling Eric's name, he moved to another room and froze.

Over a large wooden table, a medical officer stood over a soldier flanked by two orderlies, the front of his white apron soaked in blood. The orderlies were trying to hold the wounded man still as the M.O's bloodied hands probed into the soldier's open torso.

'What the hell are you doing in here? If you're not RAMC you need to get out, now!' The M.O yelled at Freddy. 'Damn it, hold him still for God's sake,' he snapped, as the stricken Tommy writhed on the table.

Freddy ran for the exit, falling to his knees and vomiting. He gulped down fresh air, oblivious now to the noise from the front. Moments later a voice asked him:

'You all right? Are you wounded?'

It was the Medical Officer, lighting a cigarette with his bloody hands.

'No ... no, I'm fine.'

'Look, it's chaotic enough in there without us having visitors,' and the officer removed his helmet, wiping sweat from a dirty brow.

'I ... I was looking for a friend. An airman ... we were patrolling together when he came down. I saw ... I saw him land and I did a pass over ... he was climbing out of his bird but he looked in a bad way.'

'And you think he might be in here?'

'This was the nearest ADS,' Freddy said forlornly.

The M.O summoned the orderly with the clipboard: 'Fraser, have we got any RFC chaps in?'

The orderly studied his clipboard.

'Just the one, Sir; a Lieutenant Jarvis; he bled out on the way here. He's with the other 'Gone Wests' round the back.'

27

Hobbs dragged himself out bed, wiping the saliva that had dribbled from his broken mouth as he slept. He peered out of his window, the sky overcast, the clouds threatening.

He dreaded rain; not because he now had to protect his 'face' from it. Rain was the backdrop to when he'd stepped irrevocably away from his life as a book keeper's clerk, crossing the rubicon into hell.

By the time he'd shaved and dressed, the clouds had lifted and the sun broke through, bathing his room in glorious, spring sunshine.

Adjusting the knot of his tie in the mirror, he wiped away a dab of shaving cream underneath his ear.

Outside, the bells of the Baptist church tower were ringing; probably a wedding or Christening later.

He checked his watch, it wasn't nine yet; plenty of time. His last act was to open the blue cloth bag on his bedside table.

Hobbs handled his mask with care, checking his tin face for marks and blemishes, giving it a gentle wipe with a clean hankie.

He'd done his best to cover the scratch on the nose using paint from a small artists' shop in town and replaced the broken glass in the spectacle lens.

Putting his mask on, Hobbs opened the door facing the room which Freddy had once occupied.

It was more than two months now since his friend had left, the only contact being that vitriolic letter.

He hoped Freddy was ok. Maybe Stan was right and there was nothing more he could have done.

Hobbs had his own life to live now … or was that rebuild?

Stan's moustached face was waiting as he descended the stairs.

'Well, look at you all dressed up. It's Saturday, the magistrates aren't sitting so someone's gone to a lot of effort for somebody is my reckoning … what's the occasion Charlie?' he asked, chuckling.

'Nothing special, Stan. There's a May pageant … a friend has invited me.'

The old soldier smiled, a twinkle in his eye.

'A friend eh? Is this the same friend you keep going out to see twice a week? Nothing gets past me, Charlie. She must be special.'

'No! It's not like that,' Hobbs snapped, feeling a surge of satisfaction at startling Stan with his reaction.

In his haste to explain, he spoke too quickly and dribbled. Pulling the notebook from his pocket he wrote instead.

'I've told you before, there is no woman. I'm meeting a friend, that's all.'

'All right, calm down, Charlie, no offence meant. It's a fine day for it anyway.'

He regretted losing his temper. Stan didn't mean any harm. But he knew the old soldier was unlikely to be so understanding if he learned his 'friend' was an eight-year-old girl.

Hobbs was aware what many would think of a twenty-five-year-old man befriending a young schoolgirl and for that reason alone he'd told no one. He'd heard the talk during the war about some men's 'preferences.'

Yet, the mere idea he could act that way towards Thirza or any child, repulsed him. It didn't stop him questioning why it was that his only friend happened to be a child though. He'd done that several times, playing Devil's advocate on the walk to and from the park.

Each time he drew the same conclusion; Thirza could empathise with his appearance, she treated him normally and yes, she reminded him of Ursula.

They didn't look alike, not one bit. But he recalled his little sister having the same maturity and common sense; how it had been her and not him, the older brother, who'd coped best when their father died.

Where had he been while his mother grieved, attempting to pick up the pieces and keep her family together? He knew the answer of course ... running riot with Bernie Stone and Johnny Beckworth, the three of them thieving and getting up to all sorts of mischief away from home.

And then the wake-up call. Johnny's younger brother seeking the three of them out under the railway tunnel where they'd set up a den to store their illicit gains.

Hobbs could still see Johnny now, repeatedly hitting his brother for going there, until finally the young Beckworth boy managed to blurt his message out.

Running home, back at the house breathless, pushing his way through family and friends crowded inside, their faces a mixture of sympathy and scorn.

Leaping the stairs two at a time, Hobbs remembered flinging open the bedroom door, his heartbroken mother sitting on the bed stroking his sister's hand.

Ursula's eyes were closed, the wheezy rasps of her slow and laboured breathing the only noise.

And then his mother speaking, her voice cracking amidst the tears:

'Tuberculosis … my baby girl's got tuberculosis, Charlie.'

The scene was so vivid, even now after all this time. He remembered his sister take her last breath and the blood curdling screams of his mother, as she clung to her daughter's lifeless body.

'Is there a parade on then? There usually is at a pageant,' Stan asked, pouring tea.

'What? Oh, yes … yes there is. And a band.'

'Oh, I like to hear a good brass band, reminds me of my Army days, marching through Cape Town.'

Half an hour later and Hobbs was out the door, the wadding underneath his mask already making him sweat.

When Thirza first asked him he'd been unsure and even now he was uneasy. But in recent weeks his confidence had grown; no longer awash with anxiety when in a crowd.

'Come on, Charlie, it'll be fun. There's going to be stalls and a puppet show,' she'd told him excitedly.

'*Then how on earth can I resist*,' he'd scribbled in reply.

There was little cloud and the cherry blossom was dazzling in the sunshine as couples and families streamed into the park. Some were spread out on picnic blankets in front of the bandstand. He passed two young women, walking arm in arm, holding pretty parasols above their heads.

Tipping his hat, they smiled, though one of them stared hard as he walked on, whispering to her friend.

It occurred to Hobbs he might struggle to spot Thirza among the crowd and he stood still, turning slowly, scouring the park for her familiar face.

He heard music from the far side of the lake and saw a parade making its way through the park led by clowns juggling coloured skittles.

Behind them a man in top hat and tails was riding a white horse, flanked either side by young girls wearing yellow and white frocks with matching bonnets. They were followed by a troupe of Morris dancers performing one of their peculiar routines.

As the parade got closer, Hobbs saw a pony and trap carrying what he guessed to be the May Queen - a blonde-haired teenage girl in a white dress, looking uncomfortable despite her smile.

Bringing up the rear was the brass band, at least a dozen men and teenage boys adorned in the same bowler hats and navy blue jackets.

Both sides of the path were lined with onlookers, who formed up behind the band so that when it arrived on the green in front of the bandstand, there was a mass of people following.

The procession passed a Maypole aflutter with pretty ribbons, before coming to a halt, the band finishing to huge cheers.

There was a tug on Hobbs' jacket and he heard a familiar voice:

'You've come, I knew you would.'

'You didn't say there would be clowns,' Hobbs replied, forcing himself to accentuate every word so she'd understand.

'I know! Aren't they marvellous.'

'Are you here by yourself?'

'No, my mother's here too. She's over there with her friends,' and Thirza pointed into a sea of people.

Of course, her mother's here; why wouldn't she be?

Hobbs had never met Mary Moran, he wasn't sure if he wanted to. He didn't even know whether Thirza had mentioned him to her mother.

'Don't worry, she's happy for me to go off on my own. Quick, come here, there's someone I want you to meet,' and she grabbed his hand, leading Hobbs to a large tree where two young boys were wrestling in the grass.

'Michael! Michael!' Thirza yelled, and the boys broke free from each other's grasp, their knees already muddy.

'Michael, this is Charlie, the man I told you about? He was in the war.'

She looked up at Hobbs: 'This is Michael Gregory. His dad is missing like mine. He wants to ask you something, don't you, Michael?'

The boy was nervous yet curious, staring hard at Hobbs. Thirza had clearly told him about his face.

He hadn't expected this and was unsure whether to say something; part of him wanted to just walk away.

Michael Gregory stepped closer.

'Is it true?'

'You cheeky sod.'

'What she says about your face, is it true?'

Thirza was mortified.

'Michael, no! I told you not to talk about that.'

The second boy was interested now.

'What you on about, Mickey, what's up with his face?'

'Thirza reckons this fella's got a tin face, lost his real one in the war.'

'You're kidding, ahhh let's see, Mister.'

'Yeh, please, Mister ... show us your tin face.'

Hobbs could see Thirza was horrified, her eyes watered and she looked at him pitifully. He was disappointed in her but most of all he was angry; angry with himself. He'd been so careful to hide his appearance, wanting to shield people from how he looked. Only for these two shits to do this.

Maybe that explained why he did it.

Lifting his spectacles, Hobbs removed the mask in one swift movement, leaned forward, inches away from the boys' faces and yelled:

'Is this what you've come to see?'

28

The steps leading down to the cell in the basement had a musty, damp smell. There was a solitary, small window up high, level with the ground outside, meaning Hobbs could see and hear whenever someone walked past.

The walls had been painted once but now the faded, white paint was flaking away, exposing the brickwork.

Hobbs could still remember the stench of stale urine and, looking at the slop bucket in the corner, was almost thankful that his sense of smell had disappeared along with his nose.

Sitting on the slatted wooden bed beneath the window, he stared at the heavy door with its tiny opening at eye level, through which he could be observed.

The last two hours had been a blur; the boys' screams alerting onlookers who simply saw a grotesque looking man with three children, two of them fleeing in terror.

Hearing their shouts, Hobbs turned to see horror on peoples' faces as they stared at the man who didn't have one.

The commotion rippled through the crowd until a constable, alerted to panicked reports of a deformed man attempting to abduct children, sprinted to the scene.

Hobbs watched the crowd part as the officer headed straight for him, whistle in mouth, truncheon in hand.

Moments later two more constables came running and he was wrestled to the ground. When one of them snatched his mask away and frog marched him through the park, his humiliation was complete.

Thirza's cries to 'stop,' 'leave him alone' went unheeded and Hobbs lost sight of her as she was swallowed by a crowd, angry and curious to see the 'child snatcher.'

Sitting on a low wall, hemmed in by the three constables, he waited for the motorised police van to collect him. No one was interested in his attempts to explain himself.

'Listen to him, he's not right in the head; you can tell that right off,' one of the officers said.

Shoved into the back of the van, Hobbs was thrown from side to side as it weaved its way through Bromley.

Now, he heard the jangling of keys and the lock turn, before the cell's heavy door swung open and a tall, thin constable stood in the doorway. He was older than Hobbs and glared at him with cautious, steely eyes, either side of a once broken nose. A thick moustache, curling into spirals at both ends, gave the officer a comic, music hall appearance.

'Out you come,' and his deep voice resonated across the cell.

Hobbs stood and the constable moved aside, motioning with his thumb for him to step out.

He was led down a passageway, passing three other cells and then up a flight of concrete steps, where he was ordered into a small, windowless room. There was a wooden table in the middle with two chairs.

Told to sit, Hobbs waited as the constable took out a notebook before staring at his face, not saying a word. 'Why am I here?' and Hobbs saw the revulsion and fascination on the officer's face as he attempted to speak. 'I've done nothing wrong.'

'We'll be the judge of that,' the constable replied, opening his notebook.

There was a long pause before he spoke again: 'I'm Constable Tunnicliffe. Do you know why you're here, Mr Hobbs? S'no good you denying it, lad, you were seen. What gets me is how brazen you were, all them people about an' all. Arrogant as well as perverted, are we?'

Hobbs felt dazed.

What the hell was he talking about?

'I've come across your sort before, lad. You get to see all kinds of scum doing this job and let me tell you sunshine,' and Tunnicliffe leaned forward: 'There's nuffin' worse than a kiddy fiddler.'

The penny abruptly dropped.

'Nooo, no that's not true,' and saliva spluttered from Hobbs's mouth. Tunnicliffe looked disgusted.

'You can deny it all yer like, but it ain't gonna help ya. We've spoken to the two boys and the girl. Yes, that's right, Mr Hobbs,' he smiled, 'we know what's been going on. Seems you've struck up quite the friendship with an eight-year-old girl. Meeting her in the park after school, going out of your way to see her too, I understand.'

Hobbs was sweating profusely, he knew where this was going but felt powerless to stop it.

Tunnicliffe was relishing every moment.

'So, I ask myself what's a twenty,' and he paused to look at his notebook, 'five-year-old man doing meeting up with a young schoolgirl in a park nowhere near his home?'

Hobbs gestured to speak but Tunnicliffe raised a hand.

'Here's what I think, Mr Hobbs. You've served your King and country, no one can deny you that. And you got banged up pretty badly, we can all see that. What was it? Bullet? Shrapnel?'

Hobbs didn't answer but Tunnicliffe carried on anyway.

'Anyhow, so you come home but you're not the same anymore are you? And what sort of a girl's gonna want to look at you in the morning, or the night before for that matter,' he chuckled.

'So, you go and get yourself one of those creepy looking masks made to try and fit in - have to say, Mr Hobbs, I'd heard about 'em but never seen one until yesterday - but you use yours to prey on young kids. Now, how I'm doing so far?'

'No! Please, it's not … '

'A man's got his needs, I understand that but kids? Really? You know, when I think of some of those boys who never came back and yet types like you made it through. Well, there's no bleedin' justice sometimes,' he said, shaking his head.

It was then that Hobbs pictured a future for himself even bleaker than the one he was already resigned to.

Across town, Mary Moran sat at her kitchen table, tears streaming down her face.

'She refuses to come out of her room, she's absolutely distraught, oh, Mother, what am I going to do?'

Evelyn Barrett held her daughter as she sobbed; the hotpot she'd been making while Mary and Thirza were at the pageant left bubbling on the stove. The last hour had been a traumatic one. Evelyn had turned down going to the pageant, she didn't like crowds and brass bands reminded her of her courting days.

Her surprise at hearing them return early had turned to shock when Thirza started screaming at her mother.

'What in Heaven's name?' she'd yelled, running into the hallway.

'Mother, it's not true ... Charlie's ... my friend, he would never hurt me,' Thirza was hysterical and Evelyn could only watch open mouthed as Mary knelt before her granddaughter, gripped her shoulders and said: 'Thirza, listen to me. What the constable said ... what that man is accused of. You're too young to understand but trust me ...'

'Noooo, I'm not too young. I've told you, he's my friend.'

'Mary, what in Heaven's name is going on?' Evelyn demanded.

But Mary's eyes had remained fixed on Thirza. Struggling to retain her composure she had taken a deep breath and said quietly: 'You are my little girl, the most precious, beautiful girl in the entire world. I love you so much, Thirza and I will never allow anyone to hurt you.'

Thirza tried to reply but Mary smiled, put a finger to her lips and continued, choosing her words carefully.

'Sometimes, people who we think are our friends, are not always honest with us. You weren't to know what this man was doing, none of this is any of your fault.'

'Yes it is,' Thirza had yelled, breaking free from her mother's hold.

'Why won't you listen to me? Charlie wasn't trying to take Michael and his friend, they just kept going on about his face, it's not fair, mother, it's just not fair!'

And then she had run up the stairs crying, Evelyn grabbing her daughter's arm to prevent her following.

She made a pot of sweet tea, things were always better after tea, and listened as Mary told the story of the monster in the park.

'It's got a lot to answer for that damned war, creating men like that,' Evelyn said, shaking her head.

But Mary wasn't listening. She was replaying the events over and over, always coming back to something Thirza said amidst her hysterical tears.

'Charlie would never hurt me, he cares for me … like Daddy did.'

Breaking away from her mother's arms, she strode out of the kitchen and up the stairs, ignoring Evelyn's calls to leave Thirza be.

Taking a deep breath, she tapped on her daughter's bedroom door. Thirza was sitting on the ledge which doubled as a window seat, looking out across the garden, her face blotchy and red from the tears that still flowed.

'All right, Thirza … I'm listening. Now tell me everything about this Charlie Hobbs.'

29

'I'm … I'm not sure, Sol, why don't we go somewhere else?'

'Come on we're here now, Freddy, we'll just have the one. If you want to go after that, then we'll be on our way.'

Unsure, Freddy relented with a nod.

'That's the spirit. Now, I'm buying, what are you drinking?'

Solomon pushed open the doors of the Railway Inn, it was still early and there were few drinkers inside. Freddy hung back as Solomon approached the bar, he hadn't been back since his run in with the landlord.

'Evening, Tommy, two pints of your finest when you're ready,' Solomon said cheerily.

'Why, Sol Wheeler, it's been too long. I was beginning to think you'd gone teetotal,' and he grinned, pearls of sweat running down his chubby face.

'No chance of that, Tommy. While ever you're still pulling pints, I'll be drinking 'em,' and the landlord laughed.

Freddy fiddled with his lighter, reluctant to step closer, but Solomon had other ideas.

'Tommy, I'd like you to meet my good friend, Freddy Lucas. More than done his bit for King and country and now in need of a beer just like me.'

Tommy lifted his gaze as he pulled beer from the pump, holding a pint jug underneath the tap. 'You know this fella?'

'Of course, he's a good friend of mine.'

'He can't drink in 'ere, Sol. I'm sorry.'

'What? I don't understand, Tommy? He's as much right to be served a drink as anybody, more so if you ask me.'

'Yeh, but I'm not asking you, Sol, am I?' Tommy snapped. 'Look Sol,' and he leaned forward, elbows on the bar: 'I gave the lad a chance, yeh, ok, I asked him to sit out back … but I can't have someone looking … well, looking like that and drinking in here. It'll … well, you know, put me customers off.'

'Your boozer's a shit hole anyway,' Freddy yelled, his scarred face scowling at the landlord.

'Freddy! Use language like that and Tommy will be obliged to ask you to leave. Now, look, Tommy … I've been coming in here for fifteen years. Have I ever given you any trouble?'

'You, Sol? No, course not, but.'

'Well, then,' Solomon said, interrupting. 'You're a good sort, Tommy, and I've always known you to be a fair guv'nor of this pub. Don't you think the lad's conscious enough as it is about the way he looks?'

Tommy's eyes flicked across to Freddy, who stood simmering behind Solomon, repeatedly sparking the flint on his lighter.

'After all he's given, the least we can all do is let the boy enjoy a pint in peace, being treated like anybody else. What do you say, Tommy?'

He didn't reply but picked up the half full pint jug and filled it to the top, the froth pouring over the rim. Doing the same with a second, he put it on the bar:

'There you go, but only cos it's you, Sol.'

Leaving a pile of coins on the bar, Solomon picked up both drinks, gave one to Freddy and mouthed a 'thank you' to the landlord. The conversation had been overheard and now the two men were attracting stares from other drinkers as Solomon led them to a table in the corner, beside a stained glass window.

'They're curious, that's all, Freddy … let it go eh?' Solomon whispered, taking a long swig of his beer.

Sipping his pint, Freddy soon realised Solomon was right. Their curiosity sated, the other drinkers returned to their own conversations, leaving the two men alone at the table.

'You know I was in here the night I … well, you know, the night on the railway line.'

'You're having me on? So was I.' Solomon replied.

They shared an incredulous look before Solomon started laughing. And then, for the first time since they'd met, Freddy did the same.

'What a pair eh?' and Solomon turned to the bar shouting: 'Hey, Tommy, you should rename this place 'Suicide Tavern.' The landlord looked bemused and Solomon and Freddy laughed out loud again.

'Now, who's going to get us thrown out?' Freddy asked, his smile exposing the gums in his mouth.

'Oh, Tommy's not a bad sort, Freddy. He's a decent enough bloke. I'm not making excuses for him or anybody else but you know … people don't know what you went through. They either don't want to confront it or they're afraid to do so.'

The smile dissolved from Freddy's face.

'Someone else told me that once.'

'Oh yes? Who would that be then? Friend of yours?'

'Charlie Hobbs is no friend of mine,' and Freddy's demeanour changed in a heartbeat.

Solomon recognised the name, recalling the letter he'd posted. He wanted to probe further but let it be.

'My old man used to drink in a pub just like this,' Freddy said, looking around.

It was the first time he'd ever mentioned anything about family and Solomon was intrigued.

'Where was that then?' he asked, taking another swig of beer.

'Nottingham, s'where I grew up.'

'Your family still up there?'

'Nah, me mam and dad are long gone. They were both killed in a house fire in Nineteen Fifteen … I'd not long finished me training and was about to join up with my regiment. We were getting ready for Gallipoli. Instead, I missed out on all that fun.'

'Bloody hell, Freddy, that's … that's tough, losing your folks like that.'

'Fire seems to follow us Lucas' about.'

'Any brothers or sisters?'

'Two; Sally moved to New Zealand before the war, she's the eldest. Married a miner who wanted to emigrate. We've lost touch, haven't heard from her in years. And then there's Dolly, she's a couple of years older than me. When my folks died she … well, she struggled to cope. Got worse and worse she did … there was little I could do being in the Army and all. She's been in an asylum for two years now.'

'Oh, Freddy, I'm sorry. Do you … do you ever visit?'

'Looking like this? Do me a favour, Sol, she's fucked up enough as it is.'

There was an awkward silence.

'Your … your injuries. From the trenches?'

'This? No, I got this flying aeroplanes. I wasn't always a soldier see. Joined up with me mates and they put me in the Manchester's; Christ knows why but when you're nineteen and have never been outside Nottingham, you don't care too much.'

Solomon stayed quiet, letting Freddy open up.

'Once I'd buried me parents I was due to return to the regiment but most of the lads I'd joined up with had 'gone west' fighting Johnny Turk. I was stationed in a reserve camp down near Maidstone when they came looking for volunteers. 'Who fancies being an observer with the Royal Flying Corps?' they asked. I stuck me hand up and was staggered when I got picked,' he continued, speaking for longer than at any other time in front of Solomon.

'Anyway, I'd have done anything to get out of those daily drills, enough to send you loopy they were. After four weeks training I joined a squadron in France and flew as an observer for three weeks before they asked me if I wanted to train to be a pilot. Well, who's going to turn down a chance like that eh?'

Solomon smiled, finishing his drink.

'I guess you've never flown have you, Sol? No, not many have, and I knew that. Incredible machines they are, really fantastic,' and his eyes lit up, Solomon catching a glimpse of happiness and wonder within.

Then Freddy sighed and swigged his beer: 'But they're shit when they're on fire.'

30

Hobbs woke to the sound of his cell door swinging open.
He must have dozed off for an hour or so because he'd
spent most of the night staring up at the light from the
street lamps glowing through the small window.

Another constable appeared, carrying a tray. Laying it on
the cell floor, he slammed the door shut. Hobbs picked up
a mug of watery tea and two slices of dry toast.

He couldn't drink the tea, not from a mug anyway. It
was Freddy who first suggested carrying a small piece of
rubber tubing to sip from. Now, he used it all the time for
drinking when there weren't any straws. But the tube was
in his jacket, taken by the police with his wallet and keys.

Ravenous, he tried eating the toast but gave up after half
a slice. Outside, the chimes of a distant clock tower struck
eight; he'd heard them at six but not again until now,
telling him how long he'd slept.

He had no idea what was going to happen or how long
he'd have to wait; but waiting was something he'd gotten
used to. And now, sitting alone, he had the same sense of
foreboding as the day his life changed forever.

The cell door opened again, it was same constable who'd brought him breakfast.

'Sarge wants to see you, follow me.'

A short walk through the station and he was back in the same room where Tunnicliffe questioned him the day before.

'Wait here,' the constable barked.

Moments later a barrel chested sergeant appeared; he was unusually clean shaven for a man in his forties – or so Hobbs assumed from the creases on his face. He sat opposite.

'Constable McElroy tells me you didn't touch your tea and hardly ate any breakfast.'

Hobbs was drained, barely able to summon the energy to speak. He wished he could write instead of trying to talk.

'I … I can't drink … without a straw.'

'You should have said something, we could have arranged that.'

Hobbs said nothing.

'Now, I've got a lot to thank policing for, Hobbs. Looking out for people and making sure those who step out of line are dealt with, well … let's say that can be very satisfying,' the sergeant said, his quiet voice unsuited to a man of his size.

'When my lads picked you up yesterday and told me what it was you were accused of, well, I won't lie Hobbs, there were a couple of them wanting a few minutes alone with you, war veteran or not.'

Hobbs was perspiring, his parched mouth desperate for a drink.

'But I don't run my station like that; others might, I prefer to let the law run its course. Not that I'm soft by any means,' he added quickly.

'I reckon if I'd have let em' have a go at you, well … I'd bet most decent folk out there wouldn't bat an eyelid, some would probably want a go themselves,' and it did nothing for Hobbs' anxiety when he began chuckling.

'But as I said, I do things by the book,' the sergeant said. He let the sentence hang and Hobbs wondered if he was supposed to thank him or say something.

'So, what regiment were you in?'

'Royal Fu … siliers … City of London,' Hobbs replied, struggling to pronounce it.

'Rifleman eh? I used to be a pretty good shot myself once upon a time; but the war came too late for me. It's a young man's game war, though from the looks of you, there's nothing playful about it.'

The sergeant was quiet and again Hobbs wondered if he was meant to respond.

'I've done … nothing wrong … ser … geant.'

'Mansell, Sergeant Mansell; You know, Hobbs, you'd be surprised how many people who end up sitting in here, tell me they've done nothing wrong,' and Mansell leaned back, a smug look of satisfaction on his face.

Should Hobbs protest his innocence again? Was it even worth trying? But Mansell held a finger up, his mouth open.

'Now, don't get me wrong, I'm sure there are some who are being absolutely truthful. And I expect you're sitting there wanting to say: 'Yes, Sergeant Mansell, and I'm one of 'em.'

Hobbs nodded vigorously.

'The problem for a lot of those people, Hobbs, is that the evidence is stacked against 'em. They plead their innocence despite everything pointing to the fact that they're guilty. Now, what also helps of course are witnesses. Witnesses are hugely important. They can clear a man … or condemn him,' and again, Mansell leaned back in his chair, savouring the moment.

'Do you believe in God, Hobbs?'

What the hell? Was the sergeant trying to trick him?'

'I wouldn't blame you if you didn't considering your bad luck in the war and that. But it seems the Gods are on your side. Or should I say the mother of that little girl? You see, she's been down here this morning to speak in your favour.'

'Oh my God.'

'It seems her daughter has backed up what you've been telling us; that nothing untoward happened and yesterday's episode was just a … misunderstanding.'

'So … so, I'm free … free to go?'

Mansell stood, opened the door and gestured with his arm for Hobbs to leave.

'Yes … yes, you are. Oh, but before you go … answer me this question, Mr Hobbs. What on earth were you doing befriending an eight-year-old girl?'

It was Hobbs' turn to stand now, emboldened at the relief of being let go.

'Because she doesn't … look at me … like you do.'

31

'All right, lads, that's enough, hand this gentleman his property back,' Mansell ordered, catching one of the constables holding Hobbs' mask over his face, mimicking his voice.

Tunnicliffe was laughing.

'Shouldn't you be out on patrol, Constable Stewart? And you too, Tunnicliffe?' and both men knew it was an order and not a question.

'Excuse the lads their bit of fun, Mr Hobbs, they don't mean any harm.'

Hobbs was too busy examining his mask to reply. It had a scratch on the left cheek and what appeared to be a dent on the side of the nose.

'Bastards.'

Mansell sensed he wanted to protest.

'I expect you'll be wanting to be on your way now, so all the best to you, Mr Hobbs.'

Making a point of putting his mask on slowly, followed by his hat, Hobbs opened the police station door, grateful to be stepping out into the sunshine.

The air was cool and he shivered, turning up the collar on his suit jacket. He hadn't worn a coat to the pageant but wished he had one now.

From across the road a nervous Mary Moran watched him from a discreet distance; she was curious to find out more about this man; no, it was more than curiosity, it was need. She *needed* to know who he was.

He paused outside the police station and looked up to the sky, his face as strange as Thirza had described it.

Then he set off walking and Mary followed, grateful to be wearing her heavy, winter coat. Despite Hobbs having no idea who she was, Mary kept her distance.

From behind, she saw a man of average height and build, appearing to walk without purpose; neither in a hurry nor taking his time.

Hobbs walked with his hands tucked into his trouser pockets; the straw boater on his head was perfect for yesterday's pageant in the sunshine but in the chill breeze, it looked out of place.

What had she been expecting? Was she angry with him? She had been … still was … wasn't she?

No, her anger had gone. Fear had replaced that; fear of what could have happened to her little girl. She wasn't afraid of him, how could she be afraid of someone who looked so vulnerable, so lost even.

And that made her mind up. Mary increased her pace, getting closer until within earshot she said:

'Mr Hobbs?'

Did he hear? She was about to call out again when Hobbs turned his head. And there he was, the man with the tin face. Thirza's description had failed to mention he wore dark glasses and, though Mary had seen them as he came out the station, up close he was intimidating.

'Mr Hobbs, my name is Mary Moran. Thirza's my daughter, I was ... I was hoping I could speak with you?'

Hobbs was so used to people avoiding eye contact that he didn't notice her unease. She had delicate features; a slim face with high cheekbones and small, thin lips. Her green eyes betrayed a nervousness Hobbs wasn't used to seeing in somebody else.

Mary had hoped he would at least say something. But she wouldn't be deterred, not now.

'There's ... there's a cafe on the high street just before the railway station. Maybe we could share some tea?'

His hand was already reaching for his notebook and pencil.

'Thank you for speaking with the police. It was kind of you. I don't want to be any more trouble, please excuse me.'

'Mr Hobbs, I ... I simply want to talk to you about ... Thirza is ... well, I mean, Thirza speaks very highly of you. She has been through so much,' and her voice tailed off.

He couldn't recall the last time a woman had spoken to him. The thought of sitting down with her excited and terrified Hobbs in equal measure.

He scribbled again.

'She is a remarkable girl. Honestly, Mrs Moran, you have done more than enough for me, thank you.'

'Thirza is terribly upset,' and Mary watched for a reaction. 'She blames herself for what happened to you; she is at home now with her grandmother, I know how much my daughter worries, Mr Hobbs.'

Mary gazed at his face, determined to stand her ground. Finally, Hobbs held out his arm and invited her to walk with him, his frozen face at odds with his chivalry.

They walked in silence for the few minutes it took to reach the café; a bell above the door jingled as they entered and they chose a table near the back.

Mary wanted to look at the other diners, could they tell there was something different about the man she was with?

And then it hit her; this was the first time she had been in the company of a man since her husband had died. What if she was recognised?

'This was a mistake, I shouldn't have come here.'

Hobbs was oblivious to her apprehension, sliding his notebook across the table.

'If you'll excuse me, I won't eat or drink in front of you, it's not something I'm comfortable doing.'

Snapped out of her unease, Mary was mortified.

'Oh, Mr Hobbs, I'm so sorry, I didn't think … you must think I am terribly inconsiderate. Please forgive me.'

Oh, how he wished she could see him smile. He sometimes forgot how cold and emotionless his tin face made him look; but not now.

'It's fine, you really … don't need … to apologise.'

'Thirza told me you didn't always write things down,' and Mary hid her surprise at hearing his voice.

She ordered tea; Hobbs was thirsty and ravenous but he wouldn't repulse her by eating or drinking.

'I'm so sorry for what happened yesterday, Mr Hobbs.'

'Charlie … please, call me Charlie.'

She looked uncomfortable at that and Hobbs regretted the informality.

'Thirza is the most precious thing in the world to me, Mr Hobbs. I can be a little over protective towards her but that's … well, that's because of how difficult her life has been.'

She paused as the tea arrived and the two of them sat awkwardly silent as the waitress took her time placing a teapot, cup and saucer on their table.

'She is a remarkable girl,' Hobbs said, stumbling over the word remarkable.

'Yes, she is. Since … since I lost my husband, we have become even closer. She has never kept anything from me. Yet,' and Mary paused, searching for the right words.

'She had never told me about you until yesterday.'

Now, Hobbs was uncomfortable.

'I don't blame you, Mr Hobbs,' she added quickly. 'After I'd calmed down yesterday - I was quite emotional when we left the park,' and she was blushing now. 'I sat down and I listened to my daughter. And she told me things that even now, sitting here, I find difficult.'

Mary delicately dabbed both eyes, taking a minute to regain her composure.

'When she was born, I saw the look on the midwife's face. Even now, in the Twentieth Century, I hear the comments from other mothers about her appearance; nonsense about witchcraft,' she said dismissively.

Hobbs understood the reference, remembering his own mother talking about the mothers of hare lip children as Devil worshippers.

'It is tough for her, looking and sounding like she does. I'm her mother, Mr Hobbs, when I look at my daughter I see the most beautiful girl in the world. But I'm not so naive that I believe other people think that.'

He remained silent, part of him listening but also wondering why she was opening up to him like this.

'She's remarkably resilience but I know that the older she gets, the harder it will be for her. And that's why I want to thank you, Mr Hobbs. You see, Thirza no longer appears afraid of her looks or her future. She says that meeting you has changed the way she thinks about herself. And for that I'm extremely grateful.'

She reached for Hobbs' notebook and pencil and scribbled her address.

'I know Thirza would very much like to see you again and I hope you will consider visiting. I dare not go back home without a yes from you,' and she smiled.

'I would like that ... very much.'

'Excellent, she will be so pleased. Next Saturday? Around midday?'

'I look forward to it.'

Mary stood and Hobbs got to his feet quickly.

'It's been a pleasure meeting you, Mr Hobbs.'

'You too, Mrs Moran.'

She was heading for the café door when she turned and said: 'Mary ... my name's Mary.'

Hobbs watched her leave before ordering more tea. Discreetly removing the small rubber tube from his jacket pocket, he savoured his first drink in hours, all the while thinking of Mary Moran.

32

Few callers ever knocked on the door of sixteen Gladstone Street. The ones that did were either pre-arranged visitors or door to door salesmen, usually war veterans who Stan Finch could never resist buying from.

When they came selling their matches, tea towels and other wares, he knew they were more likely to call in the late afternoon or evening, when people were home.

So, when there was a loud rap on the front door shortly after ten in the morning, Stan was caught by surprise.

'Hold your horses, I'm coming,' he yelled, ambling on his wooden legs through to the hallway. He opened the door to a craggy-faced man in a dark overcoat and flat cap. He was older than Stan, his greying stubble and creased face, giving him a weathered look.

'Good morning, you must be Mr Finch?'

'Aye, who's asking?'

'Wheeler, Solomon Wheeler, I'm a … an acquaintance of Freddy Lucas,' and he saw the sudden look of interest on Stan's face.

'I'm here to collect Freddy's things, well some of them anyway. He's given me a list of what he wants … the rest, well, he's told me to tell you to give them away.'

'Is he all right? Freddy, I mean?'

'Yes, he's fine, Mr Finch. He's been staying with me for some time now … he also has a job, though I'm sorry but for some reason he doesn't want anyone here knowing,' and Solomon struggled to hide his embarrassment. Remembering his manners, Stan stepped back and invited his visitor in.

'We've been wondering what happened to the boy; he just upped and walked out one morning after a row with Charlie … used to be the best of mates. Charlie's been pretty cut up about it.'

'Would that be Charlie Hobbs? I recall posting a letter from Freddy to a man with that name.'

'Aye, that's right. And that letter from Freddy, well it were poison. Charlie didn't deserve that, not after all he's been through.'

Solomon was intrigued, wanting to know more, both about Charlie Hobbs and Freddy's letter.

'You say he's living with you now then?' Stan asked.

There was little furniture in the room and what there was appeared thrown together. Solomon guessed the house was a men's refuge.

'Yes, yes he is. We met by chance a few weeks ago. I'm on my own now, my wife … she, she died earlier this year. I offered Freddy a room and he's been with me ever since.'

Easing himself into a chair, Stan shrugged.

'Well, good luck to the lad, I hope he gets himself sorted. It's tough for these boys, especially them that looks like Freddy and Charlie,' and Solomon realised Hobbs must also be disfigured.

'Fancy a cuppa, Mr Wheeler?'

'No, thank you, I've not got a lot of time I'm afraid. If you could show me to Freddy's room, I'll collect his things and then leave you in peace.'

'Well, I can't show you on account of these,' and Stan lifted his trousers; he enjoyed the look on people's faces when he revealed his wooden legs.

'But you want the top floor, room facing the front of the house. The one opposite is Charlie's.'

Freddy's room had a stale, stuffy odour that came from having its door and windows closed for weeks on end. Solomon thought of his own bedroom, had Maud's scent been consumed by the same unpleasant smell?

Again, the room was sparsely furnished; a single bed was pushed lengthways against the wall. Opposite, was an old wardrobe, a small table at the side of the bed and a chair behind the door with a pair of trousers hanging from it. It wasn't big and the sloping ceiling made it feel smaller.

The wardrobe door was sticky and Solomon had to force it open, gathering what few clothes there were. Above, was the suitcase Freddy mentioned. Lifting it down, Solomon flicked the catch, stuffing the clothes inside.

That done, he reached for a single shelf above the clothes rail where there was a book and a bundle of envelopes. The book was Arthur Conan Doyle's *The Lost World*, the title in gold lettering against a dark blue cover.

Inside, the words: '*To our dearest Freddy, with love from Mum and Dad, Christmas, 1911,*' were written in the corner of the first page.

There was something else between the pages; a family portrait. Solomon looked closely at the picture of a man and a woman, with three children. He wondered how much Freddy had resembled his father before burns had destroyed his face.

Were you as handsome as your old man, Freddy?

While the Lucas children and their mother gazed into the camera, Freddy's father looked elsewhere, his eyes fixed on somewhere beyond.

Baby Freddy was on his mother's lap and as he stared, Solomon felt sorrow for this ordinary family, riven by tragedy.

He closed the book, putting it in the case along with a bundle of letters; the top one was addressed to Mr F.M Lucas and had a New Zealand stamp on the envelope. From his sister, Solomon knew.

He didn't hear the front door open down below.

'Charlie? Charlie is that you?'

Hobbs was greeted by Stan hobbling into the hall; he was expecting the old soldier to grill him about where he'd been since the pageant.

'It's Freddy.'

'What? Is he back?'

'No, no,' Stan replied, irritated at the interruption.

'There's an old fella upstairs in his room. Says he's here to collect Freddy's things, reckons he's living with him now.'

Hobbs was about to remove his mask but a glance upstairs told him to keep it on.

'Whoa, slow down, Stan. Freddy's where?'

Stan repeated himself.

'So, what did he say? Is Freddy all right?'

'Freddy is fine,' Solomon said smiling, carrying Freddy's suitcase down the stairs.

'Freddy … are you sure … he's all right?'

'Oh yes, he's absolutely fine. As I was telling Mr Finch here, he's working now and seems to be in a more positive frame of mind,' and Solomon hoped he was doing enough to reassure the two men without breaking his promise to Freddy.

'He's living with you then?' and Hobbs noticed the old man didn't seem at all surprised by the way he spoke.

'Yes, yes he is.'

Hobbs had a hundred questions but he knew Freddy better than anyone. Instead, he simply stepped aside.

'Well, please, wish him all the best for me.'

Solomon nodded, took his hat and coat from Stan and picked up the suitcase.

'Cheerio, gentlemen and all the very best to you too.'

'Well, I'll be blowed. I never expected that, Charlie. But good luck to the lad, let's hope he's got himself sorted out eh?'

'Aye Stan, let's hope he has,' Hobbs muttered, closing the door.

33

Pacing the room, talking to himself, Freddy fiddled with the flint of his lighter, all the time running a hand over the creased, bumpy skin of his bald head.

Once or twice he pulled back the lace curtain, peering out into the street and his frustration swelled at no sign of the old man.

He stubbed his toe on the base of the armchair, yelling with pain and kicking at it with his other foot.

When the door finally opened and Solomon returned, Freddy was almost upon on him before he could get inside.

'So? Did you see him? What did he say? Come on, Sol, tell me!' and Freddy was standing inches away from the old man's face.

'Whoa, hold up there, Freddy, at least let me get in the door.'

'Fucking answer me, Sol, did you see him or not?'

Solomon dropped the suitcase, his cheerful face evaporating.

'You need to calm down, Freddy; and no one speaks to me like that in my own house,' he said icily.

The rebuke quelled the fire in Freddy, though he was still fiddling with his lighter.

'I'm ... I'm sorry, Sol. But come on, I need to know!'

'I'm assuming you mean, Charlie Hobbs? Did I see him?
Yes, I did,' and Solomon walked into the kitchen, Freddy
following.

'And?'

Filling a mug with water, Solomon took a long drink,
knowing that would only infuriate his house guest.

'And what?'

'Oh, for fuck's sake, so what did he say? No, hang on a
minute ... was he wearing it? Did he have it on?'

'I assume you mean his cosmetic mask?'

'Cosmetic mask? Fucking freak's mask you mean,' and
Freddy was so worked up he failed to see the look
Solomon gave him for cursing.

'Yes, Freddy, he was wearing it. Why is that such a
problem? I don't understand.'

'Why is it ...? Are you kidding me, Sol? He thinks that by
putting a piece of tin over his fucked up face, he's going
to be accepted ... welcomed back? 'Oh, look here comes
brave Charlie Hobbs, so thoughtful of him to cover his
face up for us,' ... what a hero, let's all applaud Charlie ...
fucking ...Hobbs.'

And Freddy started slow clapping in Solomon's kitchen,
his disfigured face contorted with rage.

'Have you ever thought he might wear it because he's
afraid? Of what people see when they look at him?'

Freddy threw his head back with a false, exaggerated
laugh, before exploding again.

'Afraid? Of course he is ... he's a fucking coward and a
fool. He doesn't get it, Sol, this is what we are now,' and
he pointed to his own face.

'We can't be fixed ... this is what it did to us. The first
thing I do when I wake up is think about how fucked up

my own face is ... and the last thing I do before I fall
asleep, before the nightmares come,' and Solomon was
surprised to hear him mention his dreams, 'is think about
this.'

'And every minute in between? This. People should be
made to look at us so they know what we gave ... if it puts
them off their breakfast, so fucking what?'

The wisest thing would be to change the conversation
but Solomon needed to know.

'I assume you were good friends once? Did all that
really end because he started wearing a mask?'

'Good friends? Who told you that? Hobbs? Or was it peg
legs, the cripple who now spends his days cooking like a
woman for blokes with no faces?'

Determined to make him answer, Solomon ignored
Freddy's ranting and tried again.

'Does it matter? I just think if you were such good
friends, why should your pal doing something to help
himself make you so angry?'

'Ahhh, fucking hell, Sol. How could you ever possibly
understand? Yes, I thought he was my mate ... we looked
out for each other, or at least I thought we did. But all that
was bollocks; all the time he's telling me 'Freddy, it's
going to be hard, Freddy, don't worry what people think,
Freddy, don't let the staring get to you' ... and all the
time, the fucking turncoat is seeing to it that no one stares
at him anymore."

And Solmon began to understand.

'Well, I don't care what people think when they see me,
Sol ... if it gives them sleepless nights, I don't give a shit.
But if I ever see Charlie Hobbs again, I'll rip that fucking
mask off his face so people can see what the cunt really
looks like.'

That was it, Solomon had heard enough. He thought of Maud, how she hated cursing, would never allow it under her roof. He glared at Freddy before pushing past him into the sitting room, bending down in discomfort to remove his shoes.

The best thing would be to say nothing, to allow Freddy to cool off. But thinking about Maud had made Solomon angry.

'You know, Freddy, you're right. I don't understand ... I never will. And yes, maybe Charlie Hobbs is everything you say he is. But if wearing a mask gets him through the day, then who am I or anyone else to begrudge him that?'

The rebuke caught Freddy by surprise and Solomon followed it with a raise of his hand to indicate he wasn't done.

'You need to find whatever it takes for you to get through the day, Freddy ... like it or not, you made it home. Are you really going to live out your days hating a man who's no different to you?'

Taking his shoes to the front door, he saw Freddy about to speak.

'Save it Freddy, I've heard enough. I got everything you asked for, it's all in there,' and he pointed to the suitcase by the front door.

34

Thirza was desperate for the weekend. This was the happiest she'd been in a long time, counting down the days until Hobbs' visit.

It was a far cry from watching helplessly as Charlie had been taken away, her inability to help him, fuelling the anger she ultimately directed at her mother.

But then things had changed; Mary had listened, Thirza had told her everything and thankfully, she was believed. The notes Charlie had written instead of speaking, her diary entries about their friendship, she'd shown them all to support her story.

They'd both cried a lot that day but her mother had wept more.

Now, halfway through the week, her excitement levels were rising. She was also secretly thrilled her mother hadn't mentioned moving to America once since the pageant.

She arrived at school with a broad smile across her face and it didn't take long for her friends to notice; or her teacher.

'You're looking very cheerful today, Thirza, I'm delighted you look forward so much to your schooling,' Grace Hesketh remarked in front of the class.

Thirza's smiled widened, her face reddening. She had known these children for as long as she could remember. Unlike some of the older ones, they didn't tease her about her lip, or the way she spoke.

She wasn't speaking to Michael Gregory though; she blamed him for everything and regretted ever telling him about Charlie. He'd tried to speak to her at least twice but had since given up, the look in Thirza's eyes enough to dissuade him.

Yet, she hadn't forgotten what it was that Michael told her he wanted to speak to Charlie about. She'd thought about it a lot; how fabulous it would be if Charlie said yes. She'd imagined that happening so many times that she'd almost convinced herself her 'happy ending' was in reach.

All she needed now was for Charlie to agree.

Grace Hesketh was also counting down the hours; though only until the end of the day. She had a date at the theatre and was struggling to concentrate as she led the children through an afternoon geography class, taking them through a map of the World, pinned to the wall.

For their final exercise of the day, she asked each of her pupils to write down ten capital cities.

'When you are finished, bring your work to the front and leave it on my desk. You may then collect your things and leave … quietly.'

A steady stream of seven and eight-year-olds duly complied with her request until only Thirza remained.

'Are you planning on staying here all night, Miss Moran? Because if you are, then you will be very much on your own as I have somewhere important to be.'

'I'm … I'm sorry, Miss Hesketh, but I … I can only think of eight.'

'Oh, Thirza, ten capital cities is really not that difficult a task … especially when we have just spent the last hour and a half studying the Atlas,' and she swiped Thirza's book from her desk, her impatience visible.

'Paris, Rome, Berlin, Madrid, London, Washington DC, Athens and Vienna … and you're certain you can't think of any others?'

Thirza's brow furrowed and she chewed on the end of her pencil.

'We talked about Russia for some time did we not? Can you recall the name of its new capital city?' prompted her teacher.

Screwing her face up, desperate to remember, a look of sudden elation appeared on Thirza's face as she squealed: 'Moscow! Is it Moscow?'

'Very good, Thirza, now, I would have thought with a name like Moran, that maybe you have relatives that come from Scotland?'

'Edinburgh … it's Edinburgh.'

'There you go … you just have to rummage around in your brain sometimes to find what you're looking for.'

'Thank you, Miss Hesketh, can I go now?'

'Yes, you can. You've been extremely cheerful today, Thirza. I trust that's a reflection of your love of school?'

'I do like school, Miss Hesketh but I'm also really excited about the weekend.'

'Oh, and what's so special about the weekend?'

'My friend, he's coming to visit. Mother says we can bake him a cake, though I'm not sure he'll be able to eat it, what with his face and all.'

'His face?'

'He was in the war, my friend I mean … but his face was damaged and now he has to wear a mask.'

'Oh, how terribly sad. You say he's a friend of yours, surely you mean of your family?'

'Oh no, my mother only met him last week; until then he was just my friend. But now Charlie Hobbs is going to be her friend too.'

Grace's blood ran cold, she felt her legs would buckle and had to grip the back of Thirza's chair to steady herself.

'What did you say?'

'That my mother only …'

'No … his name? What did you say his name was?'

'Charlie; his name is Charlie Hobbs.'

Long after Thirza had gone, skipping out of school with her carefree smile, Grace sat alone, overwhelmed by memories of Charlie Hobbs. She could still hear his laugh, see those tender eyes, remember the promises they'd both made.

But logic and reason were part of what made Grace a good teacher and she dragged herself back from an emotional cliff, posing the questions and then searching for the answers to convince her it couldn't possibly be.

Charlie Hobbs … it was a common enough name, there were bound to be other men who shared it; no, it was simply the shock of hearing his name again after all this time.

It was a strange and upsetting coincidence, that's all this was.

She packed away her things and tidied her desk before leaving, the sound of her shoes echoing through the empty building. She felt like one of her pupils, being chastised by her rational self to stop being silly.

No, whoever this friend of Thirza Moran is, it couldn't be her Charlie.

Because Charlie Hobbs was dead.

The journey home was plagued with memories of that horrific day; her mother's tears when she found her cowering in the corner of the kitchen, slumped on the floor next to the vomit her terrifying grief had induced.

She pictured the plain brown envelope with the red triangular stamp on the front, and the words 'passed by censor.'

Thankfully, she had been sitting down when she'd opened it.

'Dear Miss Hesketh, it saddens me deeply to be the one to tell you that poor Charlie has been killed. I was with him at the time he was hit and he was in a bad way when the orderlies got to him, though I don't think he was suffering. It was one of the orderlies who told me later he hadn't made it.'

'Although we've never met, Charlie spoke of you constantly. He was very much in love with you and described you to me and the other lads as 'Amazing Grace.'

'I'm so sorry for your loss and for you having to find out through a letter from a stranger. However, I know Charlie worried that if the worst was to happen, there would be no official telegram sent now that his mum is no longer alive.'

'I'm afraid I don't know where he has been buried but once I get some leave I will attempt to find out more.'

'With deepest sympathy and kind regards, Joe Winterbourne.'

But Joe Winterbourne had never written again; his own parents receiving the dreaded telegram about their own son's death a few weeks later.

With every step home, Grace was two different people; there was logical Grace, berating her panicked alter ego, desperately trying to keep calm, to think straight, to realise how ludicrous she was being.

And then panic-stricken Grace; stunned at the thought Charlie might still be alive, horrified she had given herself to another man.

'Oh my God! Sam!'

Clasping a hand over her mouth, she stopped dead in her tracks, thinking of the new man in her life. It had taken months for her to even contemplate seeing someone else. Betraying Charlie – because that's what it would be - convinced Grace she'd never marry; her virtue and solitude were the price of honouring his memory.

But the sun still came up, her doting parents showered her with love and affection, and time soothed the raw wounds she once thought would never heal.

It was strange at first, of course it was; but meeting Sam had rekindled something inside, something she thought had gone forever. Part of her waited for the guilt to come but it never did. And Grace took that as a sign.

But Sam would be calling for her later; they had a theatre date. How on Earth could she do that now?

No, she couldn't see him. Not now, she needed time to think.

Stepping on the trolley bus, Grace was oblivious of anyone or anything; lost in her thoughts, tears streamed down her face.

'Are you all right, dear?' It was an old woman, she could be her dearly departed grandmother. She had the same sympathetic eyes, the same time-worn face.

'I'm sorry?'

'You're upset, is everything all right?'

Other passengers were staring and Grace composed herself, forcing a smile: 'Thank you, I'm fine, honestly.'

It was a short walk from the bus to the home she'd lived all of her life. Her parents had liked Charlie; her mother had cried as much as Grace had, while her father would disappear for hours on his own, unsure of what to say or how to console.

What was she supposed to tell them now?

No, it was ridiculous, this could not be her Charlie, it was impossible. She decided not to tell her parents, there was nothing to tell. But she would need her mother's help. Grace couldn't see Sam tonight, however much she yearned to see Shakespeare on the stage.

She hated lying but there was no other choice. Opening the door, her shoulders sagged, shuffling into the kitchen where her mother stood at the sink, her father absorbed in his newspaper.

'Gracie you look terrible, are you all right, dear?

'No, Mother,' she lied, easing herself into a chair beside her Father. 'I think I'm coming down with something, I feel dreadful.'

'I hope it's not the flu, we've had enough of that to last a lifetime,' her father said, recalling the pandemic that swept the country a year ago.

'Well, you're not burning up which is a good sign. Maybe you just need to rest up while I make you some tea,' her mother added, resting a hand on Grace's forehead.

'No, nothing for me, Mother, I can't face anything to eat or drink,' she said, telling the truth. I … I just need to go to bed. Please give my apologies to Sam when he calls.'

She only got as far as the stairs when the tears came again, images of Charlie and Sam flashing before her watery eyes.

35

Dusk came earlier on account of the evening drizzle, coating the streets with a film of rainwater that shimmered under the gaslights. There were few people around and those who were out walked quickly, heads down in the murky rain.

Freddy did the same, his flat cap pulled low so the peak almost covered his eyes. His hands thrust into the pockets of his coat, collar turned up to cover his neck, for once he didn't look out of place. He also knew that where he was heading, he wouldn't be the only one not wanting to be seen, or recognised.

The nearer he got, the emptier the streets became until finally, Freddy was alone. Crossing the road, he turned off down a narrow alleyway running between a tobacconist's and the ironmonger's.

It wasn't lit and he headed into the darkness, unaware a broken drainpipe was spewing out rainwater above him. The freezing water splashed down his neck, and Freddy sidestepped, cursing.

A street lamp illuminated the end of the alleyway until he emerged out into the road, turning left past a row of darkened buildings.

He heard the raucous shouts and drunken laughter emanating from the Dog and Partridge and was thankful to be going the opposite way.

Another left turn and he was in a street of terraced houses where a barking dog and a baby's cries broke the silence.

Out of the shadows, two women emerged and stepped into Freddy's path. One was old enough to be his mother, her stout, buxom frame, silhouetted against the street light. Her companion was younger, slimmer and as he approached, she sauntered forward, opening her coat to reveal her underwear.

Puffing on a cigarette, the older woman blew smoke in Freddy's direction.

'Evening, dearie, you looking for some fun tonight then?'

Excited and nervous, Freddy paused; a glance at them both before shaking his head and walking on.

'You won't find better,' the older woman yelled, 'or cheaper,' said the other. When he didn't turn back one muttered 'tosser' loud enough for him to hear.

Further up the street there was someone else and Freddy's heart raced and he felt a stirring in his groin. He knew who it was, he could tell from the way she was standing, silhouetted by a street lamp, and Freddy quickened his pace.

'Watcha, Freddy, it's been a while. Thought you'd forgotten about me, sweetie.'

Her heavy coat fell open as she came up close, sensing Freddy's excitement as he stared at her cleavage, almost spilling out of her corset.

'You want the usual, sweetie? Or for a bit extra we can go to my place, it's only round the corner,' and she ran fingers up and down his chest.

'No … just the usual, Lily,' Freddy mumbled, fumbling in his pockets for a pile of coins he handed over.

'It's all there,' he said, as she counted it out in front of him.

'Oh sweetie, I've learned the hard way not to take a punter's word … no offence like,' and she tipped the coins into her handbag.

'Right, come on then, let's see if we can't sort you out, Freddy, my boy,' and she led him by the hand down a darkened alley.

Minutes later Freddy emerged with Lily following, still adjusting her skirt as she walked.

'Don't you be leaving it so long next time, Freddy, s'not good for you,' she chuckled.

He retraced his steps, walking quickly, spotting the two prostitutes still loitering at the end of the street. They scurried off into the gloom and suddenly, Freddy heard footsteps behind; two men were following.

He heard a woman's voice and then a third man appeared ahead, and walked his way. Freddy knew what was about to happen; he'd heard the stories, it was the risk punters took. But he was battle hardened and the thought of running never occurred.

Instead he slowed down, waiting until the man in front was close enough. And then in an instant, he let out a roar and lunged wildly, catching the stranger off guard.

They fell to the floor, Freddy repeatedly smashing his fists into the man's face as the adrenaline surged through him. But his assault was short lived, a violent kick in the stomach sent him sprawling in the street before hands were clawing, pulling, dragging him away.

He tried to stand but was kicked again, a heavy blow smashing against the side of his head.

And then the man he'd been punching was yelling at the others: 'Hold him, hold the bastard still.'

Freddy struggled but their grip was too strong and he was dragged to his feet, his arms pinned back.

'Jesus, look at him …. `what's up with his face?'

'It's about to be fucked up,' snarled the man Freddy had attacked and he threw a punch which smashed into Freddy's face, splitting open his nose.

There was a taste of blood as another punch came and Freddy felt the crack as a bone in his jaw splintered. And then he started laughing, hysterically, his bulging eyes gazing at his bemused attackers.

'Come on, then … do it,' he yelled.

'Go on, Sid, give the bastard some more.'

And the two men held Freddy as he was pummelled, joining in when he fell to the floor, kicking him savagely until finally, everything went black.

He heard a voice but his first thought was why he couldn't open his eyes. As his senses awoke so did the nerves that sent pain signals to his brain, raising the alarm of his battered body.

'Ere, you all right, love?'

It was a woman's voice and as the fog lifted, Freddy remembered where he was, crying out as he tried to stand. He was shivering now, wet from the rain and his own blood.

'Can you stand? Ere, let me help, ya,' and she helped him to his feet, Freddy clenching his teeth in agony. It took him so long to stand he was convinced he'd broken his leg. 'Lean against the wall, so's ya don't fall, I don't think I could pick yer up again.'

Groggily putting one foot in front of the other, he used the wall to steady himself.

'You need to get to a hospital love, you're not gonna get far the state you're in.'

Ignoring her, he stumbled along the street, his entire body racked with pain. He had no idea what time it was. His watch was missing and feebly patting his pockets, he knew his wallet and lighter had gone too. Staggering through the streets, lurching from side to side, he resembled a drunk, passing out at least once, coming round slumped on the floor in the doorway of a haberdashery shop.

Freddy clutched his side, he knew his ribs were broken, spitting out the blood that kept pooling in his mouth.

Solomon was sipping his late night mug of tea before turning in. Freddy wasn't home but that wasn't unusual; his house guest occasionally disappeared on his own in the night. He never said where he was going and Solomon never asked; not that he wasn't intrigued, he was just happy to see him doing 'normal things.'

Rinsing his empty mug he heard a noise outside; or at least he thought he did. He listened again, all was quiet and Solomon shrugged it off, getting into bed.

Then he heard it again, louder this time; someone was at the front door.

'Who's there?'

There was no reply and the old man went to the window, pulling the curtain back, feeling the cold glass against his face as he strained to look outside. Through the rainwater that ran down the window, he saw a crumpled shape at his door; it moved and the banging resumed.

Cautiously, Solomon unlocked his door and peered into the darkness.

'Oh, Jesus Christ … Freddy!'

36

Sweat ran beneath Hobbs' mask and the wadding, dribbling into his already parched mouth. Wishing now that he'd taken Stan up on his offer to use his aftershave, Hobbs could only hope he wasn't giving off an unpleasant odour.

His first tap on the door lacked conviction and he had to knock again, this time hearing it reverberate through the hallway beyond.

The sound of hurried footsteps inside, someone rushing down the stairs.

'Don't run, Thirza, you'll fall,' he heard Mary Moran say, as the door opened and Hobbs was greeted with a warm smile.

She hadn't been out of his thoughts since they'd met and seeing her again reminded him why. Mary had a graceful, delicate beauty that defied the suffering she'd endured. He thought how lucky her husband had been for her to fall in love with him.

'Charlie, you're here, come in, come in,' beckoned Thirza, brushing past her mother to take his hand and pull him inside.

Mary laughed as Hobbs stepped into the house and for a moment he was sure he could smell her scent, though he knew that could only be a memory.

Awkwardly, he handed over the small bunch of freesias he'd bought from the flower seller in the High Street, enjoying the demure smile she gave him in return, before Thirza ushered Hobbs into the sitting room.

'Thirza, take Mr Hobbs' coat for him.'

'Mother, it's Charlie ... he likes to be called Charlie, don't you Charlie?'

'Well, it is my name,' he said, whipping out a chocolate bar from his pocket .

'Yummy, chocolate, can I eat it now, Mother, please?'

'No! You can wait until after supper, now say thank you to Mr Hobbs.'

'Thanks, Charlie,' and she wrapped her arms around his waist, hugging him tight. She was still holding him as Mary returned from taking Hobbs' coat and he was suddenly uncomfortable, gently prising her away.

But as the afternoon wore on Hobbs relaxed, thanks to Thirza's infectious enthusiasm. When she appeared with a straw to drink her water, Hobbs was even confident enough to drink his tea in front of them both, touched by the gesture laid next to his teaspoon.

He declined the offer of homemade cake, asking Thirza if she would wrap him a piece so he could enjoy it later.

She skipped into the kitchen delighted.

'Thank you so much for coming today, Mr Hobbs ... it means so much to Thirza,' Mary said, perched on the edge of the sofa, hands resting in her lap. She wore a white, high necked blouse with a frilled collar and a bottle green skirt that hid her legs, and Hobbs wondered what she was thinking as she gazed at his fake face.

'I … I wanted to come, thank you for inviting me,' and he caught a brief glimpse of the bottom of her legs as she moved her feet.

'Could I get you anything else, more tea perhaps?'

'No, I'm fine, thank you.'

'Mother … I can't find anything to wrap Charlie's cake.'

Rolling her eyes playfully, Mary got up.

'Will you excuse me, Mr Hobbs.'

The room had a homely feel, everything had an order, from the vase standing on a circle of lace in the middle of the table, to the mantlepiece bookended by two simple candlesticks, a ticking clock in the centre.

There was a cabinet facing the window and Hobbs rose to take a closer look at the three framed photographs on it.

The face of James Moran stared out at him, standing proudly behind a seated Mary. She was reaching over her left shoulder, resting a hand on her husband's fingers.

They were together again in the second picture but this time Mary sat with a baby on her lap. Thirza's curls were already beginning to emerge and the split in her top lip seemed even more pronounced.

In the third photograph James Moran was pictured alone. Wearing his Army uniform, only his upper half was visible. His gaze went above and beyond the camera lens, a stare into eternity.

Beneath his cap, Moran wore a determined yet contented look, his square jaw and thin mouth unable to conceal a tenderness in his face.

'That was taken on the weekend before he returned to France. I never saw him again.'

Caught by surprise, Hobbs was thankful to see Thirza following her mother, clutching a napkin which she thrust in his hand.

'Here's your cake, Charlie, I hope you like it.'

'I know ... I will.'

He'd intruded by looking the photographs and for once was glad to be masked.

'I'd better be going soon, don't want to ... outstay my welcome.'

Thirza was crestfallen.

'Oh, please stay, Charlie, please?'

'Maybe I can come again, if, if that's all right with you, Mrs Moran.'

She smiled.

'We'd like that very much wouldn't we, Thirza?'

'Yippee,' and she dashed out of the room yelling excitedly: 'I've forgotten something, Charlie, wait there.'

'You're certainly very popular in the eyes of my daughter, Mr Hobbs.'

'I'm ... I'm sorry about before, the photographs I mean, I didn't mean to pry.'

'Nonsense, it's perfectly all right. I think you would have liked James ... and him you,' and she glanced wistfully over to the cabinet.

'Are you ... still thinking of moving overseas?'

The question surprised her and Hobbs added quickly: 'Thirza ... she told me.'

Mary invited Hobbs to sit back down.

'I'm not surprised. She was terribly upset when I first spoke about it. She ... she believes we would be leaving her father. I've deliberately not mentioned it for a while.'

Shuffling in his seat, Hobbs wasn't sure what to say but to his relief Mary continued: 'There is only sadness here for me, Mr Hobbs; this house, this town, everything about my life was with James. Now that he's gone.'

She left the sentence hanging and Hobbs was sweating again.

'But what about you? Do you have any plans? I can't begin to imagine how much your life has changed because of that dreadful war.'

It was the first time anyone had asked him about his future and he had no idea how to reply.

'Do you have family? Someone special? Oh, listen to me, asking all these personal questions, please forgive me.'

'There used to be ... not anymore,' Hobbs said.

There was a heavy silence and they were both relieved to hear Thirza hurrying down the stairs, a bundle of energy bursting into the room.

'Here you go, Charlie, you can put it up on your bedroom wall,' and she handed Hobbs a sheet of paper, her face bursting with pride.

It was a child's drawing showing three figures. One was clearly supposed to be Thirza, he could tell that by the curly, red hair.

Pencilled Thirza was holding hands with a man in a tie and they were both waving to a woman standing nearby.

'It's lovely, thank you.'

'I'm glad you like it, Charlie. That's you and me and we're waving goodbye to Mother.'

'Where are you both off to?' Mary asked, giggling.

'We're going to go and look for Daddy, and Charlie's coming to help me, aren't you, Charlie?'

37

Thank God, she couldn't see his real face.

Not that Mary was looking at him; her eyes were fixed upon Thirza, face frozen in shock.

'What? What did you say?'

Hobbs felt compelled to speak, to search for something, anything, to ease the tension.

'It's only a picture,' was the best he came up with.

There was anger in Mary's eyes.

'A picture? You think this is simply about a child's drawing? Tell me, what is going on here, Mr Hobbs? What nonsense have you been filling my daughter's head with?'

Thirza's face crumbled as she watched her mother turn on her friend.

'Mrs Moran ... I don't ... I mean.'

'You need to leave my house, Mr Hobbs. Now! And I do *not* want you contacting my daughter again, is that clear?'

She simmered with rage, her eyes fixed upon Hobbs with a venomous stare. Thirza was horrified, unable to understand.

'Noooo! Mother, please, why are you doing this? Charlie? Charlie?' she screamed.

Was this really happening again?

His first instinct was to leave but moving towards the door Hobbs stopped.

'I have done you … no wrong. Please believe me.'

Mary refused to look at him.

'Leave … now, Mr Hobbs.'

Thirza was inconsolable, clinging on to Hobbs, refusing to let go.

'Come here, Thirza! Do as you are told.'

But the little girl squeezed tighter, all the time crying and whimpering: 'Charlie, don't go, please don't go.'

Hauled away by Mary, she wriggled free, glared at her mother and screamed: 'First you lie about Daddy, then you want us to move to America and now you're taking Charlie away from me … I hate you!'

As she bolted upstairs, Mary collapsed to the floor sobbing.

The easiest thing would have been to open the door and leave there and then. Do that and he'd never see either of them again.

Instead Hobbs headed for the kitchen, filled a glass with water and returned to the hallway, kneeling beside a crumpled Mary, offering her a drink and a clean handkerchief from his jacket pocket.

Through red, puffy eyes she took the water but couldn't look at him.

'She's … she's upset, Mrs Moran … that's all.'

Mary got to her feet, refusing to let him help. She returned to the sitting room, and Hobbs followed gingerly, keeping his distance.

'She doesn't understand …'

'Doesn't she? Well, please enlighten me, Mr Hobbs, because at the moment I'm beginning to think the police were right to arrest you after all.'

He was irritated now and sat without being asked.

'Mrs Moran, your daughter doesn't believe her father is ... dead,' and he focused on making himself understood.

Mary put a hand to her mouth and Hobbs heard her gasp.

'She doesn't believe it ... because she cannot understand how a man can be *dead* if he's missing.'

'Is ... is that what she told you?'

Hobbs nodded.

'Then ... why, why didn't you tell her.'

'Tell her what? That men can vanish in an instant ... or their bodies sink into the mud never to be seen again? Should I tell her that?'

He'd gone too far, Mary's sobs told him that. Covering her face, her body shook in time to her sobs.

'I'm sorry.'

'I spent a year hoping,' she said, lowering her hands.

'Every single day for a year I hoped and prayed that he'd come home. I used to feel the same way ... men simply can't go missing, can they? How can it be that so many are lost? And then one of his friends paid me a visit and he ... he told me how James had died; and that they'd buried him close to where he fell but that in the days afterwards, the ground had been ... been churned up,' she said sniffling.

'So, yes, I know how men can go missing, Mr Hobbs; how my husband, Thirza's father, went missing. But until my dying day I will make sure my little girl never knows her daddy was shot to pieces and then his corpse blown to bits, God rest his soul.'

Should he get up and leave or say something else? There was noise from upstairs.

'I ... I should go up and see her,' Mary said.

Hobbs was tired from speaking and got his notebook out.

'If I can be of any help or, if you'd rather I go, please say.'

'One of the reasons I want us to move to America is so Thirza can get to know her grandfather,' Mary said, handing his notebook back. 'There are no men in her life, Mr Hobbs ... or there weren't until you came along.'

'I'm not trying to take your husband's place, Mrs Moran,' he wrote.

'No, you misunderstand me ... what I'm trying to say is that you have been good for her. These past few weeks she has appeared happier and more content. I guess I have you to thank for that.'

'You give me too much credit, I really haven't done that much.'

'Well, I'm not sure Thirza would agree with that. Look, I know this is asking too much of you and I would understand completely if you'd rather not, but will you stay while I speak with her? While I help her to ... understand what happened ... to her father?'

She was convinced he would say no and expected him to scribble a reply. Instead Hobbs said:

'If you think I'd be of help ... then, yes, of course.'

Smiling, Mary smoothed the creases from her skirt as she stood, sweeping her brunette hair away from her eyes.

'Thank you, Mr Hobbs and I'm ... I'm sorry.'

At the foot of the stairs she shouted for Thirza to come down. When she didn't reply it was Hobbs who suggested: 'She's tired, maybe we should wait until the morning. I could come over first thing?'

Mary mulled it over and agreed, before an awkward parting on the doorstep; Hobbs not knowing how to say goodbye, Mary just as ill at ease.

On his return to Gladstone Street, he avoided Stan and the other residents, going straight to his room, allowing his mind to wander with vivid images of Mary Moran.

He was up early the next morning, heading out before anyone else was awake. Hobbs suddenly felt drawn to the Morans, they'd become closer to him than anyone. And he couldn't stop thinking of Mary.

Why does she want me there when she tells Thirza the truth?

He had to force himself not to read too much into it.

Though it still fired his imagination.

He knew the little girl would be fine; she was resilient and mature for her age. She'd cope, he was sure of that.

Hobbs turned into the Moran's street and saw people standing outside the house. Increasing his pace, he spotted Mary, she was anxious, panicked.

'Mr Hobbs … she's gone … my little girl. She's gone!' And Mary was running towards him, the panic etched onto her face.

Clutching a scrap of paper, there was terror in Mary's eyes.

Hobbs took it and saw a child's writing:

'Mother, I'm not going to live in America and you can't make me. Sending Charlie away won't stop me finding Daddy. I know he's out there somewhere and I'm going to bring him home. Don't worry about me, Thirza, x.'

He lifted his gaze, his tin face staring impassively at Mary, a woman whose fragile world had fallen in around her.

38

'I thought you might be up to managing some breakfast, we've got to keep your strength up, Freddy.'

Solomon backed into the bedroom holding a tray.

'A mug of tea and fried eggs on toast, it's like staying at the Ritz,' the old man joked as he approached the bed.

Freddy's face was a mess, his burn damaged skin covered in cuts and bruises. The swelling over his left eye prevented him opening it; but it was the injuries that couldn't be seen that worried Solomon.

Watching Freddy painfully lift himself up into a sitting position, his face contorted in agony, Solomon winced.

He knew Freddy's ribs were broken, or at the very least cracked, but he hoped there were no internal injuries; aware how serious they could be if they weren't treated. But the one thing Freddy had been adamant about was 'no doctor.'

After dragging him in from the doorstep, Solomon managed to get him upstairs and into bed where he'd passed out with the pain. In the hours that followed he had nursed him best he could, giving him Aspro and the occasional tot of whisky from the bottle kept at the back of his cupboard.

'So, how are you feeling? Any better?'

'So, so,' Freddy replied, slowly lifting a fork to his mouth.

'Are you going to tell me what happened?'

'What does it look like, Sol?'

'It looks like someone beat the living daylights out of you; that I know! I mean, who was it and why?'

Freddy chewed his food, each mouthful an effort.

'I got jumped, Sol, that's all; they took everything I had.'

'Well, we should go to the police, report it. We can't let these thugs get away with it.'

'I'm not going to the police, Sol, I was careless, that's all. I shouldn't have been there … now I just want to forget it happened.'

'Shouldn't have been where?'

'I said forget it, Sol, it doesn't matter.'

Solomon didn't push, he knew that approach never worked on Freddy.

'I'm just looking out for you, Freddy, that's all,' and left him to his breakfast.

'Oh, I forgot to say, I found this on the stairs. You must have dropped it on your way out. Good job, or they'd have had this too.'

Freddy snatched his cigarette lighter from Solomon's hand, ignoring the searing pain in his ribs from stretching his arm out.

'For someone who doesn't smoke you're very attached to that lighter, Freddy'

He hoped Freddy might tell him why or at the very least thank him for finding it. Freddy did neither.

When the old man had gone, Freddy stared at the ceiling, allowing his thoughts to drift, coming face to face with the men who'd beaten him.

And then he closed his eyes, flicked his lighter and smiled, picturing himself exacting a tortuous revenge and watching his attackers burn.

****

'Has anyone seen Thirza Moran?'

Grace Hesketh's class shook their heads, all except one girl with her hand up.

'Yes, Martha?'

'We saw her mam yesterday, she was crying. They came to our house and spoke to my parents but then they left.'

'Thirza and her mother?'

'No, Miss. Thirza wasn't there. It was her mam and a man … a man with a strange face. My dad said not to look at him.'

'He was the man at the pageant, the man the police arrested,' Michael Gregory yelled from the back of the class.

The other children were muttering now and Grace clapped her hands, demanding silence.

'What man are you talking about, Michael?'

And Michael Gregory told the story of the pageant, beginning with Thirza confiding in him about her new friend.

'And this friend she told you about, you've met him?'

'Yes, Miss, at the pageant; but he was real scary to look at; we ran off, we didn't mean for him to get into trouble.'

'Do you know this man's name?'

'Charlie … Charlie Hobbs is what Thirza said.'

'And … and you said he was scary … to look at I mean,' Grace asked, oblivious to the puzzled faces of her pupils.

'Yeh, he was, Miss, he'd been in the war. Thirza said he was wounded in the face so now he wears this mask, to cover it up. She said maybe he could help us find our dads. I know mine's still out there, in France I mean. And Thirza believes hers is too,' he said, defiantly.

The remainder of the day dragged but when the bell for home rang, Grace knew exactly what she had to do. Grabbing her things, she didn't head for home. Instead, she turned right out of the school, walked through the church yard and into the park, heading for Thirza Moran's home.

****

'Mrs Moran, let me assure you that my officers are doing everything they can to locate your daughter.'

'Sergeant, you're not listening to me.'

'I know this is hard, Mrs Moran but in my experience, once a child gets hungry they soon come back home with their tail between their legs.'

Mary sat back, rubbing her temples:

'I can't believe I'm hearing this, it's intolerable. Sergeant, I demand to speak to your superior.'

Sergeant Mansell forced a smile.

Who was she to start demanding, missing kid or not?

'There's an inspector over at Orpington but as for here, I'm the senior officer in charge.'

Hobbs could be silent no longer.

'Sergeant Mansell … what Mrs Moran is trying to tell you is that Thirza …'

'I'm sorry, Mr Hobbs, I didn't quite catch that,' Mansell said, and the constable in the room was smirking.

Hobbs reached across the table, snatching the officer's notebook and pencil.

'Thirza has not simply run away, we believe she has gone to look for her father.'

He shoved the book back towards Mansell.

'And whereabouts does the girl's father live, Mrs Moran?'

'Her father is ... he ... died in the war.'

'I'm sorry to hear that, Mrs Moran, truly I am. But now I'm confused see, because Mr Hobbs here, he's telling me you believe your daughter has gone looking for him?'

Hobbs glared.

'You irritating bastard.'

'He was declared ... missing three years ago,' Mary said. 'But Thirza she ... she doesn't understand how that can be. Hence, she believes he is still alive and out there somewhere.'

'And by somewhere, you mean France?'

'Of course, she does!' Hobbs yelled, saliva running down under his mask.

'Let's try and remain calm shall we, Mr Hobbs?'

'Sergeant, please,' Mary said, her voice pleading now. 'My daughter is the most precious thing in the world to me. I have to find her.'

He didn't have a sympathetic face but Mansell's eyes narrowed and he stared at Mary, his bottom lip moving left and right as he pondered.

'Constable, you said a thorough search of the area was conducted and the addresses of friends were visited when Mrs Moran reported her daughter missing?'

'Yes, Sarge. We did the park, spoke to some local kids and went to the homes of those friends Mrs Moran told us about. Oh, and the grandmother.'

'How many times do I have to say it Sergeant? She's not hiding out somewhere locally,' Mary interrupted.

'All right Mrs Moran, we'll have officers go to the railway station and we'll circulate her description. Constable?'

'Yes, Sarge?'

'Contact all police stations in the county giving them Miss Moran's description; oh, and telephone the port authorities. If she is trying to get across the Channel, she'll need to get on a passenger ship.'

The constable left the room and Mary sighed heavily: 'Thank you.'

'Like I said, she'll turn up, I'm sure of it. If I were you, I'd go home and wait for news. Likelihood is she'll be home before dark.'

As they left the station, Hobbs wanted to say something comforting:

'At least they're taking it more seriously now.'

For a moment he expected an angry rebuke. Instead, Mary said: 'She's been gone hours, Mr Hobbs. I can't sit at home waiting for something to happen.'

'What? What do you want to do?'

'I know my daughter, Mr Hobbs, she'll be trying to get to France; I'm going to Dover. Will you come with me? Please?'

39

Nibbling on the last of the crusty bread she'd wrapped in a napkin, Thirza sat on the wall of Dover's Admiralty Pier overlooking the harbour. It was a dry, sunny day with little breeze and she watched with fascination the boats navigating their way in and out of port.

She had a vague recollection of being at the seaside and pictured her mother laughing, as they paddled in the sea.

But the memory dissolved as the whistle from a steamship signalled its arrival, its huge hulk looming closer.

Several warships were anchored around the port while dozens of smaller vessels weaved their way in and out of Dover, dwarfed by the steel giants they passed.

Plumes of steam wafted across the pier from trains coming and going from the line which ran almost to the edge of the sea.

For Thirza, it was new and exciting; yet, the best part was seeing Dover teeming with troops. She'd counted at least three steamers arrive, their decks packed with British and Colonial soldiers filing down the gang ways, lugging their kit bags.

Their beaming smiles and raucous laughter were heard above the noise of the docks, men happy to have made it home.

When the first ship arrived, Thirza had spent more than an hour wandering anonymously through the khaki ranks, hoping against hope that maybe, just maybe, she'd get lucky and her father would be among them.

She had even spoke to a couple of soldiers, tugging at their greatcoats to catch their attention and showing them a photo of Lance Corporal James Moran.

'Who? No, sorry, love, never heard of him.'

She was heartened at first by the sight of so many. But now the sheer size of the task depressed her. Her legs ached, she was tired.

Stealing out of the house in the early hours had been easy enough, though she wished she'd taken more food. In her small case she carried her father's photograph, some bread and cheese, two apples, a change of clothes and her teddy bear, Hugo.

Scraping together the contents of her piggy bank, along with the two bank notes from her mother's purse that she'd agonised over before stuffing them into her pocket, Thirza had gone to the railway station, finding it deserted.

But the platforms had steadily got busier and the ticket office finally opened.

Buying a ticket to Dover had been straightforward enough, though she wondered if the sour-faced man behind the counter was staring at her lip or because she appeared to be travelling alone.

Thirza loved the journey, sitting next to the window in a carriage with an elderly couple who believed she was going to visit a sick aunt near the coast.

Pulling into Dover, she sat on the promenade gazing at the enormous ships, a feeling of trepidation and excitement at the thought of crossing the Channel.

She was hungry now and sat on a wall eating the bread, saving the cheese for later. Reaching into her coat pocket, she fished out the folded letter she'd removed from her mother's special tin.

It was the telegram which confirmed James Moran was missing. More importantly, it told Thirza he was in the Duke of Wellington's Regiment. That and the date he'd gone missing - October twelve, Nineteen Sixteen – it was all she had to go on.

Before giving up her search among the soldiers filing off the troop ships, she stopped another Tommy, asking if he'd heard of her father's regiment.

His blonde hair visible underneath a steel helmet, the soldier smiled, his tobacco stained teeth and dirty face unable to hide his delight at being home.

'These lads, we're all Ox and Bucks,' and he swirled a finger around to illustrate the point. Thirza didn't understand.

'Horrocks! Oi Horrocks? Wasn't your brother in the Duke of Wellington's?'

'What's that?'

'This lass here is looking for the Duke of Wellington's … your brother was with them, weren't he?'

'Aye, but that was three years ago. He's been in Blighty ever since the Somme, got one in the knee the lucky bleeder.'

The blonde haired soldier smiled at Thirza and said: 'Sorry, love, can't help you.'

'Where's the Somme?'

'The Somme? In northern France, why you thinking of visiting?' and he laughed.

'Yes, yes I am.'

'Somme's no place for a young lass like you.'

'But my father's going to be there, I've got to go and meet him. How do I get there?'

The troops began moving out, the soldier was distracted. 'Mmm? Oh, get yourself to Amiens, good luck.'

He turned and disappeared in a sea of khaki, men jostling for position as they headed for a waiting train. Along the pier, she passed the grand building of the Burlington Hotel dominating the port.

Following a sign for 'cross channel passengers' Thirza joined a line of people waiting to buy tickets.

'I'd like to go to France please.'

Behind the glass, the ticket officer frowned at the young girl with the deformed lip.

'How old are you?'

'I'm ten,' she lied.

'Too young to travel alone I'm afraid.'

'I'm … I'm not alone. That's my father over there,' and Thirza pointed to a stranger reading a timetable on the wall.

Craning his neck to look, the ticket seller was not convinced.

'My father believes I should be independent and able to fend for myself. He's bought his ticket already and he wants me to buy my own.'

'Come on, move it along, what's the hold up?' piped up a voice in the queue.

'Well, you can't go to France, your father should have told you that,' the ticket seller said.

Thirza wanted to protest, surely he couldn't mean it?

'The only civilian route open is to Ostend. So, you'll be wanting a ticket to Ostend, right?'

'Err … yes, yes please.'

Moments later she felt the sun on her face as she gripped her ticket to Ostend. Thirza didn't even know here Ostend was.

But if it was across the Channel, then it was another step closer to finding her father.

Following a stream of other passengers making their way along the pier to a waiting steamer, she saw them directed to a gangway leading to the ship.

Steam wafted from its two impressive funnels and men in matching blue jackets and peak caps, busied themselves on board.

Thirza handed her ticket to a man at the end of the gangway, who glanced down, smiled and said:

'Hello, young Miss, welcome on board the SS Victoria.'

40

'You must try and eat something.'

'I'm not hungry, Mr Hobbs.'

Mary's gaze was fixed on the train's window and their journey resumed in silence; tea cups clinking in time to the rhythmic clack-a-tee-clack of the carriages.

It had been this way since the rolling hills of the Kent countryside came into view. Hobbs had tried telling her he was sure everything would turn out fine, but the flicker of irritation in her eyes persuaded him to stay quiet.

The green fields eventually give way to more and more buildings and the train slowed to a halt as it pulled into Dover.

'We're almost here … I suggest we go and speak with the police first, to see if there's been any news,' he scribbled.

'The police? Oh, yes, yes of course.'

Mary was exhausted; the colour drained from her face, eyes puffy from crying. Hobbs had to help her off the train, afraid she would stumble in her dazed state. The platform was teeming with soldiers waiting to board for the return journey and Mary linked arms with Hobbs, holding him close.

The gesture surprised him and he loved how it felt to have a woman so close. But the moment was brief, Mary letting go as she spotted a constable up ahead and hurrying to reach him. That left Hobbs pushing through the masses of khaki-clad men to keep up. Mary was already peppering the officer with questions.

'You're better off going to the port sergeant's office, Madam,' the constable said, pointing towards the station's entrance.

'Fifty yards in that direction, you can't miss it.'

The sergeant was sat behind a desk, chewing on a pipe. Hobbs was a passenger in this, he left Mary to do the talking and saw the excitement, the hope, when the officer confirmed he knew all about a missing schoolgirl.

But her optimism was short lived.

'I'm afraid we missed her by a few minutes. Turns out a girl matching your daughter's description was able to buy a ticket for a Channel crossing - don't ask, we've already had words with the ticket office,' seeing the look of dismay on Mary's face.

'We believe she got on board the SS Victoria to Ostend which departed at two forty this afternoon.'

Mary gasped, covering her mouth.

'Ostend? Why … why that's in Belgium isn't it? Oh my God, my little girl, what if anything happens to her out at sea?'

Hobbs thought the sergeant was either remarkably calm or uninterested.

'Now, calm down, Madam, there's plenty of staff on the ship and we've sent a telegram to our Belgian counterparts asking them to look out for her on arrival; though things are still a little … chaotic shall we say, over there at the moment.'

That did nothing to reassure Mary.

'We have to get on a ship, I have to get over there as quickly as possible. When's the next passenger ship leaving?'

'Another one is due to embark in the next hour, if you hurry you can make it. Though, wouldn't you rather wait here until we get news from Ostend?'

Mary was already out of the office but stopped at the doorway: 'No, Sergeant. I'm going to bring my daughter home.'

****

It was Thirza's first time on board a ship and standing on the deck, feeling the wind in her face, she found the experience exhilarating. Wisps of fluffy, white clouds drifted lazily across the blue spring sky, while the sun shimmered off the water as the SS Victoria steamed towards the continent.

To pass the time she treated herself to a current bun and a hot chocolate from the small restaurant on board. Happy simply to stroll around, she spent most of the voyage gazing out to sea, thrilled whenever another vessel came into view.

The fine weather drew more passengers out on the deck, keen to take in the sea air. One of them, an elegantly dressed woman, adorned head to toe in black, caught Thirza's eye.

Accompanied by a teenage girl, she reminded Thirza of her grandmother, as she tightened the lace ribbon under her chin, to keep her black, tulle-wrapped hat from blowing off in the breeze. The girl caught Thirza staring and wandered over.

'I thought I was the youngest passenger on board, how old are you?'

Thirza didn't reply, blushing at being caught looking. The girl smiled warmly from beneath her pale blue Cloche hat:

'I'm Mathilda, though everyone calls me Maddy. What's your name?'

She had friendly eyes; Thirza recalled her mother saying you could tell a lot about people from their eyes.

'Thirza … my name's Thirza,'

If Maddy was surprised by Thirza's speech defect, she didn't show it.

'Have you been on a steam ship before? This is my first time, I'm actually very excited though I have to be careful not to show it,' and she flicked a glance towards the woman in the deckchair.

'Why? I … I mean no, this is my first time too. Why wouldn't your mother want you to be excited?'

Maddy giggled.

'Oh no, she's not my mother. She's back at home in Hereford. That's Mrs Gwendoline Powell, I work for her, well the Powell family I mean.'

'Oh,' Thirza replied.

'She needed someone to accompany her to France and I volunteered. I've never been outside Hereford before, never mind France. What about you? Where's your mum?' and Maddy was looking at the other passengers.

'She's … she's not here. I'm alone.'

'What are you doing travelling alone? You can't be much older than eight or nine.'

'I'm eight and I'm ... I'm looking for my father. He was in the Army and went missing. I'm going to France to find him.'

Maddy's smile disappeared and she looked at her with pitying eyes. Thirza had seen that look before, mostly after people were told her father was dead.

'How did you get all the way out here on your own? That's very resourceful of you.'

Thirza blurted out the whole story, even the part about Hobbs being arrested.

'Gosh, that's some story; and some adventure you're on too. But how do you know ... I mean, France is a big place, I know that from the maps I've seen in Major Powell's study. How do you know where your father is?'

'Well, I know what regiment he was in ... and someone told me where they were fighting when he went missing. So, I'm going to start in Am ... Amens, I think it is called.'

Maddy giggled again.

'Amiens, you mean Amiens. That's where Mrs Powell and I are going. We're taking the train from Ostend down to Lille and then on to Amiens. I've seen the route and everything.'

Thirza's face lit up.

'Listen, why don't you travel with us? I'm sure Mrs Powell won't mind, though I'll need to ask her, what with her being in mourning and all. Oh, silly me, I've been asking so much about you, that I didn't say. We're going to visit Major Powell's grave. He died last September. Poor Major Powell; he was a first rate employer. Always looked out for us and treated us well he did.'

'I'm sorry.'

'Oh, that's all right. I miss him, we all do. But Mrs Powell ... well, she's not been the same since. Always used to be so gentle and happy; not anymore mind. A broken woman she is now reckons Mrs Faber; she's the housekeeper, back at the house I mean.'

Thirza saw Mrs Powell sitting with her head in a book.

'Come on, I'll introduce you.'

Maddy was already walking away, Thirza following.

'Mrs Powell? Let me introduce Thirza …'

'Moran,' Thirza added.

'Yes, this is Thirza Moran. She's all by herself and she's on her way to find her father.'

The old woman's eyes narrowed and Thirza felt her stare.

'Travelling alone? At your age? Does your mother know where you are?'

Thirza listened as Maddy told an abridged version of her story, impressed she'd remembered it all.

But Mrs Powell seemed more concerned about Thirza's age and the fact she was alone.

'I'm going to have to notify one of the crew. Maddy, go and fetch one of the stewards and tell him I need to speak with him right away.'

'But Mrs Powell, I was hoping she could travel with us. To Amiens I mean. That's where she's going,' and Thirza nodded, hoping her confirmation would help.

'Mathilda Dunbar have you quite finished?'

The rebuke shocked both girls.

'I am making a pilgrimage to visit the grave of my husband and your employer. Do you understand? This is not some childish adventure or a jaunt to the seaside.'

She rose from her deckchair, the two girls taking a step back.

'I knew it was a mistake allowing you to accompany me and I only wish I had insisted upon Mrs Faber making the journey. Now show some respect girl and go and fetch me the steward ... now!'

There were tears in Maddy's eyes and crestfallen, she obeyed the woman's demand, heading for a steward at the end of the deck.

'Mrs Powell ... I'm sorry," Thirza begged. 'But please don't tell anyone. I simply want to my find my father. He's missing you see.'

'Missing? What are you talking about, girl?'

'My father, James Moran, he was in the Army. He went missing ... my mother received a letter and she told me, she told me he'd died. But I know he's out there ... in France I mean. And I want to find him before we move to America. I have to find him.'

The old woman frowned and Thirza mistook that for sympathy.

'This letter, do you have it with you?'

Fishing out the telegram from her pocket, Thirza handed it over, watching her read, hopeful now she'd change her mind.

'I have school friends whose fathers are missing too,' she said, filling the silence. 'We all know that grown men simply can't go missing. That's why we know they're out there, hiding probably or maybe unaware the war's over. It's why I'm going to France, to find my father.'

That elicited a sigh from the woman.

'Oh, listen to me, child. There's no easy way of telling you this and frankly I'm surprised your mother hasn't made it more explicit. Heaven knows, there's enough confusion and myth about the war as it is.'

What did she mean? What confusion?

'Your father is *dead*. Do you understand, child? He and so many tens of thousands of others are simply listed as missing because the war was so ghastly, so frightfully savage that men were simply vapourised by bombs and shells … do you know what that means? Vapourised? It means their bodies were blown to pieces and their remains scattered to all ends of the Earth.'

Each of the old woman's words stabbed like a knife, Thirza feeling every jab and cut as Mrs Powell brutally destroyed her dream with the truth.

'Now, I'm very sorry for your loss, it's something so many of us have to bear, me included. But I'm going to have a word with the steward here and ask him to make sure you are looked after and put on the first boat back to England. I'm sure steps can be taken in advance to contact the authorities and ensure you are returned home safely where, I expect, your mother is frantic with worry.'

Thirza's body swayed, she felt dizzy and didn't see the steward come over, a downcast Maddy following. She didn't hear him agree to the old woman's instructions nor was she aware of an arm comforting her.

'Maddy, come along, we'll be arriving shortly and I want to freshen up beforehand.'

She didn't bothering lowering her voice as she added: 'What a foolish little girl.'

41

'How often does he have 'dem? T'eese ... t'eese dreams?'

'They're nightmares, Pat, and most nights really; though some are worse than others, like last night'

Solomon stood on Patricia Donnelly's doorstep. She appreciated him taking the trouble to come and apologise, though he really didn't need to. The events of the early hours were still fresh; her terrified boys running into her bedroom as they heard the screams and commotion coming from the other side of the wall.

Despite her own fears she did her best to comfort them, afraid of what she could hear and unsure what to do. Finally, as a good Catholic woman she had put her trust in God and summoned the courage to knock on Solomon's door. It had taken a few moments for him to answer but when her old neighbour opened the door she was mightily relieved.

'Oh Solomon, t'ank the good Lord you're all right. I ... I had to find out, forgive me for calling at such an hour but ... the noises you see ... they woke my boys, we ... we were worried.'

Embarrassed, Solomon had assured her he was fine and now, mid-afternoon the same day after finishing work, he'd been the one knocking on her door to explain.

'Afternoon, Pat, I've … I've bought you some mackerel, caught fresh this morning. Thought you and your boys would like a fish supper.'

It was awkward, he knew that.

'Listen, about last night, Pat.'

'Oh, Mr Wheeler, don't you feel the need to apologise, it's me who should be apologising, calling round at such an ungodly hour.'

'No, Pat, I'm the one who should be saying sorry. You were merely being a good neighbour and a friend,' and she blushed at his compliment.

'You know I've got young Freddy staying with me,' and she nodded.

'Well, he has these nightmares. I can't begin to imagine the things he saw when he was over there, Pat, and to be honest I'd rather not know. But as I say, he has these dreams and they can be quite … well, as you heard, they can be quite vivid for the boy.'

'Does he need to see a doctor?'

'Well, I'm sure there are people who could help him, medically I mean. But Freddy he's … well, he's been through a lot and I suspect he's had enough of doctors and hospitals, what with spending so much time in them. No, I think he'll be all right, Pat. He just needs to get it out of his system and get on with his life. I'm sure in time these nightmares will go away.'

Though she didn't say so, Mrs Donnelly hoped her neighbour was right. She'd only spotted this Freddy once, when he was coming from the lavatory in the yard. No wonder her boys were terrified when they'd seen him. And now they'd heard his screams in the dead of night.

She hoped his mind wasn't as damaged as his face. Next door, Solomon was surprised to see Freddy hobbling down the stairs as he came in and hung up his coat.

'Ah, Freddy, you're up and about, just be careful not to overdo it now.'

'What's with that woman next door? I heard you talking out the window, heard my name,' and he slumped into a chair, wincing.

'Oh, it's nothing, Pat was worried about us, that's all.'

'Worried about what?' and Freddy rubbed his aching ribs.

'Freddy, she ... she heard you having one of your dreams last night, she was just making sure we were all right.'

'Dreams? What dreams? What the fuck are you talking about?'

The old man never expected that and knew he had to tread carefully, choose his words with care.

'Freddy,' he said, easing himself into his armchair, 'sometimes when you're asleep ... you, well you have bad dreams.'

'Yeh, so? We all have nightmares, Sol, so what business is it of yours or that bloody nosey Irish woman?'

Solomon was not having have that. He wouldn't let Freddy bad-mouth Patricia, not after all she'd done for him.

'There's no need for that, Freddy. Like I said, Pat looks out for me, has done since Maud fell ill.'

Freddy stayed silent, but his expression was scornful.

'When you're dreaming, Freddy, you ... you shout out, scream even.'

'Piss off, Sol, scream? Really?'

'Look, it's nothing to be ashamed of.'

Solomon regretted his choice of word.

'Ashamed? Are you taking the piss, Sol? What have I got to be ashamed of? So what, if I have the odd nightmare. What fucking business is it of yours or that Donnelly woman?'

Agitated, he moved to the foot of the stairs, Solomon doing his best to placate him.

'I've told you before, Sol, if you want me to move out I will, I don't need this shit.'

'Freddy, please calm down! Having nightmares after what you've been through.'

'And what the fuck do you know about it? You haven't a clue what we went through,' and Freddy snarled, his face twisted.

'All that brave boys bollocks and land fit for heroes ... it was all a load of shit, Sol. Don't you see? We're the dirty reminders, the fucked up faces they want to forget. Well, I can't forget, Sol ... so if I wake you or the neighbours, so fucking what?' and he stomped up the stairs, his ribs burning.

She knew she shouldn't have, knowing the good Lord would never approve; but then Patricia Donnelly had always been flexible when it came to living the life of a good Catholic. Leaning against the sitting room wall, her right ear pressed against it, she listened to the rantings of Solomon's strange house guest, and her neighbour's futile efforts to calm him down.

She'd seen this volatility before, recognised the signs. This Freddy character had a temper; a temper made worse by a troubled mind.

And that worried Patricia Donnelly, who spent much of her evening thinking Solomon Wheeler had made a mistake in befriending this Freddy character.

On the other side of the same wall, Solomon was slumped in his chair, the book he'd picked up to read left closed on the table in front of him. Freddy remained in his room, a plate of liver and onions untouched outside the door where the old man had left it.

Solomon wasn't angry, how could he be? Freddy was a casualty of war, his mind altered by God only knows what horrors he'd witnessed. No, he pitied the poor man, wishing more than anything that he could do more to help him exorcise the demons within.

And then he remembered what Pat had asked: 'Does he need to see a doctor?'

He knew Freddy would never entertain the idea, and Solomon smiled imagining his reaction to the very suggestion. But that didn't mean Solomon couldn't seek help on his behalf. He recalled the house visits of Dr Lavell, becoming more frequent as Maud's condition deteriorated.

The memory triggered more thoughts of his late wife and Solomon wondered what she'd have made of Freddy. He closed his eyes, relishing how vivid she remained, hoping that would never dim. Maud was smiling, and that made Solomon smile again too, before the pain of her loss came in uninvited.

But he was used to such moments now; sometimes he gave in to them, letting the grief consume him. Other times he suppressed it, training his mind to move on.

Now, was one of those times. Memories of Maud dissolved and his thoughts turned once more to Freddy.

And Solomon made his mind up to visit Dr Lavell.

42

Despite Mary's reassurances, Hobbs was mortified. This had never happened to him before and for the life of him, he couldn't understand why it had happened now?

He remembered getting off the train, Mary speaking to the policeman, and the port sergeant's office ... and then nothing. The next thing he recalled was lying in a heap on the ground, utterly helpless as the memories engulfed him.

'Mr Hobbs? Mr Hobbs can you hear me? It's me, Mary.'

Pouring with sweat, his damp skin soaking his clothes, Hobbs' heart was racing, the cold stone of the platform pressing against the side of his face.

His mask!

Panicking, he pushed himself up, hands reaching for his face. The mask was gone, his fingers feeling the squashed, wrinkled flesh of his face.

'Mr Hobbs, your mask ... it's ... it's here.'

On all fours he turned and looked up to see Mary holding his tin face, a look of pity in her eyes.

She helped him to his feet and Hobbs checked his mask for damage, before turning away and putting it on.

'You ... you came over all peculiar when we left the sergeant's office, Mr Hobbs. Do you remember?'

He shook his head, the shame surging through him, wishing more than anything she hadn't seen him like that.

'Your breathing got faster and then you were short of breath ... you, you fainted as I was trying to help you to sit down.'

'Are you all right, mate?' a passerby asked.

'He's fine, thank you,' Mary replied.

'I'm sorry, the train it was, it was pretty warm on there. And I've not eaten much,' Hobbs lied.

She didn't believe him but Hobbs was thankful she let it go.

'I've got the tickets, we leave in thirty minutes. Are you able to go on, Mr Hobbs?'

Her question embarrassed him further and he nodded, crushed she'd seen his broken face.

They boarded the ship, making their way to the restaurant on the lower deck, Hobbs ordering tea and egg sandwiches. They were soft enough for him to eat, though he refused to do so in front of her.

Mary understood when he asked to eat alone, Hobbs taking himself off to an isolated area of the ship. Afterwards, he found her standing on the open deck, looking back towards Dover, the coastline getting smaller.

He stood beside her, looking out at the Channel, white, foaming trails snaking back towards the port. And that's when she hooked her arm around his.

'You must think it silly but I'm a little nervous about boats,' she said.

'There's nothing to worry about,' he mumbled, caught off guard by her spontaneous intimacy.

'The funny thing is, I'd never really thought about it until now. Even planning to move to America ... I'm not sure why, but I hadn't stopped to think how long it takes to get there on a ship,' and when she smiled, Hobbs fell even deeper.

'I guess it's the fear of being surrounded by all this water and a floating tin can is the only thing stopping you from drowning. They say it takes almost a week to sail to America. Did you know that, Mr Hobbs?'

He shook his head.

'No, neither did I until someone at the British Women's Emigration Association happened to mention it at a talk I went to. That's an awfully long time to be on a ship.'

'Yes, but what an adventure it will be, crossing the ocean,' Hobbs said, desperately wanting to say something with meaning.

'Maybe I should wait until they invent one of those aeroplanes that can fly to America, though I fear I'll be waiting a very long time for that day to come.'

Hobbs was struck by a fleeting memory of Freddy but it dissolved as Mary laughed. Her eyes sparkled and his insides did a somersault.

Tentatively, he reached across, placing a hand on Mary's wrist and her head rested against his shoulder. And at that moment he wished the journey would last forever.

****

Thirza was tired; dead tired. Wearily, she listened to the cross-looking man in a dark blue uniform speaking to another cross-looking man dressed the same way.

She couldn't understand a word they were saying, but both kept staring at her before one disappeared through a door and the other said:

'You are hungry, oui? You want to eat something?'

Nodding, she wiped her nose with her sleeve.

The tears had stopped now but Thirza was utterly bereft. She'd never felt more alone. Desperate to go home, she yearned to be in her mother's arms, but instead was sitting on a hard bench in the Ostend Port Authority's office, clutching her teddy bear.

Following Gwendoline Powell's intervention, she was taken into the care of the SS Victoria's crew, who sat her in a small cabin until the ship docked in Belgium. She never saw Maddy or that awful woman again.

That had been more than four hours ago. She knew because of the clock on the office wall. The port official was busy doing nothing as Thirza gazed out the small window that gave her a view of the sea.

Shivering, she squeezed her teddy bear tighter, a tear running down her cheek as she thought of home. Silently, she said a prayer, asking God to take her there.

****

The chill wind forced all but one or two hardy passengers indoors and Hobbs and Mary sat together for the final few minutes.

Surprised how well she was holding up, he prayed Thirza would be in Ostend when they finally got there.

'Would you like me to get you anything, Mrs Moran?'

A shake of the head, that smile again.

'Look, Mr Hobbs, how about we make a deal,' and she could tell from his body language, he was suddenly nervous.

'How about, from now on, you call me Mary.'

Hobbs so wished she could see him smile. The thought gave him an idea and whipping the notebook from his pocket, he scribbled, Mary laughing at his sketch of a smiling face.

'You have a deal, Mary but only … if you call me Charlie.'

'That sounds eminently sensible, Mister … I mean, Charlie. Let's shake on it.'

The familiar dread descended for him, confronted with a hand shake and he rubbed his clammy palms on the seat.

'Come on, Charlie, a deal's a deal.'

And then she saw his unease.

'Are you all right? Is … is something wrong?'

'I'm … I'm sorry, Mary. I mean no offence but I can't … I can't shake hands, with you or anyone.'

She had that look again, the one that told him she understood, that it didn't matter because he was safe now.

Hobbs briefly considered telling her the story, the withered hand protruding from the mud, the fingers curled slightly inwards as it beckoned them forwards; the makeshift wooden sign that read:

'Welcome to Hell, shake Tommy's hand for luck.'

'The war changed everything, for so many of us,' she said quietly.

A pause and then:

'So, tell me, what was Charlie Hobbs doing before the damned war got in the way?'

'I was a junior book keeper with Forsters of London. I'd always been good with numbers and my mother, well, she was determined I should make something of myself … especially after my father and then my sister died.'

'Is she still alive? Your mother I mean?'

'No, she passed away in the winter of seventeen. She never really got over losing my sister, they told me her heart just gave out one day.'

'How old was she, your sister?'

Hobbs stared at her mouth, thinking how beautiful it was.

'She was nine. Out playing one day, in bed with a cold the next and two weeks later she was gone ... tuberculosis.'

'Almost the same age as Thirza,' Mary said quietly.

And Hobbs knew what she was thinking.

43

The evening breeze whipped round her neck, but Mary insisted on waiting outside, close to the gangway, as the steamer slowly eased itself into the dock.

Hobbs was desperate to hold her but his self-doubt loomed large and convinced him otherwise.

'Are you warm enough? Would you like my coat?'

'No, I'm fine thank you, Charlie,' she said, never averting her gaze from the twinkling lights of the port.

As dusk fell they viewed the wreckage of a huge warship, sunk in the harbour entrance. Now lying dormant, its battered hulk was a roosting spot for sea birds as waves lapped against rusting steel.

They felt the bump as the ship shunted against the rubber rings lining the dock wall, the signal for two crewmen, thick ropes looped over their shoulders, to jump down and fasten the boat.

Then the gangways were lowered and the passengers filed off, Mary making sure she was among the first to disembark.

'We need to speak to the port officials, where would they be?'

Hobbs had no idea.

'Let's try over there.'

Again, she was ahead of him, Hobbs hurrying to catch up. As the other passengers followed signs for the railway station, Mary approached two uniformed officials sharing a smoke on the quayside.

'Excusez-moi, parlez vous Anglais?'

A shake of their heads.

To Hobbs' surprise she spoke again, this time in fluent French: 'Pourriez-vous me dire où je peux trouver l'officier du port?'

They were pointed further along the quayside and Mary was off, Hobbs doffing his hat to the bemused men, again playing catch up.

'It's this way …. Oh, Charlie, please let her be there.'

Up ahead was a cluster of small buildings, its illuminated sign swaying in the wind.

'Here … it's here,' Mary gasped, opening the door, not waiting for Hobbs.

'Excusez-moi, je cherche ma fille,' to the man at the desk.

And then she froze … she didn't hear the official speak, nor feel Hobbs' hand on her back. All Mary saw was her precious little girl, curled up on a wooden bench clutching her teddy bear, her eyes closed and mouth open as she slept.

Her legs nearly gave way and Hobbs steadied her as tears of relief came.

Falling to her knees in front of Thirza, Mary gently stroked the copper-coloured curls on her daughter's head.

Opening her sleepy eyes, Thirza's first thought was she was dreaming.

'Mother?' she whispered.

'Oh, Thirza, oh my baby.'

'I'm so sorry, Mother … I … I missed you.'

'Shhh my darling, it's all right, you're safe, I'm here, that's all that matters.'

They were both crying, their faces almost touching and Hobbs kept a discreet distance, watching entranced as mother and daughter were reunited. The port official smiled and said something; Hobbs had no idea what.

'I … I know now, about Daddy,' Thirza said, safe in her mother's arms.

'Huh? What do you mean, my love?'

'I … I know what happened to him,' and she was sobbing now. 'A lady, a lady on the ship … she told me that Daddy … that Daddy is in tiny pieces … and now I know he's never coming back,' and her face burrowed into Mary's chest.

She squeezed tighter, wanting more than anything to take away her little girl's pain.

'There, there. It's going to be all right, Thirza. And look, there's someone else here who wants to see you.'

Hobbs saw her blotchy face peer out from Mary's hold and her face lit up, Thirza clambering off the bench and running into his arms.

'Charlie! I can't believe you're here.'

'Where else would I be, Thirza?'

Minutes later the three of them were walking along Ostend's Digue towards the old lighthouse, needing to find a hotel now there were no more sea crossings until morning.

They passed several damaged buildings, some left in ruins, from the naval guns that had blitzed the port during the war.

Of the two hotels they found open, only one had vacancies. Much to Hobbs' relief, and he imagined to Mary's too, they managed to get two rooms.

It was while Hobbs carried a sleepy Thirza upstairs that Mary suddenly realised how she felt about this man.

She thought of the time spent on the ship, how worried she was when he collapsed at Dover, seeing his vulnerability and shame when she'd seen his broken face.

She had only known him a matter of days but already this felt different. Feelings she hadn't felt since ... well, she knew when.

Smiling, Mary watched as Hobbs carefully laid Thirza on the bed and as he turned to leave the room, she said:

'Goodnight, Charlie ... and thank you, for everything. I couldn't have got through today without you.'

She came up close and stood on tip toe, Hobbs could feel her breath and his memory searched for a scent as he imagined her sweet fragrance.

When she planted a small kiss on his forehead, he was all over the place; his heart racing, head spinning. He hadn't needed further encouragement from Mary to convince him how he felt. But now she had given it.

He took her hand, closing his own around it.

'There's nowhere I'd rather have been.'

In the privacy of his room, the first thing he did was remove his mask. He'd never worn it for so long and staring into the small mirror he saw his ruined face covered in red blotches.

But for the first time since he could remember, Hobbs wasn't thinking about his grotesque appearance; he was thinking about Mary Moran and how beautiful she was.

44

'Solomon, Solomon, do come in ... it's so very good to see you,' wheezed the doctor, his waistcoat buttons struggling to hold in his sizeable gut.

'Though I suspect if you're here, all cannot be well. So, sit yourself down my good fellow and let's see if we can't send you away from here as fit as a flea.'

Solomon liked Benjamin Lavell; the man had an optimism and cheeriness you didn't normally associate with a GP.

When nothing more could be done for Maud, Lavell had continued calling on her regularly, peering over the rim of his spectacles, his beard almost as grey as the hair on his head. Solomon thought Maud always seemed that little bit brighter when he'd left, and he'd always thank the doctor for that.

'No need to worry, I'm absolutely fine thanks, Doc. Apart from my knees giving me gyp when I go up and down stairs, I really can't complain.'

Lavell sucked on an unlit pipe, gripped between yellowed teeth.

'Delighted to hear it, Solomon; but you've not brought a bottle of whisky with you and you're sitting in my practice, so I'm guessing this is not a social call,' and he frowned.

'I have a young man staying with me, he was in some trouble but he's picked himself up and I've got him a job down at Wilson's,' Solomon explained.

'Thing is, he's ... well, he came back from the war and his face ... it's ... he was burnt, Doctor; badly burnt. And you can't help but stare at the poor boy.'

Lavell's eyebrows took on a life of their own, while his mouth chewed on the pipe.

'And now ... he's angry, I mean really angry. Blows up at the smallest thing does Freddy.'

'Well, that's only to be expected Solomon, for many of the men returning home. A good friend of mine served with the RAMC in one of the hospitals near Boulogne. He said he wouldn't even begin to try and tell me what he saw because I just wouldn't believe it. It was Hell, Solomon; literally.'

'Aye, I've heard the stories too, Doc. The thing is, it's not just his anger; he has these dreams, nightmares really. Listening to them, well they make your blood curdle, they really do.'

Lavell stared over his spectacles as Solomon continued.

'Freddy doesn't know I'm here, he'd likely hit the roof knowing I was,' the old man laughed. 'But I want to help him, Doc. Surely there's something can be done to help him?'

Lavell pulled open a desk drawer, picking up a box of matches. He lit his pipe, sucking on the end to get it burning and fixed his eyes on the smoking tobacco.

'You know, Solomon, the medical profession is divided on this. There are those who believe men can be damaged up here,' he said, poking his forehead with a finger, 'just as much, if not worse, than losing a leg or getting shot in the stomach. Some say men like that are a danger to themselves and to others, that there's no treatment and the safest thing to do would be to put them in an asylum for the insane.'

The surgery was filling with smoke, catching the back of Solomon's throat, and he discreetly coughed into his hand. Lavell was oblivious.

'Yet, others disagree, saying the neurosis is temporary, a result of the trauma they've suffered or from the horrors they've witnessed. Or, they believe these men can be treated, in much the same way that you can treat a flesh wound.'

Solomon was fascinated. Leaning forward he asked:

'And you, Doctor, what do you think?'

'It's a difficult one, Solomon. The war changed so much. When I trained as a young GP, things were a lot simpler, but medicine moves on. Look at surgery? Huge advances in recent years. But brain injuries? Neurosis caused by war? I'm not convinced, Solomon. You say this boy's face was badly burnt?'

'Yes, yes it was. He was flying an aeroplane when it caught fire … that's all I know.'

'Well, it's no surprise he's angry. He's distressed by his appearance, he knows he'll never be normal again,' and Lavell was wafting his pipe around as he spoke.

'You know, some men cope better than others. A long time ago I happened across a scene where a wall had collapsed, crushing two men. One of them lost his legs while the other was more fortunate, though he still had to walk with a stick. Guess who turned to drink and drank himself to death?'

'The man with the stick?' Solomon answered.

'Correct.'

'They say he never got over not being able to work again. But what about the poor bugger who lost his legs? He used to sell matches and trinkets outside the railway station, always had a smile on his face.'

Solomon was struggling to see the analogy.

'That's what I'm trying to say, Solomon; maybe this friend of yours simply cannot cope with what's happened to him. I'm afraid you can't help some people.'

'So, there's … there's nothing that I can do for him?' He asked, struggling to hide his disappointment.

'Oh, there's plenty, Solomon. You can start by telling the boy to pull himself together; tell him how lucky he is to have come back when so many tens of thousands didn't. You see, that's what gets me, Solomon. You hear all these tales about men coming home with shell shock and all sorts of other war neuroses, but I'm sceptical. Seems to me that many suddenly become afflicted when they find they can't get a job.'

Solomon frowned. This wasn't describing Freddy, was it?

'It wouldn't surprise me if they were the work shy ones before the war; and the ones who did as little as possible when they were over there,' Lavell added.

Solomon went over the doctor's thoughts on his walk home. Maybe Lavell was right, maybe Freddy simply couldn't cope with his appearance. It was then the old man remembered Freddy's friend … Hobbs, the man with the tin face.

He recalled their one and only meeting, how quiet and temperate he was. Not at all like Freddy.

Solomon stopped to buy a newspaper, scanning the front page before tucking it under his arm. Arriving home he was pleased to see Freddy dressed, though a little wary, as ever, of his mood. He needn't have worried.

'Hey, Sol, you're late home. I was beginning to think you must have known I was going to cook us some tea,' Freddy said cheerfully.

'Oh, believe me, Freddy, if I'd known you were cooking I'd have been home ages ago.'

'So why are you late? Oh, hang on … not my business. I've had a go at you plenty of times before now for asking me, so fair's fair, whatever you've been up to, Sol … you keep it to yourself.'

'What are we having then?' Solomon asked, following Freddy in the kitchen, washing his knife before leaving it on the drainer, like always.

'I nipped out and picked up some tripe earlier,' and Freddy saw the look of astonishment on Solomon's face.

'I got served straight away … there are some advantages to looking the way I do,' he chuckled.

'Tripe eh? Maud used to make that once a week.'

'Well, I can't guarantee it'll be better than Maud's but at least I've got some ale to wash it down with. I called in at the Railway on the way back and got Tommy to pour me a flagon of his best. It's outside in the yard.'

Solomon struggled to hide his incredulity.

'Good man, Freddy, so you're feeling better then?'

'Onwards and upwards, Sol, that's what they say isn't it?'

'Aye, that they do; and I'm glad to hear it, Freddy. Right, I'll go and change my shirt and wash up then, I'm famished.'

Freddy waited until Solomon was out of sight before picking up the old man's fish knife, wrapping it in a handkerchief and slipping it in his pocket.

45

Hobbs woke to the sound of screeching gulls and the horn of a steam ship signalling its arrival into Ostend harbour. He dressed, hoping the odour from wearing yesterday's clothes, could be masked by the soap in his room.

The last thing he wanted was for Mary to think him unwashed and he splashed cold water over his face, lathering his hands with soap.

His last act was to put his mask on in front of the mirror. Yesterday's wadding was in the bin, soaked with his sweat and he was forced to wear it without anything underneath, the metal rubbing against his skin.

When Mary emerged from her room, Hobbs was stunned how radiant and fresh she was, in contrast to his dishevelled self.

There was another hug from Thirza who was too young to notice the awkward body language between Hobbs and her mother.

'Can we have breakfast now? I'm really hungry,' she asked.

'Of course, we can, we can't go to sea on an empty stomach,' Mary replied. 'Good morning, Charlie, how did you sleep?'

'I slept well, thank you. And you?'

'Eventually; I spent a long time simply looking at Thirza.'

Greeted by the maître d'hôtel they were ushered to a table near the window, overlooking the coast.

Once seated, Mary said to Hobbs: 'You know, you can eat with us, Charlie, it's fine honestly.'

'Oh my God, I am not doing that, not here, not in front of you.'

'Thanks, maybe I'll have … something later.'

But Mary wasn't having it.

'Nonsense, Charlie Hobbs; We hardly ate anything yesterday and we've a long journey ahead of us. Now, sit and eat breakfast with us … please.'

Thirza was grinning; a look that said 'best do as you're told, Charlie.'

'Fine, I'll eat breakfast with you, but if I put you off yours, don't say … I didn't warn you.'

A waiter brought them tea, toast and jam, milk for Thirza, and scrambled eggs.

Hobbs used his straw to drink. Declining the toast, he picked up his knife and fork, acutely aware of how uneasy he suddenly felt.

'It's all right, Charlie … honestly,' Thirza said encouragingly.

And at that moment, for reasons he never understood, even when he looked back on it later, Hobbs put down his cutlery, lifted his spectacles and removed his mask, placing it on the table next to him.

Picking up his fork, he took a mouthful of the scrambled egg, doing his best to chew slowly so as not to spatter it all over the table.

Remarkably, he felt relaxed, helped ostensibly by sating his hunger and from being free of the irritation his mask was causing.

Here he was, eating at a table in a hotel restaurant, with a beautiful woman and the little girl he had come to adore. It suddenly felt the most natural thing in the world.

'Excusez-moi, monsieur.'

The maître d'hôtel appeared at Hobbs' side with a polite cough.

'Euh, je suis désolé, mais je dois vous demander de remettre votre masque ou de quitter le restaurant.'

'I beg your pardon? ... Je vous demande pardon?' and Mary dropped her cutlery loudly enough for the other diners to hear.

The maître d'hôtel was rattled.

'Ce monsieur ne va nulle part monsieur, il est un ancien combattant de la grande guerre et il va manger son petit déjeuner comme un invité de votre hôtel,' she said, and Hobbs saw she was livid.

'Do you understand me?' Mary added, reverting to English.

A hush descended across the hotel restaurant, all eyes on Hobbs. The maître d'hôtel, his balding head now perspiring, nodded.

'Je suis désolé, Madame, je voulais dire aucune infraction. Et pour vous, monsieur, vous êtes les bienvenus.'

He slowly backed away, forcing a smile before turning his attention to another guest.

'What on Earth was that?' Hobbs asked, having not understood a word.

'He wanted you to leave ... I told him you were going nowhere. He listened.'

It was Thirza who broke the silence, giggling; then Hobbs joined in, Mary's face cracked and the three of them turned heads in the restaurant again.

An hour later they were aboard a ship bound for Dover. The weather had turned and to Thirza's disappointment, Mary insisted they stay indoors.

'We don't want you catching a cold, Thirza, You know how important it is to look after your health.'

Halfway through the crossing she was allowed to explore the ship, Mary only relenting after Hobbs' reassurance.

'You know, about this morning,' he said. 'You didn't have to do that, to intervene on my behalf.'

Mary wished he'd remove his mask altogether. His damaged face gave him a fragility she'd never seen before in a man. He wasn't beautiful to look at, he'd never be that. But she knew that didn't matter.

'Well, I couldn't just stand by because you didn't have a clue what the silly little man was even saying,' she giggled.

'That's true. I thought he was asking me if I wanted more tea,' and Mary threw her head back, laughing loudly.

By the time they reach Dover and boarded a train for Bromley, the journey was taking its toll. Thirza snoozed in the cradle of Mary's arms, Hobbs carrying her the final few steps up to the front door.

Inside, an overjoyed and relieved Evelyn came running down the hallway, tears streaming down her face.

It was only later, when the emotion had subsided and Thirza was ready for bed, that he sensed the animosity coming from Mary's mother.

'Right, I think I'd better be getting back home,' he said, reading the signs.

'Thank you, Charlie, for everything,' Mary replied.

Thirza smiled at him through sleepy eyes, asking him to visit soon.

'I will, Thirza, I promise,' and he kissed his hand before placing it on the little girl's cheek.

Evelyn just wanted him to go and, hoping to distract Thirza's attention, said: 'Thirza, your school mistress will be pleased you're home. She's been very worried about you.'

'Miss Hesketh? How ... how did she know?' Thirza asked, yawning.

'She was here, she came to ask about you. I told her we didn't know where you were and we were awfully worried about you,' Evelyn replied. 'But I told her your mother had gone to find you and bring you home, along with Mr Hobbs here,' and she glared at Hobbs with mistrustful eyes.

'I ... I should go, look after yourselves,' and Hobbs headed for the door.

'Charlie ... are you all right?' Mary asked, following him into the hallway.

'Yes, but there's something I need to do, Mary ... something I need to put right.'

46

Freddy downed the last of his ale, refilling Solomon's glass, making sure the old man was drinking twice as much.

'So, what's the verdict? On my tripe?'

'Bloody lovely, you've surprised me today, Freddy.'

'Listen Sol, I know I've not been the easiest to get along with,' and Freddy raised a hand when Solomon tried to interrupt.

'It's true, I can be ... well, I can be a grumpy sod when I want to be. But you've done a lot for me, Sol. If it weren't for you they'd still be scraping me up from that railway line.'

'And me, I had the same idea don't forget,' and Solomon took another hearty swig of ale.

'Yeh, and you.'

'But I just want to say thanks ... I'm not good at trusting people, Sol and if I think people have crossed me, well ... I don't like that,' and if Solomon hadn't been drinking he may have detected the change in Freddy's tone.

'To my friend and saviour ... I won't forget what you've done for me, Sol,' Freddy said, raising his glass.

Touched by the young man's words, Solomon was happier now than at any time he could remember in the last few weeks. He was finally making progress with Freddy and that was definitely worth celebrating.

He drank some more and an hour later was snoring in his armchair.

Freddy got changed, patting his trouser pocket to check he had his lighter. A final look at the old man and he walked through the kitchen, slipping out the back door.

It was a cool, cloudy night but that suited Freddy. It would take longer to get there, his ribs still ached and he couldn't walk as fast. But the beer had helped numb the pain and, more importantly, he felt relaxed, calm.

He knew what needed to be done, he'd thought of little else since it happened. He might even meet up again with Lily while he was down there, the thought sending a surge through his groin.

Through the alleyway he turned left, there was little noise tonight from the Dog and Partridge. Minutes later and he was almost at the spot where it happened.

The street was quiet and it suddenly occurred to him they might not show.

Unsure what to do, he loitered where he'd last met Lily, all the time caressing the handle of Solomon's fish knife in his coat pocket.

But there was no sign of Lily or anyone else.

'Fuck, fuck, fuck.'

Retracing his steps, Freddy heard a noise from inside one of the terraced houses. Nothing. On he went, stopping again, where the two whores had tapped him up.

He hoped they'd show themselves again, and Freddy clenched his fists, knowing they wouldn't be so bullish this time.

But the street remained deserted. He had no idea how long he waited, he was too busy eating himself up with frustration.

There; up ahead, two figures walking his way.

'Act casual, Freddy,' he told himself, ready to exact the bloody revenge he'd longed for.

Yet, as they got nearer and emerged from the darkness, Freddy took a step back. He considered running but his ribs wouldn't let him.

And then it was too late.

'Evening, lad, you out for a late stroll then?'

Looking down, cap pulled low over his eyes, Freddy hoped they wouldn't notice his face in the gloom.

'Yes, constable … just stretching my legs.'

'Well, as long as that's all you're doing … I wouldn't like to think you were hoping to find some female company on these streets.'

'What? No! No, not at all. I'm … I'm just on my way home, good night.'

He never turned to find out but Freddy felt the eyes of both constables boring into him from behind as he trudged away.

Muttering to himself, he called in at the Dog and Partridge, almost willing the landlord to refuse to serve him or a drinker to stare at his face just a little too long.

But neither happened and two large whiskies later he stumbled outside, heading for home. He wasn't quiet when he let himself in; Solomon was still where he'd left him, mouth open, snoring loudly.

Freddy retreated to his room, armed with half a bottle of whisky. He took a long swig before lying back to stare at the ceiling, thinking of the three men utterly oblivious to being 'so fucking lucky tonight.'

The last thing he thought about before closing his eyes was that he ought to get undressed.

'Freddddddddy, Freddddddy … please don't leave me, Freddy.'

His sister Dolly was sitting in the bedroom, the one she and her sister Sally shared, with her back turned. He didn't hear himself speak but reached a hand out to take hers.

And then Dolly turned, her face engulfed in flames, yet speaking normally as her skin melted, peeling away to reveal the burning flesh and the whiteness of her skull beneath.

'They're waiting for you, Freddy, they're all waiting,' and then the flames consumed her and she stood there, Christ-like, burning.

He was falling now, hurtling to the ground as thousands of scorched, blackened hands reached out, yanking him this way and that, clawing at his flesh.

Trapped, unable to move, Freddy was lying still in a forest, thick with trees. And then Charlie was there …

'Hey Freddy, look at my face,' and Hobbs' head exploded, showering Freddy with fragments of flesh, blood, bone and brain.

'Hey Eng-lander … have you seen my Giselle? Give this to my Giselle?' and the German soldier stood in front of Freddy, his field grey tunic caked in blood and clay. Ripping open his tunic he reached into the gaping hole in his chest and removed his bloodied, beating heart.

'Take it to my Giselle,' he pleaded, blood dripping from his mouth.

He saw his parents, holding hands and smiling as they walked towards him, both of them ablaze.

'We forgive you, Freddy,' his mother said, reaching out a flaming hand.

And now he was being carried, could feel his arms and legs being held; could feel the searing heat, see the flickering flames, smell burning wood and petrol.

'In you go Freddy, time to fly,' and he was standing next to the blazing aircraft; and now he was walking towards it, climbing into the cockpit, sitting in the fire, watching fascinated as his body burned.

Lily, lovely Lily; he was on top of her, fucking her; closing his eyes he heard her scream and looked down to see Charlie, he was fucking Charlie now, while Hobbs nonchalantly picked pieces of bloodied flesh from his face.

'Freddy? Freddy, it's me Solomon,' and turning he saw the old man kneeling, a broad smile on his face as the three faceless thugs from the robbery smashed at the old man's head with bottles and staves.

And that was the catalyst for Freddy to run amongst them, blind with rage, slashing their throats and ripping open their guts, before standing triumphant, drenched in blood as the entire world burned.

47

'I wanted to put you in the picture, to let you know what's been going on,' Hobbs said, ending his story.

It took plenty to surprise Stan Finch but then, Hobbs had told him plenty.

'Well, I'll be blowed ... runaway schoolgirls, boat trips to Belgium and, if I'm not mistaken Charlie Hobbs, someone's taken your fancy,' and Stan fiddled with his moustache, grinning.

Secretly, Hobbs was pleased, it meant he could finally talk about her.

'She's ... she's amazing, Stan. The way she looks at me, the way she speaks ... and she's beautiful, did I mention that?'

'No, but I gathered as much. But what about this other lass? This Grace, the one you had ... well, you know, had everything done for,' Stan asked clumsily.

'She's met somebody else, Stan; she's moved on with her life. We both have,' though Hobbs knew that wasn't quite true.

'Well, the best of luck to you, s'all I can say. You deserve to be happy, Charlie, and if you can find happiness with this Mary woman, well good on yer.'

Surprisingly, Hobbs wasn't nervous; not yet anyway. After sleeping in, taking a hot bath and then lunch with Stan, he set off for Thirza's school.

Timing his journey so he'd arrive shortly before the school day finished, Hobbs watched the doors swing open, waiting until the children melted away into the surrounding streets.

There was no sign of Thirza. He knew Mary planned to keep her home after the excitement of the last two days.

When the playground was empty he summoned up the courage he'd need to go through with it. Walking through the gate and up the steps, Hobbs opened the door and went inside.

The Victorian building had high ceilings and every sound reverberated through its empty rooms.

Dropping the catch as he closed the door, he heard her voice.

'Who is that and what have you've forgotten?'

He couldn't disguise the sound of his heavy shoes on the tiled floor and as Hobbs reached the classroom, Grace came to the door and came face to face with the ghost of her dead fiancé.

'Hello, Grace.'

Her body swayed, slumping backwards and she crumpled to the floor, her screams and sobs echoing through the school.

'You … it can't … it can't be, you're … you're dead.'

Dead? Is that what she thought?

'No, Grace … I made it through; but not quite in one piece.'

'No … no, you're dead, … they told me you were dead!' and she was howling now, her body trembling.

'Grace, I made it through ... but my face ... it's, it's a mask; to hide what's underneath. I was knocked about pretty badly ... they didn't think I'd make it.'

Her mouth was open but she'd lost the power to speak.

Kneeling beside her, careful not to get too close, Hobbs went on.

'I was in hospital for weeks, months even. When you didn't ... I mean, when I didn't hear from you, I thought it was for the best; I didn't want you seeing me like this.'

'I thought you were dead, Charlie! Do you understand me? The letter ... I had a letter ... from Joe Winterbourne, he told me ... he told me you'd died.'

'Joe, poor old Joe.'

Hobbs thought of his friend who had joined up with him, the two of them grinning like Cheshire cats when they were accepted at the recruiting station; then having to tell their mothers, Joe's mum furious with him while Hobbs' mother only seemed resigned.

'He saw you fall, said you'd died,' Grace yelled, her face contorted in shock and bewilderment.

'He wrote to me, Charlie, knowing there'd be no official telegram because you had no family ... how could he get that wrong? How could he think you were dead when you're not? When you're here, standing in front of me after all this time?'

Hobbs had no idea. His last memory of Joe was the two of them waiting to go over; it was his last memory of anything when he'd still had a normal face.

'I don't know, Grace, really I don't.'

Finally, she began to compose herself, a hand sweeping through her hair, drying her eyes as she got to her feet, straightening the long skirt that flowed to her ankles.

'Look at me, what a mess. Your voice … is it, is it because of your injury?'

'Yes. I lost the upper part of my jaw … my nose too. I can't smell anything and I sound like a simpleton.'

She clamped a hand to her mouth, and the tears came again.

'Oh, Charlie … you poor thing.'

'I thought about you every day, Grace, truly I did.'

'And I grieved for you, Charlie. I lit a candle for you at St Stephen's on your birthday and at Christmas.'

They sat on a bench beneath the children's coat hooks, letting the silence speak for them. Then Grace asked: 'So why now? Why today?'

'Because I think you knew … or at least you suspected. Thirza Moran? Her grandmother Evelyn?'

There was the flicker of a smile.

'It was one of the children who first spoke your name. And then I heard it again from Thirza. I thought I was mad to even think it but then … then I heard she'd run away. Is she all right? Thirza I mean?'

'Yes, she's at home … with her mother.'

'I went to her house, I just had to find out. Mrs Barrett told me more about you … she's very suspicious of you by the way, Charlie.'

'Yes, I know,' Hobbs laughed. 'She doesn't trust the man in the mask.'

'Oh, don't joke, Charlie, please. I can't imagine how dreadful this must be for you.'

'It was … and still is; but it's getting better, Grace.'

'You know … you know I loved you, Charlie, I always did.'

He considered removing the mask, to reveal his true face. But that wouldn't be fair, she didn't deserve to see that.

'But I've … I've met someone else, Charlie; I hope you won't judge me or think me selfish … but I'm in love with him. And I want to be with him. Or at least I think I do … oh, I'm so confused.'

Moving closer, Hobbs put an arm around her, trying to remember her fragrance.

'It's all right, Grace. I know. I saw you with him … he looks, he looks a good man. You're the reason I'm still here. The thought of coming back to you kept me going. But I want you to remember me as I was, not pity me for what I've become.'

She held two fingers towards his tin face, touching the metal mouth that never moved, gasping as she felt. And then she kissed her finger tips and touched his face again, her lips quivering, tears streaming down her face.

Moments later, Hobbs stepped out into the sunshine, took a deep breath and lifted his head to the sky. Adjusting his hat, he sighed before walking away from his past.

48

They'd spent the morning talking, Mary ignoring her mother's advice to 'put it behind you, there's no good can come of it.'

But she knew better; her daughter deserved to hear the truth about her father; not the version told by a callous, grief-stricken old woman.

So, in the morning, after a good night's sleep and a hearty breakfast, Mary sat Thirza down and said:

'I want to tell you … about your father.'

Thirza listened as her mother described the sort of man James Moran had been; sensitive, kind, sweet, a man of integrity and morals, a man who adored his family and loved his country.

'He stood up for what he believed in and would never stand by if he thought someone was being wronged,' Mary said, stroking her daughter's hand.

'And that's why, when the war started, he knew he had to go. He loved you so very much, Thirza, he didn't want to leave us. But he told me what he was leaving behind, were the reasons he was going away. Do you understand, my darling?'

'I … I think so. He … he wanted to help people?'

'Yes, yes he did. Your father believed what was happening, in Europe, was terribly wrong,' and she paused, allowing Thirza time to absorb her words.

'The lady ... the lady on the steam ship, she said Daddy was ...'

'Thirza, listen to me, listen very carefully. What that woman said to you ... she had no right, do you hear me? No right at all,' and Thirza nodded, gazing at her mother with wide, watery eyes.

'I kept what happened to your father from you because ... well, you were young and I wanted to protect you. But you have a right to know and I'm only sorry I didn't tell you before.'

Thirza's gaze never left her.

'Your father was a soldier and he went to France in early Nineteen Sixteen, when you were very young.'

'I was five.' Thirza chipped in.

'Yes, yes you were,' Mary smiled.

'In October of that year, your father's regiment was involved in an attack. Sadly, it was during that attack that he was ... he was shot and killed.'

'But that lady, she said Daddy had been.'

'Thirza, forget what that awful woman told you. How do I know Daddy was shot and killed? Because one of the men in his regiment came to see me. He was there Thirza, when it happened,' Mary said, determined to make her believe.

'Did it ... did it hurt?'

She was struggling to hold it together now.

'I don't know, darling, honestly I don't. But I do know that it happened very, very fast. Daddy would not have suffered, I promise you.'

It was one of the hardest things she'd ever had to do but afterwards they held each other for what seemed like forever until Thirza whispered: 'Are we still going to live in America?'

'Would you like to?'

'I think so. Charlie reckons it will be very exciting; he said America is a big country with mountains and huge rivers.'

Her stomach flipped hearing his name and Mary knew she was torn; America offered them an opportunity to build a new life, one free from the shackles of grief and memories of a world long gone.

And yet, in Charlie she could imagine a future where she loved again, sharing her life with someone else.

'I really like Charlie,' Thirza said.

Mary pictured him as she stroked her daughter's hair; and she felt a longing to see him, a need for him to be there.

'I know … I like him too.'

Hobbs was desperate to see Mary too. After leaving the school, he'd even set off towards her home, getting as far as the park before stopping and turning back.

Was it too soon? Was she even interested in him that way? The nagging questions were enough to change his mind, and he turned back, heading for Gladstone Street.

He had become two people; the first, optimistic, confident, convinced that he and Mary could become something wonderful.

But the other Charlie Hobbs was a man consumed by self-doubt, pessimism and a fear of spending the rest of his life alone.

The thought of taking that path filled Hobbs with dread, and he implored himself to seize the unlikely opportunity fate had given him.

He recalled his mother believing in fate; was this fate? Either way it didn't matter. What mattered was Mary and Thirza, and Hobbs thought of little else as he walked home.

Until he opened the front door.

Stan was in the hall, excitable, animated. The old soldier looked like he could explode at any moment.

'Charlie, he's back! He's upstairs.'

'What? Who?'

'Freddy! He turned up this afternoon. Looks terrible he does; said he needs to see you.'

'What! Freddy's here?'

'Yeessss … he's upstairs, said he'd wait in your room. I don't like it, Charlie, I'm not sure you should go up there, not until the other lads come home.'

Hobbs was stunned.

Freddy was here? Why now? Was he ok? He took his mask off, not wanting to do anything that might provoke his friend.

'It'll be fine, Stan, it's Freddy. We've known each other a long time.'

'Well, if you're sure. But make sure you shout out if he starts anything though … if need be I can get up these stairs if I really have to.'

Hobbs tried to smile:

'Thanks, Stan, but relax. Freddy's not a danger to anyone.'

It was hard to believe he was about to see his old friend again, recalling Freddy's vitriolic letter and his words 'If I never see you again it will be too soon.'

What had changed his mind? Turning the handle of his bedroom door he was about to find out.

Freddy was sitting on the bed, vigorously wringing his hands. Oddly, the first thing Hobbs noticed was he didn't have any socks on.

'Hey Freddy, it's been a long time,' Hobbs said quietly, closing the door.

Freddy was scared, his face contorted with terror. His stretched, distorted skin and featureless eyes gave him a ghostly appearance. He opened his mouth to speak, but said nothing and Hobbs was reminded just how pitiful Freddy looked.

'Hey Freddy? What's wrong, what's happened?

'You have to help me, Charlie.'

'Help you? Yes, of course, Freddy. But why? What's happened?'

Still wringing his hands, Freddy replied:

'It's … it's not my fault, Charlie …I didn't know, honestly … you have to believe me. Say you believe me, Charlie,' and he lunged forward grabbing Hobbs by the shoulders, the two men's broken faces almost touching.

49

Fumbling inside his coat pocket for the key, Hobbs couldn't believe how near the house was to Gladstone Street. How on Earth had he and Freddy's paths not crossed?

His eyesight made it difficult to find the right number; he should have asked Freddy for a description, not that he was in the right frame of mind to give him one.

Solomon's home was in the middle of a terraced row of two up, two down houses on the north side of Bromley.

As he put the key in the lock, the curtains next door moved and Hobbs was sure he glimpsed a woman's face before the drape fell back. Inside led straight into the sitting room. It was cramped and looked even smaller because of a single bed next to the window.

Against the wall near the stairs was a small dining table; on it were two dirty plates, empty glasses and a flagon. It took him five strides to reach the kitchen, where a frying pan was on the stove, dirty utensils on the side. Hobbs couldn't smell the stale cooking fat.

Hearing a noise outside he peered through the kitchen window into the yard where two boys were kicking a football.

'What have you done, Freddy?'

Returning to the sitting room, Hobbs opened the door leading up to the stairs. He took a deep breath before going up

'Hello.'

At the top of the stairs were two doors, one closed, the other slightly ajar. Hobbs rapped on the closed door.

'Hello? Is anyone there?'

He entered the room, a double bed facing the door with a window to the right, overlooking the street. The room was neat and tidy, nothing seemed out of place. On the dresser against the wall, he picked up a framed photograph standing between a trinket box and a hairbrush with a pewter handle.

The picture showed a couple; the man's face was familiar, though in the photograph he was much younger.

Hobbs turned, hesitating before pushing open the second bedroom door. His heart thumping, he hoped more than anything in the world, that this room would look like the first.

Yet, it wouldn't open fully. There was something behind it and he had to push hard to get inside.

Staggering backwards, Hobbs ripped the mask away from his face, spewing vomit down the wall, unable to stop retching even after his stomach had emptied.

The pale blue bed clothes were soaked in blood, more of it splattered over the walls and the back of the door.

And then looking down, slumped against the door, he saw the mutilated body of Solomon Wheeler. The old man's torso was a gruesome, bloody mess. His arms rigid, up above his head, as though he'd tried in vain to fight off his assailant.

There were slash marks on his forearms and Hobbs saw a gaping hole in his neck, the hilt of a knife protruding from the congealed wound. Solomon's eyes and mouth were wide open, his death face frozen in shock and fear.

What could he do? What should he do? Without thinking Hobbs bent down and picked up a lamp that had been knocked to the floor, fiddling with the shade before standing it on the bedside table.

He opened the wardrobe, saw Freddy's clothes and for a moment considered taking them.

Instead, he put a hand out to steady himself, turning to look again at the old man's corpse.

'Dear God, Freddy, what have you done?'

Hobbs had seen enough death to last him a lifetime; men with no heads, limbs torn from bodies, the putrid, decaying innards of those poor souls for whom death meant no peace.

Like the others, he'd become immune to the blood and gore, oblivious to the indignity of the dead. But he didn't feel that way about Solomon Wheeler.

'I'm so sorry, Mr Wheeler,' Hobbs said aloud, forcing himself to stare at the man who had taken Freddy in, given him a home and, more importantly, hope. What price that now? He thought of Freddy, a quivering, broken wreck of a man he'd left sitting on his bed begging:

'Don't make me go back there, Charlie, please.'

So, he'd come alone, ordering Freddy to stay put, keep the door closed and not to speak to anyone. Unable to get much sense out of him, he had no idea what to expect when he got to the house. Part of him was worried Freddy was hallucinating and he'd half expected to speak with the old man, the two of them conferring about what else they could do to help their mutual friend.

Now, Hobbs couldn't help but imagine Solomon's final, terrified moments and a life ended by savage violence and brutality.

A knock on the door and Hobbs flinched, hurrying into the first bedroom, peering down from the window and seeing a woman outside. He couldn't be sure but it looked like the woman at the window.

'Think, Charlie, think.'

But Hobbs was panicking. If it was her, she had seen him open the door and go in. She knew he was inside. He had no choice but to answer.

Putting his mask back on, he took a deep breath and was about to open the door when she knocked again.

Patricia Donnelly took a step backwards, there was something about this stranger's face that unnerved her.

'Hello,' Hobbs said, a hand covering his tin mouth.

'Is … is Mr Wheeler home?'

'Er … no, no he's not.'

His speech defect only made her more suspicious.

'Must still be at work then.'

'Yes, that's right, he is. He's on day shifts this week,' Hobbs added, regretting instantly his attempt to sound plausible.

'Do you work wid' him t'en? At the factory?'

'Yes, yes I do. Mr Wheeler, he … he asked me to call round with two books he wanted to borrow. That's … that's why he gave me a key.'

Patricia Donnelly had been well schooled in how to spot a lie; the drunken father of her precious boys had been full of them in the months and years before he disappeared.

She was wary of the stranger in her neighbour's house but now she was angry. Because a man who lied was covering for something.

'Did you forget t'um t'en?'

'Huh?'

'T'e books! I saws ya on the doorstep when you got here, you didn't have anyt'ing with you - I'm not nosey but I do look out for me neighbours.'

'They … they were in my pocket, look …. I really should be going,' and Hobbs was desperate to get rid of her.

'Yes, yes of course. You must know Freddy too t'en?'

'Freddy?'

'Yes, the young man Solomon took in. A little troubled on account of the war and that but Solomon … well, Solomon likes him.'

'No, no I don't know Freddy. Anyway, nice to meet you, Missus?'

'Donnelly, Patricia Donnelly. Solomon and I have been neighbours for years. We look out for each other,' and her eyes told Hobbs she knew something was amiss.

'I'd best leave you to it t'en, Mister?'

'Winterbourne … Joe Winterbourne.'

Stepping back to close the door, Hobbs didn't see Patricia Donnelly look down. In his haste to answer he didn't notice the bloody footprints he was trailing through the house … or that the inquisitive Irish woman had spotted them.

He needed to think. But the answers never came to questions he never dreamed he would have to answer. He couldn't go back upstairs, just the sight of old man Wheeler's mutilated corpse would have him retching again.

Was this his fault? Could he have done more … he knew how fragile Freddy was. That, mixed with his volatility and anger, it was always a recipe for disaster. Why hadn't he seen that?

Or maybe he had. If anyone knew what Freddy was capable of, surely it was him. Did that make it worse? Was he an accessory to this poor man's brutal murder?

This wasn't helping, not now. Not while he was stood inside the home of a dead man. But Hobbs wasn't stupid, he knew there was little he could do to save his friend. Freddy would hang for this.

Hobbs pictured him swinging from a rope and in that moment, realised his failure as a friend was complete.

Stood in the middle of Solomon's sitting room, he knew what had to be done but couldn't yet bring himself to do it. The bed near the window, it wasn't for Freddy, so who was sleeping there

He looked around; Solomon Wheeler had lived a simple life and taken pride in his home. The few possessions there were had been cared for, the house surprisingly clean. That made the sight of a messy table and dirty pots in the kitchen an odd one.

Hobbs couldn't put it off any longer; he went to leave, taking one final glance up the stairs. And that's when he saw the bloody footprints. They were all over the stairs and throughout the rest of the house.

Cursing, he removed his shoes and ran the kitchen tap. Finding a rag on the shelf near the back door, he held it under the running water, using it to wipe the blood from his shoes. And that's when he heard thumping on the front door.

'Open up, this is the police.'

Hobbs froze midway between the kitchen and the sitting room, the door thumping again, harder this time.

'I repeat, this is the police. Whoever is in there, I demand that you open this door.'

Panicking now, he hurried to put his shoes back on, only to see a face under a policeman's helmet, peering through the window, the officer's hands shielding his eyes so he could get a better look.

'He's in there, I can see him, Sarge.'

What happened next was a blur, the front door forced open by two constables who rushed into the house, overpowering Hobbs, who was shoved up against the wall. His painful yelps were ignored as his arms were pinned back, his wrists handcuffed.

A sergeant appeared, ordering him to sit, while more constables turned up, two of them piling upstairs. It wasn't long before one yelled.

'Up here, Sarge, quick.'

Hobbs was in shock, he couldn't speak if he wanted to. He knew how this looked but was helpless to stop it.

The sound of someone else retching prompted one of the constables guarding him to glance upwards, then glare at Hobbs, almost daring him to move.

Footsteps and the sergeant emerged, quickly followed by a pasty looking constable, wiping his mouth with a handkerchief.

'We've just had a look at your handy work … you don't do things by halves do you, lad?' the sergeant said, standing over Hobbs, who lifted his head.

'What's up with your face? Christ, would you look at that. He's wearing one of them masks,' and the two constables gazed at Hobbs as the sergeant ripped it away from his face.

'Fucking hell, Sarge, look at him?'

'What's wrong with him, why's his face look like that?'

'He's a war veteran, ain't that right, lad?' the sergeant replied, staring at Hobbs with a look of revulsion.

'Well, war veteran or not, you're going to hang for what you've done, lad. I'm arresting you for the murder of Solomon Wheeler.'

50

With a sewing basket resting on her lap, Mary thumbed through reels of cotton before finding the colour she was looking for.

After picking out a needle, she reached for the tin kept in the sitting room cupboard containing dozens of buttons of all shapes and sizes. Satisfied at finding a match to the others on Thirza's school dress, she began sewing.

Mary was smiling, she had been giddy all day. Even Thirza had noticed, asking why she was so cheerful.

She told her a half truth, simply that she was thrilled to have her little girl back home; and that made her the happiest mother alive.

But there was another reason; and his name was Charlie Hobbs. The more Mary thought about him, the more she wanted to see him; and the more she wanted to see him, the more she knew she was falling for him. She secretly hoped he would visit yesterday. When he didn't, she'd hidden her disappointment. And anyway, it had only been a day.

But Mary was certain he'd call today, there was no reason he wouldn't. Hadn't they shared a moment during their frantic journey to Ostend? She smiled at the memory.

Rarely did she think of his disfigurement; when she did it wasn't about how he looked but more about the things he could no longer do ... enjoy a meal, the smell of fresh flowers, smile.

She found his resilience astonishing and it only enhanced her admiration. And she wondered what it must be like, to know that your very appearance could force people to turn away in disgust. Trying to imagine how she would cope, Mary quickly concluded that she couldn't.

No, she didn't care what Charlie looked like. She was attracted to the qualities of a man, not his appearance. And, while she would always believe James had been the most handsome man she'd ever set eyes on, it wasn't his looks that made her fall madly in love with him. It was his character.

They were similar James and Charlie, she really believed that. But also different enough that she knew this wasn't about hanging on to the past, or trying to replace her fallen husband.

A knock on the door interrupted her thoughts and she jumped up, casting Thirza's dress aside and hurrying into the hallway. How wonderful it would be if Charlie was standing on the doorstep. Mary failed to hide her disappointment when she opened the door to her mother.

'Mary, are you alone? Oh, I had to come and see you ... it's, it's awful, absolutely awful.'

Evelyn Barrett was already in the house, bustling past her daughter.

'Mother, what is it? What's wrong?'

Evelyn reached into her handbag, her face ashen:

'I went to have tea with Joyce Threlfall, you remember Joyce? Her son Oliver was at school with you?'

'Yes, mother, I remember Joyce Threlfall!'

'Well, she has a daily newspaper delivered, must be on account of Oliver working at the Chronicle. Anyway, she's in the kitchen making the tea, so I pick up the paper and start having a read.'

There was a pause.

'And?' Mary asked, exasperated.

Evelyn laid the folded newspaper on the kitchen table, pointing to a brief article running down a single column of the front page.

'I'm so sorry, Mary, but you know I always had my suspicions there was something wrong about him.'

Mary wasn't listening, she was reading the article open mouthed.

Body found in house, Great War veteran arrested

The body of a man who had been repeatedly stabbed and mutilated has been discovered at a house in Mill Street, Bromley. According to police, the murder occurred sometime in the last two days.

The dead man is believed to be Solomon Wheeler, a widower and fish filleter at J.E Wilson's & Son in the town. Police said a former soldier, who fought in the Great War, by the name of Charles Hobbs, from Gladstone Street, Bromley, was arrested at the scene of the crime.

He has asserted his innocence and an investigation is ongoing.

'No, no ... this isn't right, this can't be ...'

'Like I said, I had misgivings about this chap even before I met him.'

Mary ignored her, pacing the room, reading the article again in disbelief.

'It's a mistake ... it has to be a mistake.'

'What? Like the time at the pageant? I thought you said that was a mistake, too didn't you?'

'You don't … Mother, you don't seriously believe Charlie did this?'

Evelyn's eyes narrowed and she pursed her lips, shrugging.

'I'm just going by what the police have said and what's in the paper, dear! They don't arrest people for murder without good cause.'

'Keep your voice down, mother, please! Thirza is upstairs sleeping, she's still exhausted. Oh, Thirza …what on Earth am I going to tell Thirza?'

'Tell her nothing, just say he's gone away somewhere. The girl's too close to him as it is, it's not right.'

'Don't you dare say that! He's been … he's been wonderful for Thirza. There is nothing wrong or strange about their relationship so please don't make out that there is.'

It was Evelyn's turn to look shocked now.

'And Charlie has been a huge help to me, coming with me when Thirza went … went missing.'

There was silence between the two women and Evelyn saw the look on her daughter's face:

'You like him? This Hobbs fellow … don't you?'

'What? No, don't be silly, Mother, why would you say that.'

'Because I know my own daughter, Mary, just as you know yours. I've seen the way you look at him and I can see the hurt in your eyes now, knowing what he's been accused of.'

Mary's face crumbled and she was sobbing once more.

'Oh, you poor girl,' Evelyn said pitifully, holding out her arms as Mary tumbled into her embrace.

51

Petrified, quivering with fear, Hobbs wept dry tears; he hadn't been this scared since Flanders, yet somehow this felt so much worse. Shoved into a cell for the second time in less than a month, there'd be no Mary to save him this time.

Grisly images of Solomon's mutilated body were all he kept seeing, along with the sergeant's ominous words: 'You're going to hang for what you've done, lad.'

He was desperate for the opportunity to tell his version of events but had been left on his own for hours; the wait only increased the hopelessness.

At some point he fell asleep because when he woke he had no idea it was a new day. The cell door finally opened and Hobbs was escorted to a room eerily similar to the one where Mansell quizzed him about the pageant.

Told to sit, he was made to wait again, searching for something, anything, to focus on in the grey, sterile room, until the door opened and a suited man puffing on a cigarette came in and sat opposite.

He stared at Hobbs, who was now beyond caring that his mask had been taken away, leaving his disfigurement cruelly exposed.

Finally, he could stand the silence no longer.

'I didn't do it, I did not kill Solomon Wheeler.'

The smoking man watched fascinated, gazing at this shattered, deformed face able to speak and function.

He stubbed out his cigarette, opened a packet and lit another, blowing smoke into the air above Hobbs' head.

'Would you like one, Mr Hobbs?'

The question was innocent enough but it was laced with a menace delivered in a coarse, East End accent.

Hobbs had once smoked regularly but, like so many things, his injury now made it almost impossible. But he was suddenly craving nicotine.

Nodding, his trembling fingers pulled a cigarette from the packet and he leant forward, the man holding his light out as Hobbs lit the end and inhaled.

But he had no upper jaw and there were no muscles to hold the cigarette in place, and it fell from Hobbs' mouth.

'Having trouble with that?'

Hobbs picked it up, put it between his fingers and leaned forward to try again. But the lighter flicked shut.

'My name is Inspector Samuel Cartwright, I work in the city,' and his lips hardly moved as he spoke.

'My friends call me Sam but you're no friend of mine, Mr Hobbs so you can call me Inspector.'

'I didn't kill him Inspector … you have to believe me.'

'I don't have to do anything of the sort. When it comes to murder, evidence is the only thing I believe in, Mr Hobbs.'

Cartwright paused allowing his suspect to absorb his words while he looked for the subtle signs that convinced him he was dealing with a guilty man.

'So, let's go through some of that evidence shall we. We have a dead man; Solomon Wheeler. According to his neighbour … and she is terribly upset you know.

According to his neighbour, a nicer man you couldn't fail to meet. Recently widowed, he'd worked for the same company all his life and from all accounts, he'd do anything to help anybody.'

Hobbs was having to force himself to stop shaking.

'So, tell me, why did you feel the need to butcher the poor sod in his own home?'

Unsure whether Cartwright expected him to answer or he was going to keep talking, Hobbs stared, open mouthed, the gravity of his deformity on show.

'I didn't! I keep trying to tell you, I didn't kill him!'

Cartwright leaned back in his chair and puffed on his cigarette, this time blowing the smoke towards Hobbs.

'But here's where I'm struggling, Mr Hobbs and you're going to have to help me out see, because ... well, Mr Wheeler was last seen alive by his neighbour last evening when she spoke to him. Then, yesterday morning, he doesn't turn up for work. You with me so far, Mr Hobbs?'

Hobbs nodded.

'So then, Mr Wheeler's neighbour sees you turn up and let yourself in with a key. Is that correct?'

'Well, yes, but it's ...'

'So, in you go but Mrs Donnelly at number fourteen, well she smells a rat. Who is this creepy looking fella letting himself into Mr Wheeler's house? She's a good citizen, Mr Hobbs and Mr Wheeler's a good friend; so, she decides to check.'

Hobbs' shoulders visibly sagged.

'You are still following me, aren't you?'

'Yes, Inspector but if I could just.'

'All in good time, Mr Hobbs,' and Cartwright raised a finger.

'You answer the door when she comes knocking and there's something about your behaviour that ain't right. Shall I tell you what that was, Mr Hobbs?'

He didn't wait for Hobbs to respond before adding:

'You told her Mr Wheeler was at work and that you worked with him down the factory,' the Inspector said, not bothering to hide his glee.

Hobbs' stomach turned, knowing his lies were about to condemn him.

'But we know that's ... well, where I come from, that's a load of bollocks, Mr Hobbs. Let me cut to the chase; you're seen letting yourself into the house of a man I don't think you know. When challenged you then peddle a load of lies about knowing Solomon Wheeler, working with him and even what your name was.'

Hobbs was crying again now, though Cartwright saw no tears.

'Your bloody footprints are seen on the floor; that's right, Mr Hobbs,' Cartwright added, as Hobbs puts a hand to his forehead. 'Then when my colleagues turn up, what do they find? Mr Wheeler's mutilated body upstairs and you in the kitchen, where you've been cleaning your shoes. So, like I said, evidence, Mr Hobbs. And from where I'm sitting, I've got more than enough to see you swing tomorrow.'

Hobbs was sweating and feared he'd pass out as he did in Dover.

'Inspector,' he pleaded. 'I swear, I didn't kill him.'

Cartwright stubbed out his cigarette and folded his arms with a smile. It wasn't long before he was fumbling in his pocket and lighting up again.

'I consider myself an honest copper, Mr Hobbs, so let's hear what you've got to say for yourself.'

Taking a deep breath, Hobbs began his account:

'I'd ... I'd met Mr Wheeler once, he came to the house I'm living at, in Gladstone Street.'

Cartwright looked bored.

'He came to collect some ... some things, belonging to a friend of mine.'

'What friend?'

Hobbs hesitated: 'Freddy ... Freddy Lucas. He's ... he's a friend of mine, we met in hospital ... during the war. Freddy he ... he moved out of Gladstone Street and went to live with Mr Wheeler. I don't know why, honestly,' he added, seeing Cartwright's sceptical face.

'We ... we lost touch but then yesterday ... yesterday, he comes back and says,' and Hobbs paused briefly; was he really going to do this?

'He says he came home from a night out, went upstairs and found Mr Wheeler like that. Freddy was worried that he'd be blamed see ... what with living there and that. And he was scared too. He asked me to go over there, to see if I could do anything.'

'If you could do anything?' said Cartwright incredulously. 'Is this the best you've got, Mr Hobbs?'

'When ... when the woman next door knocked, I panicked. I shouldn't have but I knew it would look bad.'

'It does,' Cartwright muttered and Hobbs fell silent.

'You're making a bit of a habit of this, getting yourself arrested aren't you, Mr Hobbs? That's right, I've been speaking with my uniform colleagues here. What an interesting tale they had to tell me.'

'Inspector, that was all cleared up ... it was ... a mistake.'

'A mistake, eh? Well, you're becoming quite the careless type, Mr Hobbs.'

52

Freddy was restless, unable to sit still, berating himself over and over again. It had been hours and there was still no sign of Charlie.

'Where the hell was he?'

Drenched in sweat, he teetered on the edge, hands trembling, all the time muttering to himself.

At one point he opened the door, stepping out on to the landing, before hearing the voices downstairs of Stan and the other tenants of Gladstone Street, sent him scurrying back into Hobbs' room.

It was a while before he noticed his clothes; beneath his coat, the white vest turned crimson red with Solomon's blood. He had a vague recollection of scrubbing his hands, even wiping blood off his face.

Solomon, poor Solomon, and Freddy collapsed to the floor, curling himself in a ball, squeezing every sinew, silently screaming, tears and snot running down his scarred face.

He'd tried to remember, he really had; he was cooking dinner, then sneaking out when the old man was asleep, bent on finding those bastards. This was their fault, they should have been there.

What happened when he got home? It was all so hazy. Whisky! Solomon's whisky, he'd taken the bottle upstairs, drinking it on the bed. Then what? He violently banged at the side of his head with his hands, urging himself to 'think, Freddy, think!'

Sol's knife! He'd taken it with him when he went out; did he put it back? Freddy couldn't remember. And that was it; nothing else. Apart from his bad dream, he could recall some of that.

He was aware of someone there, they were struggling with him, was he being attacked again? Then it stopped. And he was awake, there was blood everywhere and poor Solomon had a knife sticking out his neck, lying in a pool of blood, eyes wide open.

He knew straight away what he had to do. Charlie would help, he always did. It didn't matter what had gone before, Charlie would forgive him, would sort everything.

And so, Freddy had gone to the house where he and Hobbs had moved in only weeks before.

Stan caught him running up the stairs but he hadn't stopped to talk. He simply needed to get to Charlie's room. It would all be all right once he was in Charlie's room.

But Charlie wasn't there and it wasn't all right. Instead, Freddy had to wait ... he'd always hated the waiting.

And now here he was, waiting again.

He should have been back by now, where was he?

And then it hit him, smacked Freddy right between the eyes. He remembered his friend's betrayal, his lies, saw Charlie wearing that ... that fucking mask, as though he could make his grotesqueness simply disappear.

And then Freddy knew.

Hobbs, the lying, treacherous bastard; he'd gone to the police, told them everything. And soon they'd be coming here. For him.

He opened the wardrobe, picked out some clothes and left his bloodstained vest and trousers on the floor.

Prising open the lid of an old tobacco tin on the wardrobe shelf, he helped himself to the few bank notes Hobbs had squirrelled away.

Hobbs' notebook and pencil were on the bedside table and Freddy scribbled a note, tore out the page and left it on the pillow, stuffing the notebook in his pocket.

He couldn't risk leaving by the front door, that old cripple would be watching out for him. Opening the window, he worked out the best way down before clambering out, scaling the drainpipe until he was close enough to leap on the tiled roof of the outside toilets.

Jumping to the ground, he hit a dustbin, its lid clattering in the yard. Freddy was panicking now, running out into the street.

Wearing Hobbs' hat, the brim pulled down low, he turned the collar up on his jacket, slowing to a walking pace, mingling with the other pedestrians.

He stared at their faces, expressionless, interested only in their own mundane lives. They reminded him of Charlie, not wanting to confront the realities of this world, and he despised every single one of them.

And then he was there. It wasn't intentional, he'd been heading nowhere. But maybe this was a sign.

Freddy pushed open the door to the Railway Inn.

'Afternoon, what can I get you? Oh, it's you, Freddy, I didn't recognise you for a minute,' said landlord, Tommy Slater.

Freddy ordered a pint and a double whisky.

'Crikey, you're on the hard stuff early. So, where's Solomon? Not joining you today?'

'What? Why would I know where he is? I'm not his fucking keeper.'

'Hey take it easy, lad. Remember who you're talking to. I was only making conversation. Now, enjoy your pint, I'll bring your whisky over.'

Freddy hated Slater; another of those who had no fucking clue. Sipping his beer, he wiped the froth from his lipless mouth. The bar wasn't busy but there were enough people to make him feel uneasy.

He headed out back, finding the small table that had once been the only one he could sit at. Slater appeared with his whisky.

'What you doing back here? You know you're welcome out the front.'

'I like it back here.'

Another round of drinks and Freddy couldn't stop wringing his hands, convinced there was blood under his fingernails.

He returned to the bar, ordering another beer and a third whisky; it was getting busier now and a barmaid served him, Slater busy changing barrels in the cellar.

Downing the whisky in one, he staggered back to his table, spilling some of his pint along the way.

'Hello, Freddy, mind if I join you?'

Freddy's mouth dropped open as Solomon sat beside him, blood oozing from his severed neck; his face and arms covered in slashes, his blood-soaked chest heaving slowly.

'Sol? Sol, I'm so sorry.'

'A fine mess you've made of me, lad; If only I could stop the bleeding,' and Solomon clamped a hand against his neck, Freddy watching the blood seep through the old man's fingers.

He had to get out of there and knocked his stool over in the rush to leave. No one noticed him stagger into the yard out back.

Why was Solomon doing this? Didn't he know he'd never meant to hurt him? The door to an outhouse was ajar and Freddy peered inside. There were crates of empty bottles on the floor, kegs of beer and an oil lamp on the shelf.

Freddy went inside, picked up the lamp and sniffed, closing his eyes, his memory recalling the pungent smell of paraffin.

He stubbed his toe against something hard, something metal, and in the darkness felt a large cylindrical tin. Brushing off the dust, he tipped it into the light so he could read what was written on the front.

And suddenly the fog lifted and the lucidity made everything clear; Sol, Charlie … all of it. He knew exactly what had to be done, he'd done it before and it helped that he found it so intoxicating.

'Burn it, burn it all down, Freddy.'

He went back inside, the tin under his arm. No one saw him pouring liquid over the tables and floor.

Tommy Slater was emerging from the beer cellar, keg on his shoulder, as Freddy flicked open his cigarette lighter, setting fire to a rag in his hand.

Dropping the burning rag, he ran out into the yard, a twisted smile on his disfigured face, as the paraffin ignited, engulfing the Railway Inn in flames.

53

Hobbs was struggling to eat the bread they'd given him. Half of it ended up on the table and using his arm he swept the remains to the floor.

His attempt to drink without a straw or tube was impossible, most of the water running down his chin, wetting his shirt.

The room was oppressive, there was little air and the eyes of a silent constable watched his every move.

He was grateful when the door opened, but that changed when Cartwright appeared and the Inspector glanced at Hobbs' wet face and clothes as he took a seat.

'Right then, Mr Hobbs, now you've been fed and watered let's continue, shall we? Tell me, why did you give a false name to Mr Wheeler's neighbour and tell her you worked with him?'

'Well … well, I.'

'I mean, if you are telling the truth, then surely, once you found Mr Wheeler's body, you should have been going straight to the police?'

Hobbs attempted to answer but was ignored.

'Or when Mrs Donnelly knocked at the door, you could have told her …yet, you decided to tell a pack of lies.'

Shifting in his seat, his clothes sticky with sweat, Hobbs feared the worst. How could he possibly get out of this?

The Inspector was right, the evidence was stacked against him.

'Inspector … please, I am telling you the truth. I shouldn't have lied to Mrs Donnelly but, but I panicked.'

'All right, let's say I believe you. So, you lie to get rid of Mrs Donnelly and then?'

Hobbs waited for the rest of the sentence … it didn't come.

'I mean, what was your plan after that? Mrs Donnelly goes away, you're still in the house with a dead man and then what? What on Earth were you planning to do then?'

Hobbs had no idea, even now he wasn't sure what he would have done.

'I … I was going to the police, to let them know what I'd found.'

Smiling, the Inspector's hands went up theatrically.

'Ah, did you hear that, constable? Mr Hobbs here was going to let us know that he'd found a man butchered to death?'

Hobbs was nodding.

'But only after you'd lied to his next door neighbour? Good, good, I'm glad we clarified that, Mr Hobbs.'

It was suffocating in there, Hobbs just wanted it to end, anything but more of this. A rap on the door and a constable's head appeared.

'Excuse me, Sir. Can I have a word?'

The interruption irritated Cartwright, who scraped his chair back on the floor as he left the room. When he reappeared, his casual demeanour was gone, replaced by an urgency that unnerved Hobbs.

'Tell me everything you know about Freddy Lucas, right now!' And Cartwright banged on the table, his face reddening.

Hobbs stumbled over his answer.

'It's a simple enough question, Hobbs … tell me about Freddy Lucas.'

'I've … I've told you, he's a friend of mine, we met in the war when we were both in hospital.'

'Yes, yes, you've said that. But where is he now? Do you know?'

Swallowing hard, Hobbs realised if he wanted to save his neck, he had to give them Freddy.

'I … I told you, he came to see me. I told him to wait there, until I got back.'

'So, Freddy Lucas is at your house? In Gladstone Street?'

Hobbs nodded and Cartwright dashed from the room, and the claustrophobic waiting resumed once more.

He had no idea how long he sat there but it was long enough to retrieve what was left of the bread and try again to drink the water.

When the detective finally reappeared he was calmer, the cockney swagger of before had gone, replaced by a look of icy contempt.

'I don't like liars, Mr Hobbs and you, well you're a liar,' he spat, his face like thunder. 'Why aren't you telling me the truth about what happened to Mr Wheeler?'

Hobbs' shoulders slumped, he was exhausted now; the effort to speak clearly, to talk for this long, was debilitating.

'Inspector … I don't know what else I can say but believe me, please … I did not kill Solomon Wheeler.'

Cartwright's eyes burned into Hobbs, it felt like he could read his innermost thoughts, his very soul laid bare.

'I know you didn't … Freddy Lucas killed him. Now, tell me, why you would risk your own neck to cover for a sick bastard like that, eh?'

Dumbstruck, awash with relief and astonishment, Hobbs' head was spinning. Had Freddy confessed? Had he been arrested?

'Even with a face like yours I can see you're surprised, shocked even,' Cartwright said. 'I expect you're dying to know. Well, how about you tell me everything and I'll let you in on my secret.'

And with that, Hobbs finally told Cartwright everything.

He talked about Freddy, how volatile he could be, the poisonous letter he'd sent after walking out. And then he described him turning up out of the blue, a quivering wreck, telling Hobbs he hadn't meant to do it.

Yes, he'd lied. But he'd done it not to protect Freddy, but because he was scared, knowing full well the fate that awaited Solomon Wheeler's killer.

When finished, head bowed, Cartwright, who had interviewed more than enough people, knew he'd heard the truth.

'There, wasn't so hard was it, Mr Hobbs?' he said, standing and heading for the door.

'Wait! Inspector … what now?'

'You're free to go, Mr Hobbs; but don't think about going too far. I've still not decided whether to charge you with interfering with a police investigation.'

Hobbs only heard half of that; he was more concerned with Cartwright leaving without telling him about Freddy.

'Inspector … you said …'

Cartwright paused, contempt dripping from his face:

'We went to your home, Mr Hobbs, but there was no sign of Freddy Lucas. Your landlord, Stanley Finch, said no

one had come down the stairs so we checked your room
… it appears Lucas climbed out of your bedroom window.
How do I know you didn't kill Wheeler? Because your
friend helpfully left a note for you on your pillow. I expect
you'd like to know what it said?'

Hobbs nodded and Cartwright opened his notebook:

*'I should have known you'd fucking betray me, Charlie. I
didn't mean to kill Sol but I'll be damned if I'm going to let
them hang me for it. I should never have trusted you, I
should have killed you. See you in Hell.'*

'All that wasted time and effort, Mr Hobbs … it appears
Freddy Lucas didn't trust you to keep his secret after all,'
Cartwright added, closing his notebook and staring at
Hobbs with disdain.

'Earlier this afternoon Freddy Lucas deliberately set fire
to a pub, killing two people and injuring several others.
Now, you're going to have excuse me, Mr Hobbs, but I
have a killer to catch.'

54

'Charlie! Oh, thank God … what the bloody hell's going on?' Stan asked, hobbling in the hallway, surprised to see Hobbs holding his mask and not wearing it. 'Bloody hell, you look terrible, how about I brew us some tea?'

Hobbs' said nothing, silently shuffling past Stan, heading for the stairs.

'The police; they were here, Charlie. They were looking for Freddy. Do you know where he is?'

Hobbs paused on the stairs.

'Freddy's going to hang, Stan.'

'Eh? Hang? What are you on about?'

His disfigured face suddenly appeared menacing and the crippled ex-soldier took a step back.

'The old man who was here? Wheeler? Freddy butchered him in his own home. They accused me, Stan … they thought I'd done it … that I'd stabbed him over and over again.

Stan could only gawp.

'He ripped him to pieces, Stan … the poor bastard was mutilated.'

'Charlie … I, I can't believe it, I'm so sorry.'

'I lied for him, Stan. Even while they were accusing me, I lied for Freddy … why did I do that? How could I protect someone who was capable of doing something like that?'

'Because … he's your friend? You've both … well, you've both been through so much together. You were looking out for him, like you've always done.'

Slumping back on the stairs, the mask dangling in his hand, Hobbs appeared crushed.

'No, Stan … I was lying for him. Freddy's a killer, I knew it and I did nothing. And now I'm as guilty as he is.'

'What? Nonsense, bloody nonsense, how can you be responsible for what the lad's done? Telling a few porkies to cover for a pal is one thing but it doesn't make you a killer, Charlie Hobbs.'

'When I sat there lying for him … even as they accused me of killing Mr Wheeler, do you know what Freddy was doing?'

Puzzled, Stan shook his head.

'He was setting fire to a pub … deliberately.'

Incredulous at what he was hearing, Stan's mouth opened wider, exposing his yellowed, crooked teeth

'Two people died, Stan. And I could have prevented that … if I'd given him up like I should have done,' and Hobbs climbed the stairs with the demeanour of a defeated man, disappearing into his room.

****

The immediate shock had worn off, but Mary remained in a state of disbelief. Her mother was imploring her not to, but nothing would change her mind. Mary's instinct was to act and that's what she would do.

'You're not seriously going? They won't let you see him, Mary, he's accused of murder!' Evelyn said, watching her daughter adjust her hat in the hall mirror.

'I have to do something, Mother! You seem to forget that he was there for me when we went looking for Thirza; Charlie has no one, he ... he needs me.'

'Do you really want this for Thirza? She's already lost her father, Mary ... do you really want to get close to a man who could ... who could hang?'

Mary loved her mother, aside from Thirza she was the only family she had left. But she'd long since stopped listening to her advice, remembering her father telling her once to trust her instincts.

'There is no way Charlie murdered anybody, Mother. How can I be so sure? Because the Charlie Hobbs I know could never be capable of that. Please tell Thirza that I love her and Mother? ... Please don't tell her about Charlie. I'll explain everything when I get home.'

Leaving the house, she walked with purpose into Bromley, rehearsing over and over what she planned to say. Her mother was right, the police were unlikely to let her see him, but at the very least she hoped Charlie would know she had tried and realise he wasn't alone.

Taking a deep breath, she walked into the police station, only to emerge moments later in a daze, stunned to hear of his release. She tried to find out more but the desk sergeant had merely smiled and said:

'I'm sorry, Madam, that's all I know.'

Only then did it occur to her that she didn't know where he lived. He'd always come to her and she'd never asked for his address. Annoyed with herself, she walked from the station into town, passing a newspaper vendor.

The article! It said he lived in Gladstone Street. Asking the newspaper seller for directions, Mary walked the quarter of a mile before spotting the street sign.

Thankfully, it wasn't a long street so she started in the middle. At the third house a man answered. Deciding this wasn't the time to be delicate, she asked him outright:

'Would you happen to know where a man with … with a disfigured face lives on this street?'

'If you mean the house for injured veterans, then you want number sixteen.'

She needed a minute before knocking on his door.

It was Stan who answered.

'Hello, I'm … I'm sorry to trouble you but my name is Mary Moran, I'm looking for Charlie Hobbs?'

Smiling broadly from beneath his moustache, Stan invited her in, shouting up the stairs:

'Charlie? Charlie, you've got a visitor.'

Turning to Mary, he said:

'I suspected it was you, when I opened the door. Told me all about you has Charlie.'

'Really?' she replied, unable to hide her surprise.

'Oh aye, he's smitten with you. And you're as pretty as he says you are.'

Blushing, Mary smiled as they heard footsteps on the stairs.

When Hobbs appeared in the sitting room, he was stunned to see her.

'Well, I'll go and brew up … tea, Mrs Moran?' Stan asked.

'What? Oh yes … yes please.'

'You … you didn't need to come,' Hobbs said.

'I wanted to. Are you all right, Charlie? The police … they said you'd been released. I knew it wasn't true, that you weren't … that you couldn't ever have done such a thing.'

Her faith surprised him and the delight at seeing her was tempered by knowing how much he'd let her down.

'I'm not the man you think I am, Mary.'

'What? What do you mean?'

'I mean, I may not have killed anyone but … but I lied, to protect someone. Someone I thought was a friend. And now they've killed again, and it's my fault.'

Mary moved closer, tenderly stroking the side of his face, her fingers brushing over skin and metal.

55

As the spring blossom gave way to lush green leaves heralding the start of summer, Hobbs could finally look forward to a future he'd once dreaded.

Cursed by a machine gunner's aim that had taken the one thing that made everyone unique, Hobbs once feared Freddy had called it right ... that his remaining years would be spent alone and unloved.

But maybe his mother had been right all those years ago, finding a teenage Hobbs crying in his room, devastated that Maggie Amos didn't look at him, as he looked at her.

'Take it from me, Charlie, it's what on the inside that counts. This Maggie girl may not know it now but one day she'll realise she let Charlie Hobbs slip through her fingers ... and she'll regret it forever.'

Putting the shame of his lies about Freddy behind him wasn't easy, but every day brought Hobbs a little closer to the man he used to be; before he learned how to march, before he learned how to fire a rifle, before he learned how to live amidst the stinking, terrifying filth that was the Western Front.

And before he'd got up from the mud that was sucking him under, to clamber forward with Joe and the boys, into the abyss that was Passchendaele.

Mary never talked about his face; it never occurred to her. This is what Charlie looked like; for her, there was no before. She never asked why he continued to wear his mask. Because she knew it wasn't about hiding or even protecting people from the reminders of war.

It was about being judged.

What was the old saying? Don't judge a book by its cover? Well, Mary knew people would judge Charlie, she'd seen them do it.

Wearing a mask was his protection from that, albeit a small one.

He was wearing it now, stroking Mary's head as they lay on the grass in the park, watching Thirza play at the water's edge.

'I don't ever want to be apart from you, Charlie.'

'You won't be,' his strange voice now the most natural thing in the world.

'Thirza,' she said, pausing ... 'I want her to know James' family; it's important she understands who her father was.'

He knew what was coming.

'I'm ... I'm in love with you, Charlie but I'll understand if you don't ...'

'Shhh, Mary, I love you too; you have given me a future I never thought I had. And you're right about Thirza ... you should move to America, it's a marvellous opportunity for you both.'

'Had he really just said that? That he loves me? Oh, my, he has ... but was he saying goodbye?'

She was confused, and could see nothing in the passive, emotionless expression on Hobbs' tin face.

'... And I'd very much like to go with you ... if that's what you'd like?' he added.

Flinging her arms around him, the joy overwhelming, Mary savoured the feeling of happiness coursing through her. They rolled on the grass, Hobbs laughing, as she smothered him with kisses.

'Oh, Charlie, do you mean it? Really? Oh my.'

'Mean what? What are you two doing?' Thirza asked, running towards the giggles.

'Thirza, we have something to tell you,' and Mary beamed with excitement.

'We're going to live in America and ... Charlie's coming with us!'

Watching from a discreet distance, Freddy saw the young girl throw herself on top of them and they laughed hysterically as they rolled in the grass. He watched the woman tickle the girl and listened to her giggles echo through the park.

The three of them went for a stroll around the lake, stopping for ice creams from the chubby faced vendor wearing a straw boater and pushing his cart.

Freddy followed them home, watching them return to the house with the blue door and the wrought iron fence.

He loathed how happy they were, how the woman clung to Hobbs' arm, the little girl holding his hand, like he was her father.

And his hatred of him grew stronger by the second, the three of them disappearing into the house. He tipped his hat to an elderly woman who passed, grinning wildly as she quickened her step after seeing his face.

And Freddy's mind began to wander, as it always did after he'd been watching them; he stared at the house, picturing the flames, seeing the smoke billow from the windows.

The door opened, breaking the vision, and the young girl emerged, skipping down the street, Freddy following, keeping to the other side of the road, his hat pulled down low.

Where was she off too?

Thirza passed the entrance to the park and headed for a grocery store on the corner, its display of fresh fruit and vegetables covered by a blue and white striped canopy.

He waited for her to come out, she was holding a bag and a bar of chocolate. Thirza loved doing errands for her mother, on account of Charlie unable to resist treating her as a 'thank you.'

'Hmmm, that looks tasty,' and she jumped hearing his voice, spinning round and coming face to face with a scary man in a flat cap.

He was smiling but looked different and Thirza was transfixed by his melted face.

'Hello, I'm Freddy, what's your name?'

'Thirza, Thirza Moran.'

'You're a good girl doing errands for your mother aren't you, Thirza Moran. I used to do errands for my mum, when I was a boy.'

Thirza didn't reply, she was too fascinated by his appearance.

'But that was a long time ago … she's dead now. She and my dad died in a fire.'

'Oh, that's sad.'

'Yes, it was. Another fire left me looking like this,' and Freddy pointed to his face. 'Terribly dangerous, fire. You wouldn't believe how quickly it can start. And how fast it spreads … once it does that, well, a fire is out of control.'

She listened puzzled.

'Do you know it's the smoke that kills most folk ... it gets in your lungs and the gases, well, they're poisonous; you pass out before you feel any pain from the flames. But some aren't so lucky,' and Freddy picked an apple from a crate at the front of the shop, taking a huge bite.

Thirza watched as bits of the fruit and saliva dribbled from his lipless mouth.

'They get trapped you see ... and the flames ... they burn the body, your skin melts and you can smell your own flesh burning.'

'I ... I have to get back, my mother ... she, she'll be expecting me.'

'Oh, I wouldn't worry about your mum ... I reckon Charlie'll be looking after her. Good old Charlie,' Freddy sneered.

'Everything all right out here? Can I help you, lad?' The shopkeeper's appearance was a relief to Thirza, but it irritated Freddy. His eyes narrowed, fists clenching as he snapped: 'No thanks, I don't like the look of any of this shit.'

They watched him saunter off across the road, where he rounded a corner and disappeared.

'Do you know that man, Thirza?'

'No, ... but he knows Charlie.'

56

Mary was furious, but Hobbs looked at her eyes and knew it was anger borne from fear; because she was petrified.

She and Thirza didn't deserve this, not after everything they'd been through and for a moment he considered asking her if she'd rather he leave.

But despite her fury, Mary never directed it at Hobbs.

'Don't you dare start blaming yourself for this, Charlie Hobbs,' she said, pacing up and down the kitchen, speaking through angry tears.

'This is not your fault. How could you possibly know that he'd ... well, that he'd do such a thing?'

Thirza had run home, breathlessly telling them about the strange man at the grocer's shop, talking about fire.

'Jesus! ... Freddy,' Hobbs said, aghast.

'Who's Freddy?' Thirza had asked, before Mary's maternal instincts kicked in and she intervened

'Oh, he's just a silly man that Charlie once knew. Now, off you go and play upstairs and I'll shout you when supper's ready.'

'But I want to stay down here and talk to Charlie.'

'There'll be plenty of time to talk to Charlie after supper, now go.'

That she managed to hold it together for that long was a miracle. Once the two of them were alone, her guard slipped and she was yelling in frustration, the tears flowing.

'I'm so sorry Mary, I … I never thought he was capable of this.'

'What does he want? Why has he been following us … he's clearly been following us Charlie.'

'I don't know. I know that he's … that he's angry with me. I told you about the letter he sent me after he disappeared.'

'What I can't understand is why the police haven't caught up with him yet? He's a wanted murderer, Charlie and now he's … he's been following my daughter, oh my God,' she gasped.

Seeing the woman he loved, the woman who'd dragged him back from the abyss, seeing the fear in her eyes … Hobbs knew however much Freddy hated him, the feeling was now mutual.

An hour later they were at the police station, dropping Thirza off at her grandmother's on the way, Hobbs keeping his distance as Mary took her in to explain. Before Evelyn closed the door, she glared at him with loathing.

If it hadn't been so serious, he would have relished the look on Sergeant Mansell's face as he and Mary walked in, arm in arm.

But whatever Hobbs had thought of him when he was being questioned, his opinion changed when they appealed for his help.

'He's got some nerve I'll say, surfacing like this. Every copper in the county is looking for him, and the city boys and ports have been notified.'

'Sergeant ... I'm afraid. What if he ... if he,' Mary couldn't finish the sentence and it chilled her blood to think of it.

'Look, Mrs Moran, we'll be doing everything we can to find Lucas. He can't evade us for long not with a face like his,' and he glanced at Hobbs, regretting his turn of phrase.

'I'm sure he won't be daft enough to try anything but I'll post an officer outside your home tonight, how does that sound?'

They walked back to Evelyn's in silence; Hobbs not knowing what to say and Mary too exhausted. Along the way he couldn't help but feel they were being followed and it put him on edge.

'Charlie, I can't let anything happen to Thirza.'

'It won't,' and he clutched her hand. 'Look, the police will find him, Mansell's right, he can't stay on the run forever. And anyway, another month and we're leaving remember? Until then, I'll protect you and Thirza ... I won't let Freddy anywhere near you, Mary. I promise.'

The walk home from Evelyn's was even more tense, Hobbs constantly looking around for signs of Freddy, suspicious of men in the distance until they got closer, visibly relieved when they walked by.

He was in awe of Mary's ability to act normally in front of Thirza, appearing to be her usual cheerful self. The three of them played charades after supper before she read her daughter a bedtime story.

When it was time for bed, Thirza hugged Hobbs, telling him to come over again soon. And then Mary surprised the pair of them.

'Thirza, Charlie's going to stay here tonight.'

The little girl was beside herself.

'You can sleep in my room, Charlie, there's plenty of room.'

'No Thirza, Charlie's going to sleep … on the sofa.'

'On the sofa? But?'

'I've slept in some very uncomfortable places, Thirza, so a sofa will suit me just fine,' Hobbs said, interrupting. 'Now, off you go to bed and get a good night's sleep. You can make me breakfast in the morning.'

'I hope … I hope I wasn't being presumptuous, Charlie? It's just … I want you here with us, you make me feel safe,' she told him.

Later, he checked the doors and windows were shut, moving the front room curtain aside, reassured to see a constable standing with his back to the house.

'I'm going up, Charlie,' and Mary was standing in the doorway. Wearing a white night gown she had taken her hair out, he had never seen her wear it down before, her brunette locks flowing over her shoulders; she'd never looked more beautiful.

'Good … goodnight, Mary, sleep well.'

'You too, Charlie.'

Alone, he unhooked his mask, savouring the relief of cool air on his face. Then the door opened, Mary reappeared, and Hobbs instinctively looked away.

'Charlie … Charlie it's all right.'

She was smiling, holding out a hand.

'I don't want to sleep alone, Charlie … come to bed with me.'

Across the street, hidden by shrubbery, Freddy peered through the darkness watching a light appear in the upstairs window.

'Sleep well, Charlie boy' he whispered.

'Sleep well.'

57

A constable remained outside the house for four nights before Sergeant Mansell turned up at the door, to say there wouldn't be a fifth.

'Why? Has Freddy Lucas been apprehended?'

'No, not yet, Mrs Moran, but there's been an unconfirmed sighting in the Midlands, we know he comes from up that way. We don't believe he poses you any threat.'

'You don't believe?' repeated Mary in astonishment.

Hobbs stepped in.

'Mary, the sergeant's right. We don't need a constable standing guard. Freddy's not going to come here, he was just trying to spook us, that's all.'

'You should listen to Mr Hobbs, Mrs Moran. I reckon he's got it bang on.'

She wanted to argue, to say no, she was certain he was going to turn up at the house. But she stayed silent. Maybe Charlie was right, maybe the fear was getting to her.

A week passed and then another and soon, all thoughts of Freddy Lucas were forgotten as Mary began the job of packing, their voyage to America now only days away.

Charlie had offered to help but he knew Evelyn was coming over. He wanted to like her, from what Mary had told him about her, Hobbs saw similarities with his own mother. But he saw the way she looked at him.

It wasn't his appearance; Evelyn didn't trust him. And after the pageant, Thirza running away, and now Freddy, Hobbs didn't blame her.

Mary was wrapping framed photographs of her dead husband, placing them carefully into a wooden crate, when Hobbs said:

'I'm going to go and collect the rest of my things from Gladstone Street. I want to say a proper goodbye to Stan too, maybe have a drink with him.'

'Are you sure you're not running away from my mother, Charlie Hobbs?'

'I was hoping you wouldn't notice.'

'I'm a woman, Charlie, of course I noticed.'

He smiled from behind his mask, making the familiar journey back to Gladstone Street and recalling the first time he and Freddy had walked through the door, both of them broken men with no future.

'But look at me now.'

Stan was thrilled to see him.

'I'll brew up, Charlie.'

'Actually, Stan, I thought we could share something a little more special,' and Hobbs produced a bottle of whisky from under his jacket.

'Well, now you're talking, lad,' Stan replied, rubbing his hands with pleasure and fetching two glasses.

'Right, first thing's first, is there any news about Freddy?'

'No, nothing,' Hobbs said, pouring the whisky.

'Bloody ridiculous him still being on the run. Makes you wonder what all those coppers are doing. If he's got any sense he'll stay well away, he must know it's the rope that's waiting for him when he does turn up'

Hobbs waited for him to finish before raising his glass:

'A toast, Stan … to brighter days and to your health. You've been a good friend, I'm going to miss you.'

'You soft sod,' Stan chuckled, downing his drink in one with a satisfying gasp.

'Pour us another, Charlie, my boy, it's been a while since I tasted this stuff.'

Later, Hobbs made his way upstairs, leaving Stan snoozing in the sitting room. He was already thinking about what he'd take and leaving the rest of his stuff to the other boys in his house, when he opened his bedroom door.

'Still wearing that fucking mask then.'

Sitting crossed legged on the chair facing the door, Freddy glared.

For a moment Hobbs considered running out and back down the stairs. But instead he stood his ground.

'Remember the last time I was in your room, Charlie? When you told me to stay put? That you'd sort everything and make it all right?'

'It's hard to put right an old man's severed neck, Freddy.'

That had the desired effect and Freddy's face sneered: 'That was a fucking accident, Charlie, I told you! Sol and I, we … we were friends, real friends.'

Desperate to appear calm, Hobbs knew he had Freddy rattled.

'Is that what real friends do then, Freddy? Slash your throat and rip your guts out?'

Freddy sprang from the chair, up to Hobbs' face, standing close enough that he could feel his breath wafting underneath the mask.

'You haven't got a fucking clue, Charlie, you have no idea what it's like for me. And don't give me that shit about feeling the same way ... this,' and he pointed to his own face, 'is the real me. It can't be fixed. Just like yours never can be ... only you think that by wearing that fucking, ludicrous mask, people will treat you normally,' and he jabbed a finger into Hobbs' chest.

Feeling sure Freddy would reach for his mask and rip it from his face, Hobbs stood ready to resist as the tirade continued.

'But you're never going to be normal, Charlie. You might fool a few people, get some to feel sorry for you ... is that what she does? I bet it is. You don't seriously think she likes you do you, Charlie?'

Hobbs bristled at that, his fear turning to anger now at the mention of Mary.

'Leave it Freddy, don't you dare talk about her.'

'She's a lonely widow, that's all. And even lonely widows need someone to *fuck* occasionally.'

Hobbs swung his arm back, driving a fist into the side of Freddy's face with a venom that sent him sprawling backwards, blood spurting from his mouth. And then he felt the excruciating pain in his hand and looked at his broken thumb.

Freddy was already up on all fours grinning, his eyes wide, mouth open, the blood visible between his teeth.

'Well, well, I never thought you had it in you, Charlie,' he said, spitting blood on the rug.

'Freddy, you need to leave and you need to leave now,' Hobbs said, wincing.

'You've never hit anyone before have you, Charlie?' and Freddy was laughing as he got to his feet. 'What you have to do, is tuck your thumb in, like this,' and he held his fist up to demonstrate before catching Hobbs unaware with a vicious punch to the side of the face.

The impact knocked his mask sideways, part of the metal cutting into Hobbs' face as he stumbled backwards, falling to the floor.

'That fuck-ing mask!' Freddy yelled, rubbing blood from his knuckles.

Hobbs saw him come closer and in the split second before Freddy's boot smashed down on his head, he thought of Mary.

58

The scraping of metal; he could hear it, wanted it to stop. Opening his eye, Hobbs' senses flickered into life as he emerged into consciousness.

'Good to have you back with us, Charlie, I was afraid you were never going to wake up,' and Hobbs lifted his head.

'I've left your tin face on because ... well, I can see how attached you are to it. But I couldn't resist, Charlie ... want to see?'

Freddy reached for the mirror on the wall as Hobbs sat slumped in the chair, suddenly aware his arms were bound to its wooden frame.

'Freddy, what are you doing?' he asked groggily, desperately trying to free himself.

Freddy ignored him, holding up the mirror.

'Here you go, Charlie what do you think?'

On the front of his mask, the one that Francis Derwent Wood had so painstakingly created to blend in with his real face, Hobbs could make out letters etched into the metal. Reading backwards through the reflection, he saw the words 'Fucking liar' scrawled on his face.

His heart sank, he exhaled deeply.

'See, that's much better, Charlie, a real improvement don't you think?'

'What do you want Freddy? Are you going to kill me? Is that it? You want me to die like Solomon did?'

'How many more times, Charlie? Sol was a fucking accident. Have you not been listening to a single word I've said? Has that fucking widow and her bitch of a daughter scrambled your brain so much that you can't ... un-der-stand-what-I'm-say-ing?'

He was laughing at his own sarcasm, the smile disappearing from his face as Hobbs asked: 'Am I going to be an accident too?'

Freddy didn't answer, instead turning his back to look out the window.

'My dad was a silversmith, Charlie ... like his dad before him. When I was a boy he'd take me to his workshop, small, pokey thing it was, no room to swing a cat.'

Hobbs strained to free his hands while Freddy's back was turned.

'I'd watch him work, see the stuff he made ... dishes, urns, jewellery. But you know what fascinated me most, Charlie?' and he spun round glaring. 'The way he extracted the silver; he'd pick up all sorts of scrap metal, copper pots and pans, lead, old coins, jewellery. Do you know how you extract silver from copper, Charlie?'

Hobbs shook his head, throbbing in agony from the kicks of Freddy's boot and the searing pain from his dislocated thumb.

'You need to refine it,' Freddy said, answering his own question, bending forward, hands on his knees.

'My old man used a furnace, sometimes he'd let me put the metals in the fire. Boy, it was hot in there, Charlie ... white hot.'

Hobbs focused on staying still, hoping Freddy wouldn't notice as his fingers probed to undo the ties.

'And then the metals would melt, turning to liquid. Now the skill; the skill is getting rid of the dross, Charlie, and extracting the pure silver.'

And Freddy put his face up close to Hobbs.

'That's what fire does, Charlie. It cleanses … purifies.'

'Is that what happened to you, Freddy?' Hobbs asked, trying to distract him. 'Were you cleansed when your aeroplane caught fire?'

'I don't expect you to understand but yes, yes I was. I never should have survived, it was retribution, Charlie … an eye for an eye and all that.'

Hobbs was confused, what did he mean? Was he rambling?

'Retribution?'

'For my parents, Charlie … do you think I wanted to go over there? Join the fucking Army? I was scared shitless, we all were, right? A pal of mine …. he'd … he'd already been killed in France. All we were hearing was how fucking hot it was. I'd have done anything not to go, Charlie.'

Freddy was animated again, pacing the room, his hands constantly rubbing the wrinkled, bald skin on his head.

'But my old man … he was like, 'Go on, Freddy,' 'time to be a man, Freddy,' 'get over there and give Fritz a kicking, Freddy. And I hated him for that, Charlie … hated him! One of the boys in the next street, his mam died two days before he was due to leave for France. He had a kid brother so they pulled him out and he got to stay home! Can you believe that? He got to stay home cos his mam died!'

Hobbs' was stunned, unable to believe what he was hearing.

'I had a kid sister, Charlie … and who'd look after Dolly if mam and dad were gone and I was in the Army? They were good people, Charlie … they were together at the end and I think the smoke would have done for them, they wouldn't have suffered,' and Freddy stared at the floor silently.

'But the fuckers still sent me over there.'

'You? You killed your own parents?'

'They made a sacrifice, Charlie … like any parent would do to protect their kids!'

'Freddy … Freddy, you need to untie me and let me go.'

'I can't do that, Charlie. It was supposed to be you and me … that's what you promised. You said we were on our own now, that we only had each other. But you lied to me, Charlie,' and Freddy was crying now.

'You fucking lied!'

'How did I lie? Because I met someone? Someone who treats me normally? Someone who doesn't see a fucking gargoyle when they look at my face?' and Hobbs was yelling now, fearing he was about to die.

'No, Charlie! Because the moment you put that fucking mask on you betrayed me and every single one of those lads who still lie out there.'

'What? That's ludicrous, Freddy, and you know it.'

'Is it, Charlie? You once told me people would never understand. And they won't … not when they never have to confront it. And that won't happen while cowards like you walk around with a fucking mask on.'

Freddy walked to the door and Hobbs heard him open it, unable to turn around.

'You need to understand what loss truly means, Charlie,' and the door closed and Hobbs was alone.

'Freddy? Freddy?' he yelled.

Forcing himself to be still, he listened for movement, for sounds downstairs. He heard voices, shouting, a commotion. And then a door slammed.

'Charlie? Charlie are you all right?' Stan's voice shouted up the stairs.

'I need help, Stan. I can't move.'

'Hang on, lad.'

Leaning back against the stairs, Stan hoisted himself up, one stair at a time, his wooden legs hanging uselessly. It took the old soldier time and he had to keep stopping to catch his breath.

'I'm coming Charlie,' he gasped and Hobbs could do nothing but will Stan to hurry.

He tried again to free his hands, but the binds felt tighter. But the thought of doing nothing compelled him to carry on.

Stan was close now, just two more stairs to go. On reaching the top, he fell back on the landing, breathing hard. Pulling himself up, using the wall for balance, he shuffled towards Hobbs' room, finally opening the door.

'I tried to stop him, Charlie, but he pushed me out of the way. Bloody hell, what's he done?'

'My hands, Stan, I can't move my hands.'

Hobbs yelped in pain as Stan untied him.

'I have to go, Stan … Freddy, he's … I think he's going for Mary.'

'Christ, Charlie … well go, GO! And don't worry about me, getting down's far easier than getting up.'

'Thanks, Stan,' Hobbs replied, ripping off his mask and tossing it on the bed as he dashed out of the room.

59

Walking home in the summer sunshine, Thirza was as happy as she could remember. Even school had become more enjoyable, Miss Hesketh doing a special class on America after it became known the Morans were leaving.

Her teacher also seemed softer, friendlier, always taking time out to ask how she was. Miss Hesketh never did that with the other children.

'It's because I'm special, just like mother says.'

Today, she didn't stop to play in the park; she was desperate to get home, she wanted to pack her crate. Mary had promised Thirza she could have one to herself and she had been planning what to put in it.

It was hard to imagine that in a few days she'd be on a ship, steaming across the Atlantic with her mother and Charlie.

Smiling as she skipped past the lake where she first met him, she hummed the Rose of Tralee, the song her father used to sing. She was still humming it when she arrived home.

'Mother, it's me, I'm home.'

Letting her satchel fall to the floor, Thirza hung up her coat, the hallway full of wooden packing crates, some marked with 'study', 'kitchen', 'drawing room.'

'Mother?'

Maybe she was in the kitchen.

But she wasn't and Thirza quenched her thirst, drinking a glass of water in one go, wiping her mouth with the back of her hand.

'Mother! Mother, can I start my packing now?' she shouted out, heading upstairs.

Behind her bedroom door Mary shuddered, Freddy's sweaty hand clamped across her mouth, another roughly mauling her breasts as he pressed himself up against her from behind.

She could feel his breath on her neck, smell his unwashed odour, and he squeezed tighter, whispering:

'That's a shame, I was just beginning to enjoy myself. Now, shhh ... don't make a fucking sound.'

The door was ajar, and through the gap Mary saw her little girl emerge at the top of the stairs, her beautiful face a picture of innocence, heading for her mother's bedroom door.

She couldn't let this happen, she wouldn't. Not her little girl, she would rather die than let anything happen to her.

Mary stamped down hard on Freddy's foot with the heel of her shoe, and he yelped in pain loosening his grip.

'Thirza, runnnnn!!!' Mary shrieked.

Her screams reverberated through the house but Thirza froze, her tiny body trembling, unable to move. Mary managed to open the door and glimpsed her little girl, but she was shoved to the floor and now Thirza screamed as the man with the melted face appeared from nowhere, dragging her into the bedroom.

Freddy threw her to the floor, Mary crawling on her hands and knees, flinging herself protectively over her daughter.

They were hysterical as Freddy closed the door, moving over to the window, his eyes searching.

'Shut up! The pair of you, keep fucking quiet. He'll be here soon, if I know Charlie, it won't take him long.'

'Please … please, don't hurt us. Just take what you want, Mr Lucas,' Mary said, stroking Thirza's head buried into her chest.

'Mr Lucas? Well, aren't you all manners … most folk just call me Freddy. But I like that, I like being called Mr Lucas.'

He was sitting on the windowsill looking out on to the street.

'To answer your question, I'm waiting; for Charlie. There's no point starting without Charlie.'

'Think Mary, think!'

She took deep breaths, shuffled to get more comfortable and said: 'Charlie … Charlie's not here. He's gone back home … he won't be back for some time.'

'Oh, now you're starting to sound like Charlie. Been around his fucked up face a bit too long haven't we. No, he's on his way, take it from me, no one knows Charlie better than me,' and Freddy grinned, the same wild, manic expression that Thirza had seen outside the grocery shop.

Out of breath, his hand throbbing, ribs racked with pain, Hobbs fought his body's urge to stop running.

He had been caught in two minds - go to the police or straight to the house. He decided on the latter, gasping for breath, pausing for just a minute, bent double against a lamp post.

Back at the house Mary was listening; Freddy had left them alone for the last five minutes and she was straining to hear.

'Mother, why is that man here? Why does he want to hurt us?'

'I don't know sweetheart but I won't let anything happen to you, do you hear me?' and she did her best to force a smile.

They heard clattering downstairs before Freddy was in the doorway.

'The crates? What are they for?'

'We're ... we're moving, we're going to live in America.'

His eyes darted from side to side, muttering to himself.

'And Charlie? Is Charlie going too?'

Mary had no idea what the right answer would be; she went with the truth:

'Yes, yes he is, Mr Lucas.'

'The bastard ... that treacherous bastard. I fucking HATE yooouuuuu, Charlie!' and his screams filled the house, sending Thirza into hysterics.

Slamming the door, he left them again and for a fleeting moment Mary thought he might go. Then she heard him talking to himself and the cellar door opening, its hinges creaking.

And then she could smell it.

Thirza could too, her tears subsiding, as she lifted her gaze.

'What's ... what's that smell, Mother?'

Mary knew exactly what it was; paraffin.

'Thirza, listen to me. We have to get out of the house, we can't stay here. Do you understand me?'

'Yes, Mother, but that man ... he won't, he won't let us, will he?'

'No, but we have to go. Now, listen to me carefully.'

Summoning every ounce of energy he had left, Hobbs kept running, past the school, through the churchyard and into the park. He stopped again, retching this time, throwing up against the park railings. Not far now, he was almost there.

Freddy returned to the bedroom and found Mary alone. 'Where is she?'

Petrified, convinced she was going to die, Mary glared at him with defiance.

'She's gone, Mr Lucas, you should have kept more of an eye on us.'

Howling with rage, Freddy hurled Mary's dressing table over, as she cowered, protecting her head, as he stood over her yelling:

'You lying cow, you lying fucking cow!'

Grabbing her hair, he wrenched her arms away and smacked her in the face with back of his hand, Mary falling, clutching her reddened cheek.

And then, to her astonishment, he left the room again. But this time, she was ready. Leaping to her feet she slammed the door, grabbed a chair and jammed it underneath the handle, wedging it tight so it couldn't open.

Then, she coaxed Thirza out from her hiding place inside the wardrobe and the two of them clung to each other, stifling their sobs.

The paraffin tin was only three quarters full but Freddy knew there'd be more than enough. He splashed it over the floor in the hallway and kitchen, making sure to douse the curtains and sofa in the sitting room.

Then, for good measure, he slopped more over the packed wooden crates containing Mary's memories.

So what, if the little runt had done a runner or was hiding somewhere; no matter, she'd burn like her mother.

Throwing more liquid over the stairs, he poured the final few drops on the landing, shaking the tin before hurling it downstairs, summoning the memory again of its pungent odour.

Mary heard the tin clatter against the wooden floor, knowing she didn't have long. Sliding the window open, she was frantically throwing sheets, blankets and pillows on to the grass below.

'Thirza, listen to me ... I'm going to lift you out and then you have to jump, do you hear me?'

'Mother, I'm scared, I don't want to, please, Mother,' and the tears came again.

She wanted to say it was ok, that everything would be fine. But they heard him at the door.

'You cow! Open this fucking door ... now!'

He tried kicking, forcing it with his shoulder, Mary and Thirza praying for the chair to hold. It did and Freddy screamed:

'A locked door's not going to save Charlie's girls.'

He felt in his pocket for the lighter that had once belonged to his dad; the one he'd used to start the fire that torched his family home, listening to his parents' screams as he hid in an outhouse.

Freddy relished the sound of the flint striking the steel plate, gazing at the flame ignited by the vapour.

Holding it against a paraffin-soaked rag, he inhaled slowly, in awe as always at the way fire took hold. He held it until the tips of his fingers burned and then dropped it, the rag consumed in flames, fire engulfing the landing.

60

Hobbs turned the corner into Mary's street, his lungs ready to burst, stumbling again and having to break his fall with his injured hand.

Wailing in agony, he forced himself on, he could see the house now, there were people gathering outside, pointing.

And then he saw Mary, she was at the bedroom window and ... 'oh my God.'

Mary was dangling her daughter from the window, Thirza holding on to her mother's hands, her vivid, red curls standing out against the brickwork.

'Nooooo!' Hobbs yelled, coughing as the acidic saliva filled his mouth.

He watched in horror and heard the screams of people below as Thirza fell from view.

There was smoke coming from the house now; dark, swirling wisps that toyed with the building before dissipating into the summer sky.

He was almost at the gate when he saw Mary at the window, she was looking down and Hobbs pushed past onlookers, relieved to see the little girl sitting up on a pile of blankets on the front lawn.

'Charlie, Charlie, get Thirza,' Mary cried.

More passers-by gathered as the fire grew in intensity, flames now visible inside the house, the smoke getting thicker, darker.

He tripped, falling next to Thirza and he scooped her into his arms, carrying her across the road.

'Please, take ... care ... of her,' he gasped to a crowd, stroking Thirza's curls.

He ran back towards the blaze, standing beneath the window.

'Mary, jump. You have to jump.'

She nodded, tentatively leaning out the window, and Hobbs saw terror etched on her face. And then the chair gave way, the door flung open and Freddy stood against a backdrop of flames.

He was at the window before Mary could react, shoving her out of sight, before sliding the window shut. Hobbs could only stare in horror as Freddy gazed at him, a sneer across his face.

'Ma-ry! Ma-ry,' and he sprinted for the door.

Holding his arms up in front of his face, Hobbs ran through the choking smoke and heat. The stairs were ablaze but it didn't matter, nothing mattered, as the flames licked around him and he felt his skin burn.

He made it to the top of the stairs, a ring of flame around Mary's bedroom door. It was getting harder to breathe and he saw his trouser leg ablaze, desperately beating it with his hands to snuff out the flames.

But Hobbs' desire to reach Mary overcame everything and he surged towards the door, his shoulder colliding against it as he crashed into the room, sprawling to the floor.

'I knew you'd come Charlie, I fucking knew it,' Freddy yelled, grinning with excitement.

But he took his eyes off Mary and she shoved with all her might, sending Freddy hurtling into the wardrobe.

Hobbs was on his feet, grabbing Mary's hand, pulling her towards him. Throwing his jacket over her head, he clutched her waist and yelled:

'Don't let go of me.'

Together they dashed out the room, through the flames on the landing and down the stairs. Hobbs used his body to shield her and felt the searing heat against his skin, until finally, they flew out the open door, collapsing on the grass, gulping in air.

Smoke was coming from Hobbs' jacket, Mary's dress aglow with orange sparks, as help came from neighbours, patting them both down.

'I'm … I'm all right, where's Thirza?'

'Mother, Mother, I'm here?'

'Oh Thirza, my baby.'

'Are you all right, love? The fire brigade … they're on their way,' asked a woman.

'Charlie? Charlie?' and Mary turned this way and that, frantically searching for Hobbs.

And then she screamed as the same woman's voice told her:

'He … he's gone back inside.'

The house was fully ablaze now and Hobbs could see nothing but thick, acrid smoke. He crawled on all fours feeling for the stairs.

'Freddy! Freddy,' he yelled, coughing.

With his coat over his head, he leapt through a wall of flame on the stairs and then up to Mary's bedroom.

Even in the fire, he could see the door was closed and he sprinted towards it, smashing it open a second time.

Freddy was sitting in the chair and he stared at Hobbs open mouthed. Hobbs was bent double, coughing and spluttering, and he slammed the door to buy precious time.

'You came back ... you came back, Charlie,' said an incredulous Freddy. 'This is how it's meant to be, Charlie, you and me ... together, like you said.'

'We have ... we have to go, Freddy,' Hobbs gasped, smoke filling the room, billowing in from under the door.

'We are, Charlie ... we are,' and he put a comforting arm around Hobbs, the two men gazing at each other through their broken faces. Freddy was smiling:

'It won't hurt, Charlie, I promise you.'

'Freddy, no, we have to get out,' and he wriggled free, going over to the window and yanking it open.

The sudden influx of fresh air was fuel for the fire which was now burning through the door, flames licking the bedroom walls.

Putting a leg up on the sill, Hobbs yelled: 'Freddy come on, we have to go now!'

Flames broke through the door, the wood crackling and disintegrating as it burned and Hobbs heard the shouts from people below, the distant bell of a fire engine.

Finally, Freddy was coming towards him.

'That's it, take my hand, Freddy, we'll jump together.'

He was next to him now and he smiled broadly.

'I love you, Charlie,' and he shoved Hobbs out the window.

Hobbs heard screams, coming round on the grass, his leg broken, the pain excruciating.

The last thing he saw before blacking out was Freddy closing the window, his disfigured face peering out from the glass as the room was consumed by fire.

Epilogue - 1928

The air was warm in the sea breeze and the woman stood holding the rails, staring down at the swirling mass of foam leaving trails across the ocean surface.

Thick, grey cloud drifted over the horizon, the remnants of yesterday's storm.

She remembered her fear and that of other passengers as the liner lurched from side to side, hearing huge thunder claps, feeling a shiver as she peered out of the porthole window into the blackness beyond.

But then the comforting words of a young steward, calmness personified as he addressed the nervous passengers seeking solace in the bar.

'Ladies and gentlemen, please try not to worry, this ship can handle storms much worse than this,' he'd said smiling.

'It's what she was made for.'

And so, she'd sat nursing her gin, picturing the liner as a great, hulking beast, surging through the sea, steely and determined, thwarting the storm, defying the angry sky.

Beneath the covered, wraparound deck, she took a flight of stairs up on to the open deck above, avoiding the men playing shuffleboard.

There, passengers lazed on deck chairs, some reading, others lying out in the sun. One young couple had pushed their chairs close together, the woman nestling in the man's arm as they shared a cigarette.

Thanks to the weather, this was the first time she'd ventured outside, in awe at the sheer size of the Atlantic Ocean.

There was nothing but water, as far as the eye could see, and the huge RMS Franconia was dwarfed by the vastness that surrounded it.

The sea was calm and the liner glided effortlessly through it.

Back down more stairs, passing beneath the huge mast that dominated the forward deck, she finally reached the bow of the ship.

There was less noise here; the ship was heading into the wind and the steam blew backwards, billowing out of her huge, single funnel.

She spotted the three of them gazing out to sea, smiling as they held hands. For a moment she simply watched, deciding this was what true happiness felt like, and she wished to capture it, savouring the moment forever.

But the young boy saw her, breaking away from his parents to come running over, grabbing her arm.

'Where have you been? Come on ... we've been waiting for you, it's so amazing up here,' he yelled, giddy with excitement.

'Steady on, Jimmy, I don't want to end up going overboard!' and she laughed as he playfully yanked her along.

'There you are. We were beginning to think you'd got lost!' her mother said, and the two of them embraced.

'I'm sorry, Mother, but I didn't sleep well because of the storm and I had … well, I had a headache when I woke up.'

'Too much gin? Me too … though it was medicinal.'
'Charlie Hobbs, you should not be showing a young woman the ways of alcohol … you're incorrigible,' Mary said, smiling at Hobbs.

'What's in-corr-gerbil mean?' the little boy asked.

'It means your father will never change, James,' Mary replied and Hobbs saw that impish smile, the one that told him his wife loved him dearly.

'Your mother is quite right of course, Thirza. Though, I think she forgets that it was *her* who first introduced *me* to the ways of gin!'

Thirza laughed out loud at the shocked expression on her mother's face; Mary raising her eyes in mock indignation.

'I'm hungry … can we have lunch now?' James asked, looking up at Mary with pleading eyes.

'Yes, my darling, yes we can. Thirza, why don't you and James go on ahead and get a table? We'll be along shortly.'

She recognised that look on Mary's face.

'Come on, Jimmy, let's go and see what cakes they've got for afternoon tea later,' and James' eyes lit up at his sister's suggestion.

Hobbs and Mary watched their son hold the hand of his half-sister, as she took him back inside.

'I can't believe my little girl's not little anymore,' Mary sighed, leaning against Hobbs as they looked out to sea. 'It makes me feel old.'

'If it helps, you don't look old enough to have a daughter of eighteen. You look more like sisters.'

'Charlie Hobbs, you're such a charmer,' and she kissed his cheek, oblivious now to the defect that affected his speech.

She'd thought this day would never come, that her dream of moving to America had gone forever. First the fire, then waiting for Hobbs to recover from his injuries, had delayed them going. Then it was her mother succumbing to a sudden illness and the long months nursing her until finally, Evelyn's death was a blessing and Mary was grieving again.

They should have gone then but suddenly Mary was undecided. A few months later Hobbs proposed, they were married the following summer and a year later James was born.

They couldn't emigrate with a baby, at least that's what she told Hobbs. Let's wait until he's older Mary suggested.

Then, the news that Howard Moran had died. And now here they were, six years later, heading to Boston where a widowed Laura Moran would meet her son's daughter for the very first time.

Mary would never have gone without Thirza; but her daughter was as excited about the prospect now, as she was reticent as a child.

They were days away from a new life, in a new country and Mary squeezed Hobbs' hand a little tighter, and he gazed into her eyes and nodded.

It was in her handbag; she'd checked again before leaving the cabin, though it had never left her side since they'd left Liverpool.

Reaching inside, she removed the small cloth pouch, handling it like it was the most delicate thing in the world.

Loosening the drawstring, Mary put a hand inside. Despite being covered, the metal still felt cold. Removing it carefully, she handed it to Hobbs. One of the spectacle arms was missing, along with the lens of the right eye. The nose remained intact, though the paint was beginning to flake off, exposing the tin beneath.

On the cheek and mouth were a series of deep scratches, though he could still make out some of the letters underneath that they were intended to hide.

Hobbs saw his tin face staring up at him, feeling the memories stir. He glanced at Mary, who smiled encouragingly, and then tossed it over the side, watching the mask disappear as it sank into the murky depths.

Acknowledgments

The devastating legacy of the First World War continues to this day. My interest, and fascination with such a tumultuous and catastrophic period in our recent history, is largely thanks to my dad.

Together, we've made countless visits to the battlefields of the Western Front where the cemeteries of the fallen hold such a revered place in the hearts of so many.

Thanks to the astonishing work of the Commonwealth War Graves Commission, the dead and missing of the Great War will rightly, never be forgotten.

But for those who were 'lucky' enough to make it home, they found a country tired and scarred by war, with the result being so many veterans were forgotten, ignored, and in some cases shunned.

We now know so many men suffered terrible psychological effects which they endured alone, a belief that locking those memories away was their only option.

For wounded veterans — men like Charlie Hobbs and Freddy Lucas — shutting the war away was never an option.

I was inspired to write *We Are Broken* after reading about visionary sculptor Francis Derwent Wood's devotion to helping young men with dreadful facial injuries.

Derwent Wood used his artistic skills to create lifelike facial masks for hundreds of disfigured veterans.
Sadly, little if any testimony remains from the men who wore them.

Imagining how life must have been for these men, who would have felt incredibly vulnerable and self-conscious about their appearance, is what prompted me to write this novel.

The face on the cover of this book belongs to someone known only as Rifleman Moss. He's wearing a mask much like the one worn by Charlie Hobbs and his photo was very much the catalyst for this story.

My apologies if you find references to Thirza's 'hare lip' offensive. Terminology, treatment and understanding of a condition we now know as 'cleft palate' is much better than it was in the early Twentieth Century when sadly, there were still those who believed in nonsense about Devil worshipping being to blame.

My thanks go to Natalie Young whose expert insight and suggestions helped make this a much more compelling and readable story and Jelena Mirkovic for her fabulous cover design.

And to my family; my wife, Jo and daughters, Grace and Ella (who I look forward to becoming my publicity agent when she's old enough, such is her belief in her dad's writing) I love you.

This book is dedicated to my Mum and Dad, who set the bar ludicrously high when it came to parenting. They remain my inspiration.

If you've enjoyed reading *We Are Broken* it would be fabulous if you'd consider leaving a review on Amazon.

All authors rely on book reviews — but for independent publishers, positive reviews and feedback are absolutely essential.

Why not also find out more about me and my writing by visiting my website **www.paul-coffey.com**

Finally, thank *you* for investing the time to read it. The biggest compliment an author can have is for someone to take the time to immerse themselves in a world they have created, investing in its characters.

That is both richly rewarding and incredibly humbling.

Also by
Paul Coffey

SHADOWS OF THE SOMME

A name on a headstone … a century of secrets

'Harrris looked up at the sky, crystal blue and cloudless … closing his eyes, he put the whistle to his lips and blew.'

July 1st 1916 and in the French countryside tens of thousands of doomed British soldiers are being killed and wounded as the bloody Battle of the Somme begins.

A century later and Tom Harris has no interest in the First World War. For him it's a conflict from another age. But during a visit to the battlefields he becomes fascinated by a headstone in a British war cemetery showing his namesake.

Desperate to learn more Tom begins to delve into the past where he discovers ordinary men consumed by extraordinary times. And in doing so he unearths a remarkable and moving story.

Available now on Amazon